A Rose for Ana María

A Rose for Ana María

a novel by

FRANK YERBY

THE DIAL PRESS
NEW YORK
1976

Manufactured in the United States of America

Third Printing 1976

Book design by Holly McNeely

Library of Congress Cataloging in Publication Data

Yerby, Frank, 1916–
A rose for Ana María.

I. Title.
PZ3.Y415Ro   [PS3547.E65]   813'.5'4   75–45143
ISBN 0–8037–7248–3

A NOTE TO THE READER

This novel was written during the spring and summer of 1974, and is as true to the observed facts of recent Spanish history as it was then possible for the writer—with twenty-one years of continuous residence in Spain behind him—to make it. But due to the inevitable time lag between the writing and the publication of a book, many events have occurred since, among them the death of Francisco Franco and the crowning of Juan Carlos I. The writer makes no claim to either omniscience or prophecy; he asks only that this novel be judged upon the basis of what was known in 1974, and not upon the conceivably very different basis of what has come to light, or has happened, since.

FRANK G. YERBY
MADRID
DECEMBER 1975

The boy, Diego Fernández, lifted the woman's stocking he was wearing over his face just high enough to free his left eye. Thin as the nylon was, seeing through it on a dark Parisian street at two o'clock in the morning wasn't easy. Breathing through it wasn't either, especially when you were dog sick and shaking and trying not to throw up.

"*Merde!*" he said to himself in the French that, because of that monstrous accident of history called the Spanish Civil War, was his native language, instead of the Spanish that should have been. Of course he spoke Spanish, too—his Republican refugee parents had seen to that—but badly. He looked up and down the street in both directions. No one was in sight. 'Oh, hell!' he thought. 'Why doesn't this species of a cretin come on?'

But he still didn't see his helper: the *type* he'd called from the Clichy-Levallois group—which was about as far from his own activist cell in the Fifth Arrondissement as it was humanly possible to get and still remain within the municipal boundaries of Paris—to come and back him up in this mission. He didn't even know the name of the comrade the Clichy-Levallois cell had assigned to him. When the *type* showed up finally, he wouldn't ask it. And both of them would keep their stocking masks down over their faces, so that neither of them could describe the other to the *flics* if either was captured.

That was the way it was done. That was Party discipline. And it made sense. You never worked on jobs like these with anyone from your own cell, or with anyone you knew, even slightly. So no matter what the CRS or the ordinary *flics* did to you when they'd got you down to headquarters, or even before that, en route in the *paniers à salade,* as he, like the born Parisian that he was, called the police vans—the outcome wouldn't depend upon so uncertain a factor as human valor.

"*Le courage,*" he told himself. "The courage I haven't got. I've thrown up three times in the last hour. And I probably will again if this *sale type* doesn't show up soon. And I'm shaking. I'm shaking like a *clochard* who hasn't been able to promote himself a bottle in two days. *Et pourquoi?* Why?"

"Because," he told himself slowly, "I killed him. A man. *Un brave type.* Gallant. *Avec vrai noblesse.* A gentleman. *Merde!* What am I doing using bourgeois terms like these? Only they —fitted him. A gentleman. *¡Un auténtico caballero español!* A *Spanish* gentleman. And hence, the best. So I didn't mean to. *Et quoi?* So what? For him it arranges things enormously that he died at the trembling hands of a cowardly murdering bungler instead of by anyone's deliberate intent, doesn't it? The hell it does!"

Then he heard the footsteps of his assigned helper coming on. He jerked the stocking down over his face. Waited. The comrade from the Clichy-Levallois group came up to him. Said, his voice muffled by the stocking mask, "*Numero Sept.* Number Seven."

"*Treize,*" Diego said. "Thirteen." He thought: 'Thirteen's bad luck. Another bourgeois superstition! But all the same——' He said, "Did you bring the stuff?"

"*Le voilà.* Here it is," Number Seven said.

"All right. Let's get going, then. Give me the lock picks."

That was Party policy, too. The one who had to wait never had the tools, the explosives, or, for that matter, any kind of incriminating evidence on him, in case the police picked him up before the helper from another cell got there. Which made sense, too, since it cut the time of danger down to the unavoidable minimum.

Seven passed the lock picks over. Diego turned to the car. It was a Renault Sixteen—a vehicle modest enough not to attract too much attention. It had a Star of David pasted inside its windshield. Which meant it belonged to a rabbi. That was why Diego had picked it out from all the other cars. Since where they were, in the rue Greuze, was in the Sixteenth Arrondissement, it was almost certain that the Renault belonged to the rabbi of the big synagogue at number 69 rue d'Auteuil, which would only compound confusion if the guards before the Israeli Embassy in the avenue de Wagram got the *matricula.* As they probably would. The Israeli guards were the best in Paris. These days, they had to be. And that was why the Israeli Embassy was going to be the most dangerous of the three on his list. At two thirty in the morning, there wouldn't be any guards before the others, he was sure.

He got the lock open in a shade under two minutes. "Too long!" he told himself grimly. "The *flic* on this beat is sure to come along any minute now . . ."

He slid under the wheel. Pulled the hood release. Seven stuck his fingers under the hood. Freed the safety catch. The spring-loaded hood bounced open. Seven bent over the motor. Diego knew what he was doing: hooking a jumper wire across the opened contacts of the key they didn't have. Diego pulled the handchoke all the way out as he heard the starter whirr. Pushed down on the accelerator. The motor caught at once. Number Seven came around to the right front seat.

"No," Diego said. "You drive, Seven. I've got things to do." That was true, but it wasn't the reason. The reason was he didn't trust himself to drive. His nerves were shot, and he knew it.

'Maybe,' he thought, 'this will straighten me out. Action usually does. And this is—necessary. They're all on the list Ernesto gave me. Only he doesn't expect me to hit 'em all the same night. So I will hit them all. That's crazy. Absolutely insane. Insane enough to maybe work. So that when Ernesto asks me—the ice-cold swine!—why I blew it, cost the Party the millions the Spanish government—or his family—would have paid for the Vice Consul, I can balance that with this. With *three* embassies. The offices of Turismo Español; the main office of Iberia Lineas Aereas——'

"Where to, chief?" Seven said. Only he said it in Spanish: *"¿A donde, jefe?"*

"Don't speak Spanish, imbecile!" Diego said. "Not even when we're alone. You'll get into the habit, and——"

"D'accord. Où allons-nous, alors?"

"Turismo Español. In the place de l'Opéra, first. Then Iberia."

"Merde!" Seven said. *"Vous êtes fou, vous!"*

"Yes. Sure. I'm crazy. That's why what I do works. Did you bring the timers?"

"Yes," Number Seven said.

"I'll set 'em for half an hour. By the time the soup blows, we'll be at Objective Number Two."

"And that is?" Seven said.

"L'ambassade des États Unis; numero deux, avenue Gabriel," Diego said.

"Good!" Seven said. "That one I like! We'll give it to 'em good, eh? *Ces cochons americains!"*

"Shut up and drive, will you?" Diego said. "I've got to arm these timers."

"All right. But one question, comrade: Where're you going to put the soup? In the garbage pails?"

"No," Diego said slowly, "too risky. They pick up the

garbage early in some districts. Especially in la place d'Opéra. And garbage collectors are—human beings, comrade. Workers.''

"*Negres,*" Seven said. "*Bicôts.* Or are you going to invite them to breakfast, like Monsieur le President Giscard did?''

"Niggers and Arabs," Diego said. "They are, aren't they? The garbage collectors. Street sweepers. Sewer and *pissoir* cleaners. People who have to do all the dirty, stinking jobs we French refuse to——"

"*You* French," Seven said. "I'm Spanish, damnit! *¡Y tanta honra!* And so are you, Thirteen!''

"Am I?" Diego said. "Am I—anything? Even a human being? Or didn't I—resign from the human race two—three hours ago?''

"*Tu m'enmerde!*" Seven said. "That's no way to talk, *Treize*! Especially not when we've got a job to do. . . .''

"*D'accord.* Right. Turn here. Don't go straight into l'Opéra. Detour. Two rights, one left, another right—''

"I know how it's done, Thirteen. But calm down, will you? Nobody's following us.''

Diego got out of the car. He had a newspaper in his hands. A pot of glue. He coated a place on the window of the Spanish Tourist Office with the glue, spreading the thick white mess over an area slightly smaller than the newspaper's pages. Slapped the newspaper over it. Waited. Then, taking out an expensive diamond-tipped glass cutter, he marked a circle just below the newspaper's free, unglued borders, biting deep into the glass with the tool. Holding on to the newspaper's protruding edges, he punched the center of the circle with his fist. It broke very cleanly and soundlessly around the scribed line. He pulled it outward with the newspaper that was glued to the glass. Pushed the five sticks of plastic explosive and the small clockwork timer through the resulting hole. Turned, walked back to the stolen car.

"Iberia," he said to Seven.

"Voilà!" Seven said. *"Comme vous êtes professionel, vous! Quel expertise! Ça va, hein?"*

Diego shrugged. "I do this all the time," he said. "When I'm not killing people, that is. Get this heap moving, will you?"

They were crossing the place de la Concorde just before entering the avenue Gabriel where the American Embassy is, when all the night roared, vomited fire. Once. Twice. From behind them. From up the rue Royale, the boulevard Madeleine, the boulevard des Capucines, from, surely, the place de l'Opéra.

Seven grinned at Diego.

"Ça-y-est!" he said. *"Ça va, comrade!"*

"Give me the blowtorch," Diego said.

Seven passed it over. Diego got out of the car. Crossed the *trottoir* until he came to the big iron gate of the American Embassy. Took out a small container filled with butane gas under pressure. Fitted it to the blowtorch. In forty-seven seconds the big chain looped through the iron bars of the gate dropped to the ground, its burned-through links glowing a dull, grayish rose. Behind him, from the place de l'Opéra, he could hear the *Whooop-huh ooooh* of *les pompiers,* the firemen, and the shriek of police sirens.

The big, old-fashioned lock on the gate was child's play. He stepped into the embassy garden, walking soundlessly. Three minutes, twenty-six seconds later, he was back in the car.

"Where to now?" Seven said, grinning at him.

"The Spanish Embassy, number thirteen, avenue Georges Cinq," Diego said. "After that, the Israeli, one forty-three, avenue Wagram. Then *l'ambassade d'Irak, dix, place des États Unis——"*

"*Irak?*" Seven said. "Isn't that against Party policy, Thirteen? We're supposed to *love* the *bicôts* these days."

Diego looked at him, thought: 'You filthy racist. Goes against all the Party's doctrine. But leaving the Party out of it, I still hate *types* who use words like that. *Bicôt*—billy goat.

Couldn't he just say Arabs once in a while, for God's sake?'

But he didn't say that. It just wasn't smart to get Seven's back up. He had to depend upon him too much now. He said, mildly: "It *is* against Party policy—which makes it one sweet cover-up. The comrade chief will understand that when I explain it to him. Besides, we won't use *le plastique* this time. A couple of Molotov cocktails only. The Iraqis can afford to repair damages from a small fire, can't they? With what, thanks to them and other beturbaned friends, *essence* costs these days——"

"You can say that again!" Seven said. "I've been leaving my heap at home and taking the métro to work ever since the last price rise. Only a millionaire can afford gasoline now, and they're——"

"Exploiters of the people, and dirty swine," Diego said wearily. "Now, come on!"

That night, the police and the fire departments of Paris were driven to a state bordering upon insanity. From Opéra to Concorde, from there to the Sixteenth, both Georges V and Wagram within minutes of one another, and then, finally, the squad cars screaming down Kleber and d'Iena both to come screeching into the Plaza of the United States from both ends of it, to find the Iraqi Embassy not blown apart by that hideous explosive the French call *le plastique*—as by then the American, the Israeli (though to the Israelis' credit, they at least had pumped one good long burst of submachine-gun fire into the back of the terrorists' car, without, *malheureusement!,* hitting either its tank or its tires), and the Spanish embassies already had been, not to mention the offices of the Spanish Tourist Agency, and those of Iberia, the Spanish airline—but blazing merrily enough; and they, *les pompiers,* anyhow, unreeling their hoses and taking out their axes and going to work, had no sooner begun to pour their hard white streams into the burning Embassy when once again the sky flared into artificial day and still another jagged slamming crash followed by the slow rolling boom of the echoes rode in upon them.

A police lieutenant in a squad car picked up his radio telephone. Listened to the voice crackling over it. Screamed: "My God! It's the rue du Faubourg St. Honoré! Perhaps even the Élysée Palace itself! And *Monsieur le President*—"

"Is out with a blonde, *comme d'habitude*!" his colleague said. "But *Madame la Presidente et ses gosses* are sure to be there, so——"

The squad car burned rubber taking off. Not that they needed to. Close to twenty squad cars were pouring into the rue Faubourg St. Honoré by then.

But it wasn't the Élysée Palace, residence of the presidents of France. It was the Embassy of Great Britain at 34 rue du Faubourg St. Honoré. . . .

"Quel coup de tonnerre!" Seven said. "A true master stroke, Thirteen! Now they'll sure as hell think its the IRA instead of——"

"The ETA," Diego said wearily. "The Basque Liberation Movement—whom they'll normally blame instead of us. Now drop me off in l'Étoile, will you?"

"Okay. *D'ac.* But what'll I do with this heap? Those Hebe bastards really messed it up, didn't they? It's a miracle they didn't get us . . ."

"Don't think they were really trying," Diego said. "Cause them too damned much trouble if they killed a Frenchman—terrorist or not— in France. Take this shot-up wreck and park it in front of the synagogue at *numero soixante-neuf* rue d'Auteuil. Since those guards in front of the Israeli Embassy sure as hell got its license number, that will exercise the Arabs and the Jews, both . . ."

He started towards the métro entrance, walking halfway around the vast circular place de l'Étoile, watching tiredly the changing angles of the Arc de Triomphe as he did so. He hoped he wouldn't meet a *flic.* Explaining to a policeman what the hell he was doing in the place de l'Étoile at four o'clock in the morning after someone had wrecked half the embassies in Paris would be too much of a chore. The worst of it was that even if he made it downstairs to the subway, he hadn't the slightest idea where he could go. Home was out. For, although he was absolutely sure that the police hadn't, and couldn't have connected him with the murder of Señor Don Enrique Ximenez, the Spanish Vice Consul, or the job he and Seven had done on the embassies, Ernesto could. And would. And knew where he lived.

'I,' Diego thought morosely, 'would—by long odds!—rather explain things to the *flics* than to Ernesto . . .'

To a *flic,* he could say, "Look, *m'sieur l'agent,* I tied one on last night. Got drunk. *Sous. Ivre.* Picked up a *poule*——"

He stiffened suddenly. That was a thought! Because if checking into some fleabag without baggage would call far too much attention to himself after that night of flame and thunder, the same act would evoke a weary yawn if he did it accompanied by a whore. What better place was there, after all, to hide than the kind of dingy hotel room a *poule* would lead him to? Where *she* was known, and her clients didn't need to be? Not that he needed a woman with that tiredness in him, that sick, bad sadness pulverizing his very bones beneath its weight. He was aware, even then, that after what the sight of the Vice Consul's blood and brains splattered across his uneaten lunch had done to his nerves, he would be incapable with the loveliest, most sexy creature alive. Besides, all the really high-class articles who drove around the Étoile in fancy cars would be gone by now, leaving only—

The kind of raddled public garbage who was approaching him now. Sixty, if she was a day. No, say a well-used fifty—or perhaps even a disastrous forty-five . . .

" '*Allo, beau gar,*" she breathed throatily. "*Vous avez du feu?*"

The standard routine. Ask for a light, and then——

He said, contemptuously: "*Combien?* How much? *C'est à*

dire pour toute la nuit? For all night long?"

She stared at him.

"Ambitious little fellow, aren't you? That will be—" she hesitated, estimating his shabby worker's clothes and his bearing that contradicted that shabbiness completely—*"quatre mille?"*

"Trois," he said. "Three thousand."

"Trois, cinq," she haggled. "Three thousand five hundred—"

"D'ac," he said. "Okay. C'mon."

She led him up the avenue Carnôt to a fleabag in the rue des Acacias. He knew the routine. Being young and human, and—largely because of the kind of things he did for the Party —very lonely most of the time, he had occasionally been forced by that loneliness, by his anguished need, to make use of a whore. So he paid the five hundred francs for the room without grumbling and went up those stairs. He could afford the money. Like all Party specialists, he was well supplied with cash. Only he was forbidden to use it on himself in ostentatious ways.

But once inside the room he put it to her frankly: *"Voilà tes trois mille cinq cent—y pour rien.* For nothing. I need to sleep. I haven't for a long time. And I'm giving you a break, *bébé.* You can sleep, too. You've got more than enough to throw his share to your *mech,* haven't you? So there shouldn't be any problem—"

She stared at him a long time. Said: *"De ma part, pas de problème. Mais——"*

"But what?" he said.

"How far behind you were the *flics* when you picked me up?"

"Far enough," he said quietly. "Fact is they don't even know that I'm the *type* they're after. So there's no money on my head if that's what you're counting on. . . ."

"Wouldn't take it if there were," she said. The absolute sincerity in her tone, quiet, understated, unmistakable, made him stare at her.

"Voilà la poule avec le coeur d'or!" he said.

"No," she said wearily. "I haven't much of any kind of heart left; and what I had, never was of gold. I'm a dirty bitch, like all the other dirty bitches in this racket, *beau gar*. But I've learned to be a little less stupid than the rest—"

"Meaning?"

"Those bombings. All over town. Spaced out just right so that the *flics* and the *pompiers* had to run their poor, miserable asses off, from one end of Paris to the other. That called for—organization. *Expertise. Professionalité.* And—numbers. No one poor little blond *gar* did *tout ça,* all by himself . . ."

"So?" he said.

"So I turn you in, and *tes amis* pay me a little visit. At best they do a little fancy razor work on my face. At worst, the *flics* find me floating in the Seine. My face isn't much, but it's *la seule que j'ai. Ma vie—aussi. Cette très enmerdeuse vie.* This very shitty life. Bad as it is, I cling to it. *Tu me comprends, n'est-ce pas?"*

"Perfectly. In fact I feel the same way," Diego said. "Now lie down. You look tired. And I'm beat. Let's sleep . . ."

Then it was broad daylight again and he still hadn't slept. He had lain there beside her, turned away from her so that her cheap perfume and her unwashed female stink wouldn't make him throw up again, and thought about the man he had killed. About Don Enrique Ximenez Calvo, Vice Consul at that same embassy on the avenue Georges Cinq he'd also blown up. Which was overdoing things a little, but there it was.

The trouble was that Don Enrique had got to him. Had shaken the pristine purity of his Marxist faith. Finished shaking it, that is. Because working with Ernesto had put the first cracks in the wall supporting his life, long ago. His revolutionary zeal had all but vanished even before the twenty days he'd spent guarding that mundane, highborn, humorous, and quixotic Spanish gentleman the Party had kidnapped, knowing that, as all such things usually were, the crime would be blamed on the ETA, on *Euzkadi ta Azkatasuna,* that stark-raving band of fanatics dedicated to the absolutely insane proposition that *Las Vas-congadas*—the Basque Provinces in Spain—could be liberated from the Spanish and become an independent nation. Free *Vasconia*. Which was what *Euzkadi ta Azkatasuna* meant in *Euz-kadian* or *Vascuence*, the speech of the *Vascos*, the Basques, and the oldest language in the world.

But those twenty days had finished wrecking Diego's life for him. Because, during them, he had conceived an admiration, a respect, even a fondness for Don Enrique that was practically indistinguishable from love. Not, of course, a homosexual love; he had, he thanked the God he didn't believe in, none of those tendencies that frightened and disgusted him in Ernesto, but a filial love, say. He'd come to love Don Enrique the same way he did his own father. No, more; because Don Enrique wasn't the weakling that Jaime Fernández was; so that *burgesa, capitalista, Falangista* though he was—bourgeois, capitalist, member of the Spanish Falange, the only surviving fascist party left in Europe since the Greeks had thrown out their colonels and the Portuguese had staged their magnificent *Revoluçoã dos Cravos,* their Flower Revolution—Don Enrique had been, nonetheless, entirely admirable, and Diego's feeling toward him, therefore, undiluted by the necessity for pity.

And now, he, Diego, had killed him. Killed the man whom he had come to admire and respect more than any other he had ever known. He hadn't meant to, of course. He could legitimately call it an accident. But Enrique Luis Ximenez Calvo was dead, all the same. Dead with his blood and his brains splattered across—God!

He got up. Dressed. Moved by a sudden pity at the gray weariness in the face of the whore, he put still another thousand-franc note on the pillow beside her. He stood there a long moment, staring at her. Seeing the lines of fatigue, self-loathing, pain relaxed by sleep, he reduced her age still further, cutting it back to the thirty-eight or -nine she actually was. Then he got out of there.

The streets were literally crawling with *flics*. But that didn't bother him too much. At that hour quite a few poor working slobs would be on their way to their daily grind. And he actually held down a job in the Sixteenth. At the Peugeot garage in la rue de la Forge, only a few streets away. Besides, there was no reason for the police to stop him. They had no description of the man who had killed Enrique Ximenez, and still less of last night's terrorist bomber. Even if they did detain him, his papers were in order and his alibi letter-perfect. No, it wasn't the Police de Ville, nor even the CRS—the Compagnies Républicaines de Sécurité—as brutal as those unmitigated bastards were, nor, for that matter, the only police he really feared—the crack, first-class *agents de la Sûreté*—he had to consider now; but Ernesto. Comrade Chief Ernesto. And he had cost Ernesto, and the Party, a cool three million francs, the ransom they surely could have collected for Enrique Ximenez, if he, Diego, fool that he was—clumsy, bungling, murderous fool!—hadn't got rattled and killed him.

Would Ernesto accept his explanation? Would his liquidating in a single night all the objectives he had been given for a whole year, plus two that hadn't even been on his list, make any difference? He didn't know. He honestly didn't know. There was no telling with Ernesto. Diego had seen him pardon the most heinous offenses against the Party with a soft and gentle smile. And he had also known comrades to disappear forever —surely at Ernesto's orders!—over what any normal man would have considered trifles. Ernesto was a character straight out of Kafka. Nothing he did had any rhyme or reason except to Ernesto himself. And yet he was the most valuable man the Party had. The obscurantist twisting of his icily evil mind came up with the absolutely damnedest plans that somehow always worked.

'In fact,' Diego thought, 'my throwing in the British and the Iraqi embassies last night is first-class Ernesto. Drive the *flics* straight up the nearest wall. By their fingernails at that. The

Spanish Embassy, Iberia, Turismo Español? Why ETA, of course! Who else? But the American Embassy? Everyone hates the Americans. Bet they'll round up every Cypriot Greek in town as today's most likely suspects. The Israelis? *Al Fatah;* Black September—or any of two hundred other Arab terrorist groups. Or *one* crazy Arab, and his crazier Japanese pals! The Iraqis? Either the Israelis or French Jews pissed off by the French government's wooing of the Arabs. But the British Embassy could only have been the IRA, the Irish Republican Army, a group never before known to operate in France! Damned good with bombs, those *salauds.* So—doctrinaire Ernesto-type tactics; the *flics* falling all over their size fifty-two feet, hauling in hundreds of suspects for a multiple, top-flight job done by two kids in a stolen car. Ernesto will appreciate this. If I ever get to explain it to him. If his *pistoleros* let me live that long . . .'

But he thought Ernesto would listen to him. The reason he thought so was rather unpleasant. Ernesto was clearly fond of him. Too fond. And it was whispered in Party circles that the short, thickset, glossily bald little monster was a secret homosexual. Sometimes Diego believed the rumors, and at other times he didn't. With Ernesto who could tell? What was certain was that Ernesto had never touched his hand, except to shake it with a surprisingly firm grip. Nor his cheek, for that matter. Or embraced him, Spanish fashion, in that entirely male bearhug that Spaniards call *el abrazo.*

Anyhow, he'd have to chance it. In an hour, he could go home. By then his mother, Libertad, would have left for work. And she wouldn't come home for lunch. With this new family she worked for as *une bonne,* she wasn't allowed to. So he'd be all alone in their tiny, miserable flat in the Third Arrondissement and wouldn't have to face her questions. He could call in sick to the garage. André Spanelli, the Corsican brigand who ran it, would accept that. He had to. Diego was the only really decent mechanic he had.

He stopped at a sidewalk cafe and had coffee. Nothing else. He knew nothing else would stay down. Then he took the métro to la place de la Bastille. Got off. Walked the rest of the way home.

As he put the key in the lock, it came to him what he was going to do next. Absolutely the last thing on earth anyone would expect him to do. It would keep him safe for the rest of the day. Not even Ernesto would think of looking for him there. But that wasn't the reason he was going there.

The reason was he had to.

At three thirty that same afternoon, Diego Fernández stood on the edge of the sidewalk of the rue de Roquette where it runs into la place de la Bastille and stared at the traffic pouring in a rumbling, roaring, screeching stampede around the base of the monument, and at the *agents de la Police de la Circulation* who were dancing and waving their white batons and shrilling through their whistles and going crazy trying to direct it. As usual.

He half-raised his arm to signal one of the many taxicabs that had their green roof lights on and the cardboard *Libre* signs placed behind their windshields, which meant they hadn't been able to pick up a fare yet. Then he jerked his arm down again. Looked at his watch.

"No," he said aloud, talking to himself, knowing that was a bad sign, that it meant something, a breaking point reached, maybe. "I won't take a taxi. Passy's too far. It would be over before I could get there. And cabfare would cost the eyes out of my head—a factor to consider after all the ready cash I blew on that young, sweet and delicate creature last night. I mean this morning. It was after four o'clock, wasn't it? At least I don't have to worry about having caught a dose—or about anything else but Camarada Ernesto, considering what's in the afternoon papers. Gave the poor *flics* a hard time. Sorry about that, *messieurs les agents!* Next time I'll leave my calling card when I blow up half of town."

He paused. Thought: 'Come off of that, Diego! This is no time for cheap bravado. You know what you have to do. Go up there. Do I? Yes. I've got to go. I owe him that much, don't I? Or do I? Fat lot of good it'll do him now . . .'

He moved off around the circular plaza, walking fast. His gait was loose jointed, slouching, easy. There was even a certain grace about it. When he moved, he didn't look awkward anymore. He caught a fleeting glimpse of his reflection in a window of a passing autobus, saw that his sandy blond hair was a mess, as it nearly always was. He put up a big red hand and pushed it through the thick curly mop, trying to comb it out with his fingers.

"You," he told himself, "look like a German or a Swede. Blond hair, blue eyes. Tall. *Tú. Jodido bárbaro del norte, tú.* You fucking northern barbarian! Which is why the Party uses you for these things, surely. Harder to trace. Someone fire bombs the offices of Iberia, Lineas Aereas. A *type* wrecks the show windows of Turismo Español. So whom do the *flics* look for? A black-skinned Andaluzian bastard with patent leather hair, slicked down with shoe polish, maybe.

"Figures. The French police have never even heard of the *provincias* of Galicia and Asturias, that's sure. Where our ancestors were Celts and Teutons. Where we kept the Moors out. Didn't get tarbrushed like the rest of Spain. Until 1934, anyhow. Until Franco, himself, sent them in along with the Legion under Colonel Yagüe. But as a member of the Chiefs of Staff of the *Republic,* it is useful to remember! Ask Tía Juana about that. She could tell you. If you could get her to talk. If anybody could. To talk—or do anything but sit there and stare."

He kept on walking, hopping, skipping, dancing between the murderous avalanche of cars, until he got to the entrance of the métro. He went down the stairs. But, before going to the ticket window, he slouched over to a huge map of Paris and looked at it. Then he gazed down at the row of push buttons beneath it until he found the one he was looking for. Pompe. The rue de la Pompe, where the church was.

He pushed that button and two strings of colored lights came on. The first string was blue and flashed an azure glowing row up the line that ended at Porte de Neuilly, but not all the way, for the lighted bulbs only went as far as the station Franklin Delano Roosevelt, leaving the rest of the Neuilly line dark. But from the Roosevelt station, another string of lights flickered in a southwestward direction past the Trocadero station to a smaller circle called Pompe. But these were green, which meant another line altogether. Following the green glow with his gaze, he saw it ended at Pont de Sèvres. So now he knew how to get to where he had to go: from Bastille to Roosevelt on the Neuilly line, get off at Roosevelt, walk down stairs to the lower level, and then take the Pont de Sèvres line to Pompe. Simple enough, even as confused and gut sick and tired as he was.

He went over to the ticket window and bought a round-trip ticket on the first-class cars. It was the first time in his life he had ever done that. Usually he rode second or third class. But he didn't feel like standing up all the way to the Passy residential district. Usually there were seats to be had on the first-class subway cars, while second and third were sardine cans. He needed to sit down. He hadn't eaten since day before yesterday. And he wasn't sure he could stand the collective aromas of his at least official compatriots from those social strata who rode second and third class on an empty stomach. He'd have to eat soon, he knew. If he could manage it. If he could get food down. And afterwards make it stay.

There were two or three empty seats. He slumped into

one. Noticed at once that the other passengers were staring at him, their mouths tightening, becoming grim and disapproving. They were all well dressed. Groomed. Coiffed. Some of them were almost elegant. Almost. Because really elegant Parisians don't ride the métro. They drive, or are driven in damned expensive cars. He groped for one of his mother's more biting expressions:

"¡Quieren y no pueden!" she always said. "Would be's if you could's!" her voice dripping pure Iberian scorn.

But, he realized, riding the first-class cars while dressed in blue jeans, a blue denim shirt, and a black leather jacket just wasn't smart. Not under the circumstances he found himself in now. His clothes branded him as a worker, or a hoodlum. The black leather jacket was the uniform of Paris's juvenile delinquents, giving them its name. *Blousons noirs,* people called them. People like these. Rich, reactionary bourgeois bastards. Bloodsuckers, one and all. "Public shitters!" he snarled at them under his breath. "Fuck off, will you? I paid my fare. I've as much right as you to . . ."

He closed his eyes. Leaned back against the seat. Tried not to think. To stop remembering.

But he couldn't manage it. He couldn't at all. Even after he had changed trains at Franklin Delano Roosevelt station, and settled into his seat in another first-class car on the Pont de Sèvres line, he went on seeing in appalling technicolor upon the tridimensional widescreen cinéma of his mind that bloody hulk that had been a human being, a brave, gay, bright human being, lying there sprawled out on the floor and——

He shuddered. Opened his eyes. Closed them again almost immediately. Or they closed themselves. Not sleep, but his own weakness overcame him. He felt the train go rocketing past several stations. Then it slowed. Looking out, he saw that it was drawing into the big and imposing Trocadero Station, so he got up and went to the doors. But he didn't get off there. Instead he remained standing just inside the double pneumatic doors until they hissed closed again, and the train rocked and clicked

and clacked and glided through the dark tunnels until they got
to the next station. Smaller, less imposing. *Pompe,* the signs said.

Then he did get off. Went up the stairs. Stood there blinking into the afternoon sun, trying to get his bearings. The
Spanish Church was at number fifty-one *bis,* rue de la Pompe.
He started walking up the street until he came to it. Stood
outside of it, looking at the glass-enclosed bulletin board, with
the black plastic letters that could be moved about to spell out
whatever message the *cura* wanted to convey to the faithful.
Today the message was written in Spanish and read:

MISA DEL CUERPO INSEPULCRO. SOLEMNES
FUNERALES POR EL EXMO SR. DON ENRIQUE LUIS
XIMENEZ CALVO, VICECÓNSUL DE ESPAÑA EN
PARIS, VILMENTE ASESINADO POR LOS ENEMIGOS
DE LA PATRIA. SU VIUDA, LA EXMA. SRA. DOÑA
MATILDE GIL-PATRICIO DE XIMENEZ, SUS HIJAS, PI-
LAR Y MARTA, Y SUS AMIGOS DE LA COLONIA ESPA-
ÑOLA DE PARIS, RUEGAN UNA ORACIÓN POR EL
ETERNO DESCANSO DE SU ALMA.

He put that into French, slowly. He was very tired, and
when he was bone-weary, defeated, whipped as he was now,
things came to him more easily in the language that he had been
all but born to, that he thought in most of the time, that he used
every day and everywhere, except at home. At home he spoke
Spanish. His mother insisted upon that.

'A Mass for the Unburied Body,' he translated inside his
mind. 'Solemn funeral for the Most Excellent Gentleman, Sir
Enrique Luis Ximenez Calvo, Vice Consul for Spain in Paris,
vilely assassinated by the enemies of the Fatherland. His
widow, the Most Excellent Lady Matilde Gil Patricio of Ximenez, his daughters, Pilar and Marta, and his friends of the
Spanish Colony in Paris, entreat a prayer for the eternal repose
of his Soul . . .'

Diego stood there, blinking at those words. They didn't

mean anything, of course. They couldn't. They were part and parcel of stupid bourgeois superstitions, designed to enslave the unwary with their pious cant. And yet——

And yet he stood there with them blurring out of clarity before his suddenly scalded eyes because their stately solemn *Spanish* majesty had moved him so.

"Thou!" he howled almost aloud. "Thou unsayable of all bad milk! It was *not* my fault! And wherever thou art thou knowest that! I had no wish nor desire nor even will to kill thee even though thou hadst destroyed every certitude I had! Oh thou thing of evil cunning. Oh decadent *cabrón* of a bourgeois. I this unto the milk of thy mother. I that upon the tomb of thy father. I——"

But cursing the dead man did no good, not even in so awesome a vehicle for cursing as Spanish is. So he stopped it. Bowed his head. Crept into the church.

From where they stood, fifty meters from one another on the *trottoir* across the street from the church, a vantage point far enough away from it so that they could watch all the approaches to it with ease, the two plainclothesmen from the Sûreté saw him go inside. At once they started converging upon the church doors at a dead run, drawing their Browning automatics as they came, and cursing themselves under their breaths because they had already made a mistake, a very gross error, in not moving in the moment this boy had stopped to read the bulletins before l'église espagnole.

They hadn't for two reasons: seeing his shabby worker's clothes, they'd assumed that he'd only paused out of idle curiosity; and his blond hair had convinced them that he couldn't be Spanish. But nowadays, who could tell? There was a whole internationale of terrorists who aided one another. No one had expected those three Japanese at Lod Airport near Tel Aviv to start shooting either, since they obviously were not Arabs. Could not a blond Irishman from the IRA be doing his bit for the Basque Liberation Movement, the ETA? And if this long, gawky type of an imbecilic *salaud* had even one grenade in his pocket, just one—all those sleek, dark exquisite Spanish women who had been giving them both a testicular ache all morning would be *foutues* et *fichues,* not to mention their own careers and any future promotions!

By then they were there. One of them paused in the big double doors. Nodded to the other, who raced around back of the church. The Sûreté man in the front entrance waited until he was sure his colleague had had time to cover the back door. Then he moved in quietly, slipping his pistol back into his shoulder holster, but keeping his hand on it, just in case.

Then he saw the boy. He was kneeling in a back pew with his big, red hands folded in the attitude of prayer. He had lifted his face towards the altar. From one of the stained glass windows beyond him the morning sunlight streamed down and made multicolored jewels of the tears on his face.

The *flic* took his hand off his gun. Relaxed. He had had much experience of political terrorists by then. They danced, whooping with delight around the mangled, charred bodies of their victims. They gave the V for victory sign. They crowed, boasted of their crimes, no matter how fiendish, how irrational. But they *never* cried. Or showed any signs of either shame or remorse. Or—of grief . . .

He studied the boy quietly. A pretty lad for all his awkward, gawky looks. Perhaps *M. le Vice Consul espagnol* had been a pederast. And this boy his lover.

He shrugged. He'd question the boy, of course. But he didn't expect to find out anything useful anymore. The killers were hundreds of kilometers away by now. Safely back in Spain likely. Aside from a bit of spicy gossip to drop into *sa* Berthe's eager ear, he'd get nothing of value from the odd encounter, he was sadly sure.

Diego knelt there. What he was trying to do was say a prayer. But he didn't know any prayers. He had never been christened or baptized. His mother had prevented that. She was very religious about her politics, very pure. And it came to Diego that in this it had been his father not his mother who had been right. "There are times when you *need* a prayer, *hijo*," Jaime Fernández often said, "not to save the soul you may not even have; but your sanity, your reason, your identity, your sense of who and what you are. And the questions of whether that prayer is meaningful or meaningless, or whether there's anyone up there to hear it or not, matter less than what the mule leaves behind him on the road, as long as it eases all the places and the ways you're hurting. . . ."

The Spanish priest who preached the funeral sermon was very old—a relic, surely, from the Civil War. And, as such, he was naturally choking with rage. He called down heaven's wrath upon the heads of the dastardly assassin who had deprived Spain of the services, and this weeping family of the love and protection of so good and just a gentleman. The longer he preached, the more violent his language became until finally his very fire-breathing curses upon—as always—"*¡Los Rojos!*" "The Reds," began to comfort Diego.

They did that because they reminded the boy of the book his father was writing, or more accurately, compiling. It was called *El Libro de las Abominaciones, The Book of Abominations.* And it was going to be, Jaime Fernández Quesada insisted, the only 100-percent fair book ever written about the Spanish Civil War. Because on one page, his father placed the most fiendish crimes he could find committed by the Republicans, and then on the page opposite it, an equally fiendish crime, as similar to the first as he could dig up, committed by the Franquistas. So in one page, if he put the murder of Asalto Teniente Jose Castillo by Jose Antonio Primo de Rivera's Falangist bully boys before the very eyes of his new bride, on the next he described the murder of Calvo Sotelo, the Fascist leader, at the hands of the Republican Assault Guards in revenge for the first killing. The execution of young Primo de Rivera by the Republic was balanced by the revenge execution of the young son of Largo Caballero, the Socialist leader, by the Franquistas, and so on.

It made sickening reading. And it left one with an appalled sense of the implacable Grecian nature of the Spanish tragedy. Diego had stopped reading it long ago. It made life, and human destiny, seem too damned hopeless.

But now, suddenly, the old priest's spluttering vituperations reminded him of two of the best stories, verified, as were all his father's stories, by impeccable eyewitness accounts, of the Catholic priest who made wounded Republican militiamen in Extremadura, including a bleeding fifteen-year-old girl, dig their own graves, and then buried them—alive. Or how the same priest blew out the brains of the militiamen, gut shot and dying, who had taken refuge in a church in Badajoz, before the very altar of Him who had taught forgiveness, preached mercy. . . .

But the minute he remembered that, the opposite page crashed into his mind: How the Republican militiamen at Navalmorales, hearing the parish priest say he wanted to suffer for Christ, stripped him, scourged him, put a crown of thorns on his head, tied a load of wood to his back, gave him vinegar to drink, then offered him his life in exchange for one good, hearty blasphemy. But when the priest refused, they merely shot him, saying crucifixion would honor him too much . . .

He bowed his head, shuddering. Murderers one and all, and now, he——

Then he heard the rustle of silk. Smelt that perfume. Looking up he saw a girl coming toward him, not from the back of the Church, but from the front, from among the more intimate circle of the mourners. She was a thin little thing, with a pert and perky turned up nose of the kind that always got a girl called *chata* in Spain, and a mouth much too big for her bony, emaciated face. Her lips were shockingly thick. Thicker than those of some black Senegalese girls he had known. He could see the bones in the hollow of her neck, and across her upper chest, because her black silk dress was simply too big for her, in spite of the modesty of its cut.

'Borrowed,' he decided; then he saw her eyes.

They were a shade as close to pale violet—actually lavender, he realized with sudden wonder—as it was possible for
human eyes to get, which made them almost as startling as her
mouth in her deeply tanned face. Her hair was jet black, and
close cropped into a short gamine's cut. Like a boy's. But there
was nothing boyish about her. Even as thin as she was. Even
with those tiny breasts her tunic showed.

Then something about the dress itself caught his attention.
It looked rather like the kind that pregnant women wear. He
stared at her belly. But the dress was too loose; the church, too
dark. He couldn't be sure.

By then she was beside his borrowed pew. So close he
could see her nostrils flare, read what was in those oddly—for
a brunette—wrong-colored eyes. Hatred. Bottomless, quivering, total. 'Why,' he thought, 'she'd kill me if she could!'

"Move over!" she hissed in French. "Make room for me!"

Dumbly he moved. She slid into the pew, all boneless
grace. Bowed her head, murmured wordless sounds. Crossed
herself. Said, her lips unmoving, her voice flat, controlled, tone-
less: "Ernesto wants to see you. The usual place. And that's an
order, understand!"

"Yes, comrade," he said softly. "I understand."

"Don't call me comrade, damn you!" she said.

He shrugged.

"Very well mademoiselle," he murmured. "Or is it—
madame?"

"Neither—to you!" she spat; and then her voice drowned.
He could see the sobs she was locking in by sheer will swell and
quiver and torture her throat.

"What's wrong?" he said. "What passes with you,
mademoiselle? What is it that to you arrives?"

"Him," she got out, her voice a grate, a scrape, a long,
slow tearing. "I loved him, you comprehend that? He was—my
man. Not *hers!* Not ever of that stupid aristocratic machine for
making babies! You put in *deux sous* worth of *saucisson et—voilà*

—*un bébé!* Oh damn Spanish women anyhow! That's all they're fit for! To breed! Never to be—lovers. Never to pant—and scream and die and burst and explode and go to heaven and to hell as he could make me do every time! And you—you grubby, unwashed, lowbred murdering swine, you've killed him!"

"*Ça, oui,*" he said sadly. "That, yes. But with an infinity of regrets, and with a sorrow insupportable. I think it will render me mad if——"

She turned then. Stared at him.

"You cried," she said accusingly. "*Vous avez pleuré! Pourquoi?* Why? I saw you!"

"I know," he began; but then he saw that the service was over and that mourners were filing past the open coffin to gaze down into the dead Vice Consul's face. He got up. Took her arm. Said: "Come."

"No!" she hissed. "Not with you! We mustn't be seen together. You cretin! Go ahead—I'll follow you."

He stood there staring at that too-still face. At the white bandage around the top of the dead man's head. The 9 millimeter parabellum bullet had mushroomed after tearing through the back of the Vice Consul's head. Had made an exit hole coming out you could shove your fist into. Had showered the upper wall and part of the ceiling with bone splinters, thick globs of blood, and grayish-pink brain tissue. Splattered more of the same as he fell into the plate where his lunch——

A shaking got into Diego. Tears burst, exploded from his eyes. A hard, rough hand reached out and took his arm. Shoved him ahead.

"*D'hors!*" the man's voice said. "Outside! *Filez!* March yourself!"

But before they had had time to growl anything more—in their *si exquise voix de flics*—than: "*Vos papiers! Documents. Carte d'Identité!*" which he produced at once, gave to them, because like those of all the Party specialists who did what he did, they weren't even false but real and legal and he had a provable cover for every word they said, a tall woman came through the door. A hauntingly beautiful woman in her early forties—even with her eyes red and swollen almost shut she still was—followed by two younger, but much less beautiful duplicates of herself.

"Let him go, *messieurs les agents,*" she said quietly. "*He* had nothing to do with it. Of that, I am sure."

"But, *Madame la Vice Consul,*" the Sûreté agent said, "how can you be so sure?"

"He cried," she answered. "Murderers don't cry, *m'sieur l'agent.* At least not the kind of cold-blooded political assassins who killed my husband."

"There, you may be right," the Sûreté man said, "but all the same . . ."

"Then let *me* question him," the Vice Consul's widow said.

The Sûreté men stared at her. At each other. Shrugged.

"*Comment vous appellez-vous?*" the Vice Consul's widow said. "What's your name?"

"*Me llamo Diego,*" Diego said. "*A servirla, mi señora.*"

"Spanish!" the two Sûreté men roared. "Why—"

"*¿Y tus apellidos?* And your family names?"

"Fernández. Lluis-Puig," Diego said.

"That's an odd combination," Señora Ximenez said. "Your mother was Catalan, then? And your father?"

"Asturiano," Diego said.

"Tell me, *hijo*—why did you come to my husband's funeral? And—what made you—cry?"

"He was—my friend," Diego said simply. "My patron, too —but more my friend. You see—"

"Could not all this be said in French?" the Sûreté man said.

"*Oui. D'accord,*" Diego said. "His Excellency, *M'sieur le Vice Consul,* was my patron. And my friend. You see, I work at the Peugeot repair shop in la rue de la Forge. Near the Étoile. And one day, he brought in his convertible for an overhaul. A five-oh-four, motor of injection. Nice *bolide,* that. We got to talking—the chief of the shop was home sick that day. I heard his accent and addressed him in Spanish. He—was pleased. Asked me details of my parents——"

"Refugees?" the Sûreté man put in. "Republican refugees?"

"Yes," Diego said simply, "but I was born here, in Paris, *m'sieur l'agent*. I am a Frenchman. I have no part in quarrels settled long before I was born. My mother—remains bitter. Her first husband was shot by the Franquistas after Oviedo was taken. My two half-brothers and my half-sister were destroyed by the bombs the German Kondor Legion dropped on the port of Barcelona after she had gone back there with them near the close of the war. But my father, having been a prisoner in Russia until 1948, renounced his Communist beliefs because of what he experienced there. He has rejoined the church. Goes to mass twice a week. I—I go with him sometimes—"

" *Which* church?" the Sûreté man rapped out. "What is the name of the priest?"

"Sainte Roquette. In the street of the same name, near the Place of the Bastille. Père Dubois," Diego said.

The Sûreté man came out with a notebook. Wrote that down. But he knew it would check out. The boy hadn't even hesitated.

"But why did you come to the funeral?" Matilde said.

"He was—kind to me. Treated me—almost as an equal, señora. Talked to me, listened to my views. Corrected my mistakes in Spanish. Whenever he had to pass through l'Étoile and had a few minutes to spare, he would detour into la rue de la Forge and chat with me. Three minutes. Five. I—I—" Diego's voice choked up on him. "I loved him. Like my own father. No—more. He was so—good-natured. So—happy. So—kind. . . ."

"Oh, let the boy go!" Matilde said. "Can't you see he's telling the truth? That's just the way Enrique was. A democrat. A lover of the people. A real one. Spanish aristocrats quite often are, you know." She turned back to Diego.

"Thank you for coming—son," she whispered.

"No hay de que, señora," Diego said. "Don't mention it." Turned to go. Stared straight into those pale, pansy-colored eyes. They were unsettled now, troubled. There seemed to be a little less hatred in them.

"Yeux de fleur," he murmured. *"Lèvres de negresse. Visage de singe. Mais, comme même——"* "Flower eyes. Lips of a negress. Monkey face. But, all the same—"

Then he moved away from there, slouching along, his gait easy, casual, neither slow nor fast.

But all the time, as he went, until he was out of sight of the little group of people before l'église espagnole, and even after that, he could feel those flower eyes burning holes in his back.

The moment he got to "the usual place," a Left Bank quai-side bookstall, run by a German Jewish immigrant who, naturally, was also a member of the Party, Diego saw Ernesto coming up the quai towards him.

And, as always, he felt sick. Gut sick and cold and more than a little afraid. Camarada Ernesto. Or, as he had been known in Cuba, where he had been—among other things— liaison man between the Soviets and the Castristas at the time of the missile crisis, Ernesto "Rubles" Raminez. Which wasn't his name, either. His name, Diego's father swore, was Ernst Grünwald. And he was, maybe, a Czechoslovakian. Maybe. What he was, really, was a robot. A cybernetic robot, existing at absolute zero, as far as anything remotely resembling human warmth was concerned, out of whose mouth poured, in five or six different languages, none of which showed any trace of a foreign accent, a stream of Party directives, followed immediately, of course, by his own calmly expressed, closely reasoned interpretations and explanations of those directives.

It was, Diego realized now, these explanations and interpretations, rather than the directives themselves, that were true masterpieces of creative literary art. For so wonderfully were they designed to still the qualms of the lower and middle hierarchy—to which by then, Diego, through sheer competence and devotion, legitimately belonged—over the meanderings of the Party line, over its not infrequent flat contradictions, that it had taken Diego months to realize the simple fact that close to 90 percent of Camarada Ernesto's weighty and subtle directives in support of each and every party position, regardless of its importance or its lack of it, maintained not even a nodding acquaintance with either logic or common sense.

But Diego had resigned himself to that finally, just as a good Catholic eventually must to the dogma of his church. And for much the same reason. In fact, he had even known, vaguely, but in a strange way, truly, what that reason was. Up until he had met the Vice Consul, anyhow, he had accepted—with reservations—the basic syllogisms of Marxist dialectics; but Enrique Ximenez had made him doubt them, had torn him loose from —or chipped out from under him!—the few bleak and barren bedrocks to which he anchored his world. Which was an agonizing thing, not easily to be borne.

"I *need* the Party," he told himself now again, trying once more to find something solid enough to cling to in a suddenly terrifying world that was dissolving all around him. "Without it, what am I? Nothing. *Merde.* A poor bastard. A member of the proletariat. While with it, *within* it, I am—somebody. I pull a little weight. Not much, but—some. People—comrades— respect me. They know I'm good at what I do. That I can be relied upon. Even Ernesto respects my—competence. But is this enough? No. It's not. As Don Enrique pointed out, I am neither blind, nor a fool. The Party is—far from blameless. Still, what it does—its *aims,* anyhow, its goals—must be carried out by someone, some organization. The someone—me. The organization—it. Even though its methods are ripping my guts to bloody shreds. So I've got a bourgeois conscience. *Merde alors!* Why not? What's wrong with a bourgeois conscience? Better a bourgeois conscience than no conscience at all. Maybe the Party *will* end the social injustices of capitalism, someday. Then comrades like me—with my *sacré* bourgeois conscience!—will be necessary to overthrow the new *socialist* injustices people like Ernesto are busily putting in the old ones' place. Worse injustices, likely. Which is why Papa was wrong to—desert. To concern himself about his hypothetical soul. Better to stay. When the Revolution comes, we're going to need decent comrades to keep people like this fat, white, bald, utterly repulsive slug from enslaving the whole *enmerdeur* world . . ."

He said now, aloud: *"Hola,* Ernesto . . ."

"¡Hola, matón!" Ernesto said.

Diego stared at him. But, apparently, Ernesto wasn't being sarcastic. He was even smiling. That, "Hello, killer!" had been approving, then? Or had it? With Camarada Ernesto one could never be sure.

"Let's walk," Ernesto said, and took Diego's arm. Diego didn't say anything. They moved off, together.

"Good show, that of our aristocratic little Spanish fascist," Ernesto said. "Of course, we *could* have used the money, but——"

"But what?" Diego said.

"A most exemplary aristocratic corpse is not to be sneered at either. Induces confusion among the enemies of the people. Even—fear . . ."

Diego didn't say anything.

"But there's one detail I confess I don't understand—that eludes me, shall we say?" Ernesto said softly.

Hearing his tone, his voice gone low and tender as a lover's, Diego's breath turned to ice in his lungs. His genitals contracted. Tried to crawl up into his belly. Perform an autocastration on him. Because Ernesto always sounded that way when he was contemplating the liquidation of an erring comrade. One who had fallen by the wayside, gone soft, betrayed the Party. Or—simply failed.

"And that is?" Diego said. His voice didn't go reedy. Or

shake. He was glad of that much, anyhow.

"How the gentleman—*el ilustrísimo caballero*—got out of those leg irons. Could you enlighten me on *that* point, camarada?"

"Of course," Diego said. "*I* unlocked them. Took them off."

"So?" Ernesto said.

"*¡Maldita séa!*" Diego exploded. "Goddamnit, Ernesto, he was bleeding! Those cuffs had rubbed his flesh raw. And I was given the strictest instructions—from *you,* I was told, camarada! —were they?"

"That he was not to be ill treated? Yes. They were. But from there to unlocking the leg irons, camarada?"

"There, I admit to a mistake," Diego said. "Not in taking off *las esposas,* because he'd have got gangrene and died if I hadn't. But in taking them *both* off at the same time. I should have removed one, dusted his wounds with sulfa powder, bandaged it, and put the cuff back on, before going on to the other. But I didn't. He seemed so—harmless—"

"And?" Ernesto said.

Diego turned his left cheek towards Ernesto. The blue bruise was beginning to turn yellowish now.

Ernesto smiled.

"I see. He had to prove his *machismo,* his *hombria,* his valor, his fiery Spanish blood?"

"Yes," Diego said.

"And then—you shot him?" Ernesto said.

"Yes," Diego said, his voice the silence, beneath all sound.

"A fact which you now—regret?" Ernesto said.

"Yes!" Diego said defiantly. "It wasn't necessary! I should have hit him over the head with the gun barrel. Or——"

"Only you—got rattled?" Ernesto said.

"Only I got rattled," Diego said. "So? Am I up for disciplinary action? Do I have to present an autocriticism of my conduct before the cell?"

"No," Ernesto said gently. "Your instincts—are sound, camarada. Only you retain a stronger residue of bourgeois sentimentality than I had thought. Your father's fault, likely. Poor Jaime! Not enough iron in his soul, I sadly fear . . ."

"You leave my father alone, Ernesto!" Diego flared.

"*Mais oui! Mais certainement! Pourquoi pas?* He's no danger to us. He is—unfortunately—a finished man, *ton père.* Let him go to church, beat his breast, weep his mea culpas! Such a one can never harm us. I, camarada, am more disturbed by the faint traces of rot I begin to see in you. You were one of our best. You can be again. Only you'll have to work at it. . . ."

"And if I don't? If I *won't?*" Diego said.

Ernesto shrugged. Smiled softly, tenderly.

"Don't force me to answer that, camarada," he said.

"They will find me floating in the Seine," Diego grated. "With a bullet through the back of my head."

"Or perhaps they will *never* find you," Ernesto said. "The possibilities for corrective action are—limitless, camarada. Oh come now! Let us not be morbid! And to spare you unnecessary worry, Comrade Diego, allow me to tell you that I was opposed to the tactic of kidnapping Vice Consul Ximenez in the first place . . ."

"You *were?*" Diego said.

"Yes. I don't believe in threats. Only in action. Holding a man for ransom puts us on the level of the Mafia, say. Threatening to blow up an airplane if money is not paid, or some idiots are not released from jail, who, by the very fact that they got caught in the first place, have demonstrated their uselessness as operatives for any serious organization. But terror—implacable terror—is quite another thing! Keep your enemy wondering if he's going to be alive tomorrow. Or if his wife and his children are. Or if his beautiful home is going to remain standing. Or —if the Embassy of his country is—shall we say?"

"Ernesto——" Diego whispered.

"Those things undermine his efficiency, make him—and

his cause—far more prone to failure. But in the case of *su excelencia, el ilustrísimo caballero,* Señor Don Enrique Luis Ximenez-Calvo, I was overruled—by *my* superiors in the Party hierarchy. With the result that we find ourselves in a most unsavory mess—thanks, in part, to you, camarada! Now, tell me: Why did you go to his funeral?"

"Well—" Diego floundered. "I—"

"No, don't. You waste my time—and yours. The truth is, you really don't *know,* do you? *Why* you went, I mean?"

"No," Diego said. "I really don't."

"Doesn't matter. Only, unfortunately, it has blown your cover. Or come uncomfortably close to blowing it, at any rate. And *that* you can scarcely afford at the moment— *¿verdad?* Not after playing with fireworks all over Paris last night."

Diego licked bone-dry lips.

"Ernesto—" he said.

"Of course I knew it was you!" Ernesto said. "You—my creation. Your tactics were absolutely brilliant. Used timers, didn't you? So that when the police were rushing in to apprehend the terrorist at one explosion, you were already engaged in blowing up something else on the other side of town. Oh, yes. Brilliant! Or rather, without false modesty, *my* tactics were. You have been a good pupil, camarada! Quite the best I've ever had . . ."

"Yes," Diego said. "I only had to remember all the the things you taught me, *camarada jefe . . .*"

"But your application of them wasn't half bad," Ernesto said. "No, to give you your due, they were very fine indeed. Even—splendid. Which is why I have forgiven you for that of the Vice Consul. Forgiven you completely. In fact, you've a nice little vacation coming up. To rest your shattered nerves, say. In Spain."

"In Spain!" Diego said.

"Yes. Why not? Lovely country, Spain. I enjoyed my stay there—nineteen thirty-four through nineteen thirty-nine. I found it quite—lively. Of course I don't remember it any too well. I was very young then. Younger than you are now."

"Ernesto——" Diego said.

"I'm not joking. I'm even sending a comrade along—to keep you company. The dear little creature who passed along my message to you in church this morning. You see, I *knew* that's what you'd do . . ."

"You knew I'd——"

"Go to the funeral? Yes, why, yes; of course. Romantic sentimentalists are *so* predictable, camarada."

"And that girl will——"

"Go with you. She will be—your wife for the occasion. A pair of emigrant workers returning to *la patria* out of sheer nostalgia. Touching, isn't it?"

"Ernesto, I don't think——"

"You never think, I sadly fear. Incidentally, you may use her as such if she'll let you. *That* should calm your nerves enough for what you have to do in Spain. . . ."

"A—a job?" Diego said.

"Yes. Not for us, though. For our dear, dear friends of the ETA, *Euzkadi ta Azkatasuna—Vasconia Libre . . .*"

"They're fools!" Diego said.

"Of course! But such useful fools, camarada. They maintain, at great cost to themselves, an unrest that otherwise *we'd* have to supply—at the price of blood. So, whenever we can, we oblige them—"

"What's the job?" Diego said.

"You cross the frontier with your lovely, blushing bride. Oh I take that back. Ana María's hardly lovely, is she? But she *is* a sexy little piece. Obsessional behavior. Compensation for her inferiority complex. 'Even if my poor little tail is bony, at least I know how to move it, lover!' That sort of thing . . ."

"A nympho?" Diego said.

"No. I wouldn't say so. In fact, I doubt there is any such thing. One man's nymphomaniac is another man's frigid wife. Haven't you found it that way?"

"Yes," Diego said. "Not that I'm anybody's *tenorio,* but——"

"Then she'll be good for you. I'll wager she'll crawl all over you *before* you reach the frontier."

Diego shrugged. Then he remembered something.

"Tell me, camarada—is she *Spanish?*" he said.

"*De los cuatro costados.* On all four sides," Ernesto said. "Why?"

"Something she said. She cursed all Spanish women. Violently. And vilely. In French."

"Fits. A part of her self-hatred. Maybe you can cure her. . . ."

Diego stared at him.

"But—the job?" he said.

"Quite simple. Our friends in Madrid will give you a package. You will deliver that package to a certain place. After that you will come home. Without dear little Ana María, of course. She'll be staying a while. With her parents, los Condes de Casaribiera. . . ."

"What!" Diego said.

"Why yes, she's an aristocrat. And a traitor to her class. Out of conviction, which makes her a *very* good operator. Her connections are of the best. She is related by blood to the class of people who, when invited to *el Pardo,* the residence of the Head of State, can, and *do* refuse to go. And get away with it. The ones who no longer speak to the Duke of Cadiz since he married Franco's pretty little granddaughter—though I honestly believe he did it for love. A charming thought, what? Oh, yes, our little Ana María will be useful in Spain. Very!"

"Ernesto——" Diego said.

"Yes, camarada?"

"The job, Ernesto. The *job.*"

"I've told you. You receive a package. And deliver it. That's all."

"As once someone delivered a similar package to—the Admiral?"

"Camarada, it is *unwise* to know too much. What you don't know, not even those gorillas at *la Dirección General de Seguridad* can beat out of you."

Diego looked at him. Said: "I am to do this thing out of Party discipline, then? And to prove to you, *camarada jefe,* that I have not gone soft?"

"No. You are to do it because it is necessary. And because their *Segunda Bis* knows every operative that ETA could send. The personage in question is *very* dangerous. To ETA and to *us.* He is in the sense that he has both the will and the intelligence to take the reins in a strong hand when the *Caudillo* dies. He alone could prevent the chaos we're counting on from taking place. He could squelch the bickering between the various idiotic bands of Monarchists, halt the palace intrigues against Juanito in favor of the Duke of Cadiz, and of the Carlistas against them both. He would smash the Old Shirt Unmovables, dreaming of not only keeping the clock stopped, but actually turning it backwards, putting into practice the retarded adolescent's ravings of their martyred dilettante leader—flatten them like the fat, sluggish worms they are without a qualm. He will not even favor Opus Dei, although he belongs to it. With him in power, ETA will get *nowhere.* Nor the Catalan separatists with their mad hope for an independent Cataluña. And waiting in the wings to mop up the blood—*our* classic tactic—will be worse than useless. In fact, it will be futile——"

"The President of the Government?" Diego said. "I've heard he's *very* strong . . ."

"You do not know. You will never know. It is not useful for you to know. All that you do know is this: If you do your work well, it will contribute towards Spain's being freed finally of the longest-lasting political, intellectual, and moral slavery that the twentieth century has yet known. And perhaps the deepest, the most stifling. Is this not reason enough for you to act, camarada?"

Diego thought about that. A long time. A very long time.

Lifted his grave blue eyes. Let his gaze rest upon Ernesto's face.

"Yes. It is enough. And I will do it, camarada," he said.

Before he started home to his mother's grubby little flat in the rue de St. Gilles just off the Boulevard Beaumarchais in the Third Arrondissement, he had it all—every detail, committed to memory, since, as always, his instructions from Ernesto had been verbal. He was not to leave at once but to wait until la Sûreté had finished investigating him. *Le garagiste* in la rue de la Forge would give him a clean bill of health: *bon gosse*; good worker, quiet, never in trouble so far as he knew. Why yes, the Spanish diplomat used to stop and chat with the kid; but surely *messieurs les agents* didn't believe——

And the priest at the church his father went to. He was young, and of the type called *prêtres ouvriers,* worker priests; sometimes even, *prêtres rouges,* Red priests. He'd give anyone a clean bill of health in order to frustrate *les flics,* at whose hands he'd suffered; and whom he cordially hated. And Diego had completed his military service with—acting on the strictest orders from the Party—an exemplary record. "Apolitical," his ex-officers would honestly swear. *Bon gosse. Sage.* A good kid.

But only after that could he leave for the frontier. To bolt now would convince the police that he was, after all, afraid of something; that he was running away.

"You will be advised—by telephone," Ernesto had said. "We will check with your employer and the priest. Both are sympathizers of ours—fellow travelers, you might say. With the army, of course, we cannot check, but knowing how la Sûreté works, we will simply allow four additional days. Meanwhile your behavior must be scrupulously normal. Go to work. Hang out at your usual places. You might even go to mass with your father next Sunday. That would be a nice, reassuring note to the police. . . ."

"And—the girl? Ana María? I am not to see her?"

"Of course not, you cretin! She lives in Passy. In one of

those obscenely luxurious apartments on the avenue Foch. That would really blow things, *camarada*! If you're that hard up, I can advance you the price of a *poule.* Even a sleek, expensive poule —of the type that drive around the Étoile at night in Jaguars. Or at least they used to. With this of the price of *essence* these days I cannot say . . ."

Diego looked at Ernesto.

Did the thick, short, glossily bald little comrade *ever* make use of a woman? Or was he a homosexual as was sometimes whispered in Party circles?

Neither, Diego decided. Camarada Ernesto had no emotions at all beyond his all-encompassing devotion to the Party. He was in many ways—a monk. A Red monk, and Communism was his religion. He even sounded like one, having the soft, blurred, occasionally reedy voice of the at least emotionally castrated that all priests and monks seemed to have.

"No, thank you, comrade," Diego said shortly. "I haven't yet been reduced to buying it."

"Why not?" Ernesto said. "It's a commodity like any other. And purchase—outright purchase—would seem to be wiser. Avoid emotional entanglements that way. Unless you're the type of abject sentimentalist who falls in love with whores . . ."

"I don't fall in love—period." Diego said. "Women are an encumbrance. In the service of the Party, one can't afford excess baggage . . ."

"Good!" Ernesto said.

"But how am I to pick up your little Red *condesa*?" Diego said. "Drive up the avenue Foch and park before her door?

"Of course not. The night before, she will leave her expensive flat, with absolutely no luggage at all, except her purse, and an ordinary plastic shopping bag. In that bag she'll have a poorly made, cheap, badly cut dress of the type that working girls buy at Galeries Lafayette."

"The plastic bag had better *not* have Galeries Lafayette's

name on it," Diego pointed out, "or the taxi driver might notice that fact as odd. The name of some boutique on the rue Faubourg St. Honoré, say. But then they don't pack in plastic bags, do they? A cardboard box—a damned good one, with expensive nylon cords, and the name of the boutique embossed in gold."

Ernesto nodded his glistening bald head admiringly.

"Good! Ve-ery good!" he said. "Knew you'd snap out of the blue funk you've been in! But still—a plastic bag. From one of the in-between shops near the Madeleine. Rich girls *do* shop in 'em, you know. Because the sort of box you mention, while tactically correct, would cry out to be noticed, while the taxi driver might not remember a plastic bag at all."

"I see," Diego said. "And you're right. Go on, comrade."

"She'll ask to be driven somewhere—to Café de la Paris, for instance. Get out. Walk. Until she gets to Galeries Printemps, say. Go in. Do a little shopping, toothbrush, soap, Tampax, perfume; the cheap kind of perfume she'll need. Go into the women's lavatory. Into a pay toilet. Change there. Put her good dress, her expensive shoes, her smart purse into the plastic bag. *Et voilà!* Out comes *une petite midinette*—on her way back to work after lunch . . ."

"And?" Diego said.

"She goes down into the métro. A taxi at this point would be too dangerous. Takes a third-class car up to le Gare St. Lazare. Enters a dingy hotel where a room has already been reserved in her name, and where her luggage for the trip will be waiting. And *yours,* for that matter . . ."

"Isn't that risky?"

"No. We *own* that hotel. Just as we own a half interest in the garage where you work. Or did you think that *votre patron* was a benevolent sentimentalist?"

"Go on," Diego said.

"She will call you at your home . . ."

"No," Diego said. *"You* call me, Ernesto. Or have someone else do it. A man."

"Why?" Ernesto said.

"My mother is, as you know, of the Party. But she is also Spanish. *Very* Spanish. She would question me all night if a girl called whose voice she does not know—"

Ernesto smiled at him.

"Does she know many female voices?" he said.

"Almost none. I have forbidden them to call me at the flat. And they are very few, anyhow."

"Good!" Ernesto said.

"Go on, camarada—please."

"A man will call you. Give you the name and address of the hotel. You will descend from your mother's flat. A 'special' will be parked before your door. You will enter it, using the keys you will have received by mail a day or two before, drive to the hotel where your blushing bride will be awaiting you, and the two of you will leave Paris by any route you choose— as long as it heads south by west. *Voilà toute.* Any questions?

"Yes. How am I to know the 'special'?"

"You will recognize it at once: It will be an ancient two-oh-four. So old, in fact, that you will doubt that you can arrive in it to the next corner. But under its hood will be the motor of a five-oh-four injection. Hotter than Ana María's *'tite queue malpropre*—"

"Doesn't she wash?" Diego said, because Ernesto's argôt phrase meant, "Ana María's dirty little tail."

"Excessively. I only make a joke, camarada. The tires will be Michelin, radial, with steel wire cording, and racing treads. The suspension will be special too—a bit uncomfortable I'm afraid, but so stiff that you will be able to outcorner absolutely anything, including a D.S. twenty-three Pallas. As for speed only a jet plane could catch you, and it only with difficulty. I need not remind you that none of these odd characteristics of that ancient wreck are to be displayed unnecessarily, do I?"

"No. And the brakes?"

"Racing-type discs on all four wheels. Double hydraulic lines to each of these. Plus mechanical linkage to the back pair.

I do not wish you dead, camarada. Fortunately you drive well. Any other questions?"

"Yes. One. How in the name of Camarada Mao are you going to find a place to park the 'special' before my door? Or for that matter, *anywhere* in Paris including atop the Eiffel Tower?"

"A good question. Just before your special arrives a tow-truck bearing the sign of a well-known repair service will remove whatever vehicle is parked before your door. After you have departed, they will bring it back. The only element of risk is the possibility of the owner's awakening and catching them at it, *before* you descend to the street. Should that happen, he will suffer a blow of a blackjack to his cranium, I sadly fear. But since he will presently wake up in the back seat of his own auto, safely parked again just where he left in the first place, and with nothing missing, he will very likely begin to doubt whether what he thought he was witnessing actually occurred at all. So I shouldn't worry about even that contingency if I were you. Besides you can surely prevent such an unfortunate contretemps from ever happening by getting out of your place fast enough and soon enough. Four A.M. sharp. *D'accord?*"

"Yes. *D'ac.* ¡*Salud,* Camarada Ernesto!" Diego said.

When he got back to the flat he shared with his mother, she was already there, waiting for him. She was sixty-four years old now, having been born exactly one year to the day after the tragic risings of July 1909 in Barcelona, and having given birth to him at the ripe age of forty.

"Diego, *hijo*," she said at once, "tell me—"

"What, *Madre?*" Diego said. At home, he spoke Spanish. He had to. Or else Libertad would have given him no peace.

"This of last night. All those bombings. Were any of them —yours? I mean, were you involved in any of them?"

"No, *Madre*," Diego lied, thinking: 'You worry enough about me now, ¡*pobrecita de mi alma!* So I hope I can pull this one off. I'm not good at lying to you, *Madrecita mía.* And I don't like having to do it. But today, I must. For your sake. For your own comfort, I simply must . . .'

She studied him.

"You look like the bad death, my son," she said at last. "Didn't you sleep last night—wherever *los demonios* it was that you were?"

"Badly. My *maldita* stomach again. And I wasn't with a *chica,* if that's what you're thinking. I haven't a girl. You know that. At least not such a one as I could spend the night with. I haven't since——"

"That last *idiota de una francesa* threw herself into the Seine over you. Then where were you, that you didn't come home all night?"

"At a meeting. A special meeting. We were just finishing when those bombings started. So Ernesto thought it wiser that we stay there 'til daylight. So the *flics* wouldn't pick any of us up. And so we could plan a defense when they accuse us of it —as they will. . . ."

He rubbed his hand over his middle. His stomach *did* hurt. As always when his nerves were shot to hell. Libertad saw the gesture.

"Oh, damn the Party anyhow!" she said. "You must eat at better restaurants. They should allow you that . . ."

"It would blow my cover. A garage mechanic couldn't afford to eat in the kind of places I'd have to in order to cure my busted gut. Besides, it's mostly nerves, anyhow . . ."

Libertad stared at her tall, blond, much too thin son.

"Sure you weren't mixed up in those bombings, *hijo?*" she said.

"Quite sure," Diego said. *"¡Segurísimo!"*

"Good. You're all I've got, you know. Since *los aviones* of the Nazis and the Italians slaughtered your half-brothers in the bombing of Barcelona."

"Don't think about that, *Madre,*" Diego said.

"I think about it all the time," Libertad said. "I will think about it *hasta mi propia muerte.* 'Til the day I die. And I shall have no peace until they are avenged, finally. They and all the children of the people—those of Durango, for I was there and saw their tiny, broken bodies, like dismembered dolls, *hijo,* except that their blood was red!—and those of Guernica, and Irun and San Sebastian and Madrid, itself, and a hundred places more—who were slaughtered so that the *señoritos* and the *militares* could continue to enjoy their privileges, could feed like the *antropófagos, los caníbales* they were, upon the corpse of Spain. . . ."

"Then you will know peace, and soon, *mi Madre!*" Diego said, and sat down at the table.

Libertad went into the kitchenette and came out bearing their supper. They were poor, so they did not eat meat very often. That was Party policy, too. For although both Diego and his mother were very valuable operatives, the Party considered that to maintain their "cover" they had to live as poorly as possible. This had been explained to them very carefully, and they had accepted it. Later on, when they had risen in the Party hierarchy, they would be well provided for, they had been promised. They believed that too, because they had seen it happen. Even now, a month ago, Diego had been formally presented to the *Camarada Secretario General del Partido Communista Español,* Santiago Carrillo, as "one of our brightest young men—and, incidentally your namesake, *Camarada Secretario!*" This, by Ernesto, himself.

How had Ernesto found out that his real name was Santiago instead of Diego? He didn't know. But it was characteristic of Ernesto. He missed nothing, not even the smallest, seemingly totally unimportant detail . . .

Libertad put his plate down before him. He sat there staring at it. As usual it was *tortilla española,* Spanish omelette, which is nothing more than boiled chunks of white potato folded into an ordinary omelette of three or four eggs. It was greasy, tasteless, filling, relatively cheap, and if you'd been born with a Spanish stomach, as, fortunately for him, Diego had, digestible enough. But at the mere sight of it today, a scald of green nausea hit the back of his throat. He clapped his right hand over his mouth, and exploded up from his chair. He barely made it to the sink in the kitchenette. The toilet would have been too far. It was down at the end of the hall, and served all four families on that floor.

Libertad stood beside him, wiping his mouth, his forehead. "Something—I ate—for lunch," he got out. "With—what—I have to spend—the places I've got to eat in—ugh!"

"It's all right," Libertad said tenderly. "Go lie down. I'll fix you a consomme——"

"No, nothing! Nothing, *Madre*, for God!" Diego shuddered.

He couldn't tell her the truth. He couldn't. Not her—nor anyone. There was no way to, although in one way, the truth was very simple: When you've seen a potato omelette that has been knocked to the floor, stepped into, and then had human blood and brains splashed across it like tomato catsup, say, you aren't very likely to eat potato omelette again.

He lay there on his narrow cot in the cubbyhole that served him as a room and stared at the ceiling. From her own room, Diego could hear his mother's voice.

"I will call them, and tell them that I cannot return to work this evening," she was saying, "that my son is sick and——"

"No, go!" Diego said. "Do not make an enormity over a thing which has no importance at all. I have an upset stomach, true. But then I have often had an upset stomach. It is one of the diseases of the poor—though a better one than hunger, I think. All I need is rest, *Mamacita.* Believe me, I will be all right. . . ."

"Are you sure, *hijo mío*?" Libertad said. "You may even have a poisoning from tinned sardines which, as you know, can be very bad, and——"

"I ate no sardines," Diego said shortly. "And I shall be all right. If you do not get out of here and leave me in peace I shall start speaking French to you. Or bring—" he hesitated, then chose a name she was sure to know—"*ma petite* Brigitte here to share my bed——"

"Brigitte *who?*" his mother said.

"Bardot, of course," Diego said.

"Both too French and too old for thee, my son!" his mother said cheerfully. "A faded *viciosa* of forty is no prize. Bring Sophia Loren instead. Italian women are much like us, anyhow——"

"At least they yell as loud and give a man as big a headache," Diego said. "Truly I am fine now, little Mama. Getting rid of it helped. In a little while I am going to get up, and——"

"Go to see your father, doubtless," Libertad said, her voice become both frost and flint.

"With thy permission, *Madrecita*," Diego said.

"Or without it! Oh go to see that spineless eunuchoid! That witless, drunken sot! But do not betray him with that *puta gastada* of a *francesa* of his, as *she* has been trying to get you to do for years!"

"I do not believe that Lilyan is either used up or a whore," Diego said. "Though that she is French, I have no doubt. And why should I *not* help Papa a little with his homework? He is both old and tired and—"

"*¡Sin vergüenza!*" his mother yelled at him. "Shameless One!" Then, her voice softening, "If I did not know how much you love that weak and witless old fool, with his brains pickled in alcohol by now, I'd suspect—"

"What, *Mamacita?*" Diego said.

"Nothing," Libertad sighed, "thou art too much *his* son for that, and, besides—you love him . . ."

"And thou—*Madrecita*," Diego said softly, as she came into his room to kiss him good night, "thou dost not?"

She stared at her son. Nodded, slowly.

"Yes. And I, too," she whispered. "Thy father is lovable in the same way that small animals and crippled birds and all things tiny without defenses are. If he had not been idiotic enough to fall into the clutches of that used-up whore so soon after we parted, I——"

"But, *Maman!* He waited five long years!"

"Not enough. He should have waited ten," Libertad said, and kissed him. "Sure you'll be all right, *hijo?*"

"I feel fine. I feel enormous. So enormous that I shall make the not so used-up Lilyan enormously happy," Diego said.

"Take care you do not give her an enormous belly," his mother said. "Sleep a while, my son. Rest. I go. . . ."

S ome women," Lilyan said, as Diego came into his father's neat little flat, "have all the luck!" Of course she said it in her native French so it came out in a much more complicated fashion, as things generally do in that language; but that was what she meant, more or less. Though rather a bit more than less, Diego often thought. She said that every time he visited his father's place. And squeezed him, hard. And kissed him in a way that only a blind man would have described as motherly.

"Who, for instance?" Diego said, also as usual. So much of life was made up of games and rituals.

"Ta mère," Lilyan said. "Thy mother. Who else? To have a *beau garçon* like thee around *all* the time!"

"But you have Papa," Diego said, his tone abstract, remote, very nearly absent, really.

"Which means, in effect, that I have nothing at all!" Lilyan said tartly. *"Ton père! Voilà un homme!"*

"¡Hola, Papa!" Diego said, bending over, kissing his father. He was relieved to note that the old man didn't smell of wine. At least, not yet.

"Hola, hijo," Jaime said. "I must say you look like the bad death tonight——"

"Oh, no!" Lilyan said. "Speak French or I am going to anger myself very much and——"

"Thee and thy anger!" Jaime said, and smacked her across the buttocks, hard. But he switched over into French all the same.

"What is it that passes with thee, my son?" he said.

"Nothing. A bad stomach. My pay is poor and all the halfway decent restaurants cost too much these days. . . ."

"And, additionally, the cooking of thy mother would erode a stomach lined with brass," his father said. "Libertad has many virtues, but cooking is not one of them . . ."

"How affectionately you speak of her always!" Lilyan said. "Why don't you go back to her, then?"

"I would, if she would have me," Jaime said calmly. "But she won't, so the question becomes academic, does it not? I am stuck with thee, *ma chère* Lilyan. And thou with me. A fitting punishment for us both, is it not so?"

"Papa," Diego said, to change the subject, "I'll call for you Sunday. At ten thirty. That we may attend eleven o'clock mass together."

Jaime stared at his son. When he spoke, a little quaver of something—worry, fear—had got into his voice.

"Thy stomach?" he said. "It is—grave then, *mon fils*? You have seen a doctor?"

"Oh no, Papa!" Diego said. "My stomach has nothing that an improved diet would not cure. It is just that—that I have these moods of—of sadness, and I thought——"

"That taking the church, and our religion with something more of seriousness might help?" Jaime said. "It might. But then it might not. That depends. Upon so many factors——"

"It has helped you," Diego pointed out.

"That, yes. But then I am old, and tired—and—defeated," Jaime whispered. "Therefore I have become as a little child again. Ready and willing to—distrust my reason, knowing how ill it has always served me. Of how little value mere *human* reason is, anyhow. But tell me, why are you sad, my son? *Une fille?*"

"I have no girl. Not seriously, anyhow. It's not that. I listen to *Maman*—"

"*Merde alors! Cette femme!*" Lilyan exploded.

"I am all she has, Lilyan," Diego said softly. "And women *need* to be listened to. Don't you?"

"*Ça, oui,*" Lilyan said. "But she shouldn't use you to——"

"Nor should I," Jaime said sadly. "But I do, don't I, Diego? All the children of Spanish refugees have been—emotionally crippled by their fathers' pouring out upon their defenseless heads their memories of that *maldita* Civil War which was the great trauma of our lives. All of our remembered horrors. All that we suffered, endured. The bile of all our unavenged injustices—I am as guilty of that as she is. *¡Basta ya! Ça, c'est assez!* I won't any more, I promise you."

"No, Papa," Diego said. "Please tell me—your things, too. I need them. To—to balance the things of *Maman, tu vois?* Or else I shall have only an unformed and prejudiced point of view, and——"

"And you have not?" his father said. "How is it, then that you *remain* a member of the Party?"

Diego stared at his father. When he spoke his voice was very low. And strange.

"Papa," he said, "why do you hate the Party so?"

Jaime studied his son's face. A long time.

"Something has happened to thee, my son," he said. "Something—grave."

"What makes you say that, Papa?" Diego whispered.

"Because you do not leap to the defense of your sacred Party. You do not point out to me that Communism has made Russia the most powerful nation on earth, a leader in all the sciences, all the arts. You do not remind me that it has raised

China from starvation to a world—and a nuclear power in little more than a generation. That single-handed it halted the Nazi hordes, that——"

"And so forth and so forth and so on," Diego said. "Perhaps I grow weary of propaganda, Papa. Anyone's propaganda —even the Party's."

"Because of—this?" Jaime said, and picked up the newspaper from the table.

"Police admit failure. Terrorist killers of Spanish Vice Consul believed beyond our frontiers——" the headlines read. "No link between Murder of Consul and Embassy Bombings, La Sûreté Declares . . ."

Diego raised his eyes to his father's face.

"Why should that have anything to do with it?" he said.

"I thought—no! I'd hoped that this would have shocked you into the recognition of what the Party does, and therefore *is*."

"ETA," Diego said. "More their sort of thing, wouldn't you say?"

"ETA—yes. The Basque Liberation Movement. Them, of course. Some of those bombings, anyhow. The Spanish ones. But ETA, Fifth Assembly. Does that say nothing to you, my son?"

"No," Diego said. "Should it?"

"Yes. The Fifth Assembly is a subgroup within the general Basque Liberation Movement. A *Marxist* subgroup. It is widely believed to be Maoist in its political leanings. It loudly proclaims itself to be Maoist. Too loudly."

"Hence you believe——?" Diego said.

"Hence I am certain that it is not. And the evidence supports me—"

"Would you like something to drink?" Lilyan said. *"Un pastis? Une bière?"*

"No—nothing, thank you," Diego said. "Wait—if you don't mind, Lilyan—I'd like a cup of tea. With a slice of lemon in it, not milk."

"Mon anglais!" Lilyan cooed. "Very well, milord! Coming up!"

"You were saying, *cher* Papa, that the evidence——"

"Supports me in my belief that ETA—*Quinta Asamblea*—is a Stalinist organization, if not actually supported by the PCE—*el Partido Comunista Español*—and the Soviets, themselves. You have followed the case of the late, unlamented Admiral Carreo Blanco, President of the Spanish Government?"

"Not really. Only the broadest points. The sight of a two-ton Dodge thirty-seven hundred flying over the top of a five-story building must have been quite something, eh, Papa?"

"It was—impressive. Too impressive for ETA. When have those Basque idiots ever done anything that *maldita* smart? I say, *hijo!* With all that hair, you look just like Our Lord. Or one of the twelve Apostles . . ."

"I got a haircut two months ago, Papa," Diego said with mock contrition. "No—come to think of it, it was three—"

"Or four, or five," Jaime snorted. "Doesn't matter! You're not really an effeminate, despite your looks. Or the police wouldn't have had to pull that last *'tite amie* of yours out of the Seine—fortunately with breath still in her—"

"She was a fool," Diego said darkly.

"All women are," Jaime said; then, noting that Lilyan was back with the tea: "and *French* women to a superlative degree. They only think with those greedy little gape-mouthed brains they wear between their thighs . . ."

"Salaud!" Lilyan said. *"Cochon! Bicôt!"*

"You see?" Jaime said wearily. "She confuses the whole animal kingdom. And yes, *ma très belle et si gentille Lilyan,* I *will* have a cup of tea, *moi aussi . . ."*

"You will wait, won't you, *mon amour,* until I put a little arsenic in it?" Lilyan said.

"Why, yes. Yes, of course. Arsenic *and* ground glass. But, on second thought, put them in some wine, not in tea. Tea is for the English, and other effeminates. I prefer to die happy!"

"Pa—pa!" Diego said reproachfully.

"*¿Que?*" Jaime said. "Oh, I see. Thy mother sent thee over here to molest me by remote control. I shall not drink to excess, *hijo mío.* But then, there is no such thing as excess, is there? Excess does not exist. To drown *my* sorrows, there is not enough wine in all the world. Bring me some wine, dear Lilyan. A bottle of *Spanish* wine. Who knows? Perhaps if it warms my blood sufficiently, I may overcome the repugnance that you awake in me and *te faire plaisir*! Pleasure you a little—"

"What were we talking about, anyhow, Papa?" Diego said. "Aside from my long hair, I mean?" He thought: 'Maybe, if I can get him to talking, I can head off the usual war . . .'

"If this *idiote* would stop interrupting me for as long as two minutes, I should arrive at the point . . ."

"Oh, so you have a point?" Lilyan said. "I was commencing to doubt it. I thought it had atrophied from lack of use!"

"But it had not occurred to you that *mon petit point* was merely a trifle discriminating, is it not so?" Jaime shot back. "That it prefers *une clientèle plus distinguée,* shall we say? Those who wash themselves occasionally!"

"Papa! Lilyan!" Diego protested. "If you start a fight I shall go home! At once. Both my stomach and my nerves are unequal to it, tonight."

"*D'accord, beau gar!*" Lilyan said, and kissed him again. "I shall be patient. I shall only assassinate this old goat *after* you have gone!"

Diego held onto her a second; hissed into her ear: "Don't bring the wine! Maybe he'll forget and——"

But she didn't understand him, or pretended not to. She went out and came back with the wine. 'Perhaps when he's drunk, he *can,*' Diego thought.

"I thank you, most sincerely, my dear!" Jaime said. "But one more question, *hijo*: Were you, by any chance, playing with fireworks last night?"

He cackled happily, not even waiting for Diego's reply. "Little boys who play with *petardos* and firecrackers wet their beds, you know!"

"No," Diego said shortly. "And my bed is quite dry, thank you!"

"I am glad," Jaime said. "I was at least hoping that the Party would not introduce you to the gentle art of political assassination. Leave murder to the ETA. They're good at it. Look what they did to the Café Rondo. Thirteen dead. All innocents with no political connections. And right across the street from *La Dirección General de Seguridad* at that!"

"Les Espagnoles," Lilyan said, *"sont des sauvages!"*

"Yes. We are," Jaime said. "Especially when we're drunk. And when my good and gentle son has gone home, I will savage thee to thy entire satisfaction. So shut up, will you? *Ta gueule,* Lilyan!"

"So?" Diego said sadly, noting that his father had polished off three quarters of the bottle already, which meant that the evening was sure to end badly—a fact which he already knew.

"So, this of the bombings last night. Perhaps not—Ernesto. That did lack his habitual *finesse.* But the case of our little Vice Consul? That *smells* of Ernesto, Diego!"

"If so," Diego said slowly, "someone crossed him up. *Nothing* was served by Señor Ximenez's death, Papa. Except to give whoever was responsible for it—some Maoist splinter *groupuscule,* I'd guess—a bad name. And I don't mean among rightist, reactionary circles, for they don't matter. But among wiser, cooler heads among the Left itself. This has hurt us, Papa. This has hurt us badly."

"I," Jaime said, "am glad to see that you are thinking at last, my son. But it distresses me that you regard this peculiarly cruel and heartless murder as merely a matter of politics——"

"Isn't that the level we were discussing it on, Papa? What is war except the extension of politics by other means?"

"Von Clausewitz. He was right. It is. But on human terms it is also—mass murder. You have often asked me why I hate the Party. That's why. I cannot think of human beings as pawns in a game. In even the great and seductive game of—power. The most seductive of all games. Because it is the one lust we have that lasts throughout our lives——"

"I'm glad *one* does!" Lilyan said.

"Oh God!" Jaime groaned. "Go take a walk, will you? Around the Étoile. Leading a poodle. That's how it's done these days when *essence* costs too much. I was saying, son, before this steam-heated species of a would-be *putain* interrupted me again, that I cannot regard human beings as pawns. To me— they are real. They hurt. They cry. They moan. They bleed. They die. They die very badly, sometimes. I have seen that— all of it—much too close, my son—all the ways there are of hurting, bleeding, dying. Even the various ways there are of going mad. You see, I knew an Ernesto, once. No—not this one! He would have been much too young in those days. But such a one as he—expert, efficient, cold—*un tal Camarada Martín. Not* his name, of course. What they call themselves are never their names, is it not so? I should be grateful to him, I suppose—"

"But you're not?" Diego said.

"Yes. I am grateful. He made *you* possible, *hijo mío,* by saving my life. But only for that. What has the life he saved been, after all?"

"Papa—" Diego whispered.

"*¡Una mierda! Merde!* Shit!" Jaime said. He was very drunk now.

"Papa, you're wrong! I—"

"Even in my old age, having elevated my balls to the space between my ears once occupied by my brains, I fall into this— cunt. This piece of tail. Unwashed tail at that—"

"This I will not permit!" Lilyan shrieked. "I'll kill thee! I'll *trancher ta gorge!* Slit thy throat!"

"While keeping my manly attributes pickled in alcohol— to play with them?" Jaime laughed. "Forgive me, my sweet! I love thee. Truly I do. Especially thy little unwashed cunt. Now, be quiet, and later on, when Diego has gone home, I shall reward thee. . . ."

"Why don't *you* go home," Lilyan said, "and leave *him* here?"

"Because then Libertad would kill both thee and me," Jaime said, peacefully. "Which would be *un grand tour de force* except that the thought of her being guillotined over two such lumps of stinking *merde* distresses me : . ."

"*¡Papa, por favor!*" Diego said.

"All right. I missed much of our sacred Civil War, did you know that, *hijo*? I was in Russia, being trained in advanced political tactics. After Camarada Martin had got me out of Asturias in nineteen thirty-four. Before our sweet little Caudillo's Moors and Legionnaires could catch me——"

"I know about *that*," Diego said.

"Do you? The truth, I mean? That the miners of Asturias were the best-trained, best paid, most pampered workers of all Spain? That, in comparison with the rest of Spain, we had no grievances at all? The uprising was purely political. Its aim—to establish a workers' soviet. Its means—dynamite and—atrocities."

"Now, Papa!" Diego said.

"Now, Diego!" Jaime mocked. "You have heard the other side—what they did. How the Moors raped little boys, baby girls, pigs, goats, and even chickens. How the Legionnaires crushed the testicles of their captives between big wooden nutcrackers of the sort they make in the villages. How they whipped men to death, violated women. And, due allowance given to our native Spanish propensity for gross exaggeration, all this was true. True enough, anyhow, for officers of the Legion to murder the journalist Luis Sirval when he returned to reveal it. But what *we* did, you have not heard. Less than they; but still—atrocities. The burning of churches, convents. Blowing up the bishop's palace. The University of Oviedo. And we should not have. If as we claimed, our cause was just, we only dirtied it by our action . . ."

Diego sat there, staring at his father. 'You don't want to

hear this!' he thought, something close to pain rising in him. 'You've troubles enough, doubts enough. And you *need* the Party! You need——'

"It was—a lark to them," Jaime whispered, "a game. I—was the schoolmaster. I had taught their children. I was an—intellectual. A man of words. And among the doers of deeds, men of words are forever suspect. *Nuestra hombría.* Our man-hood—"

"Ha!" Lilyan said.

"They have much right," Jaime said morosely, "and so have you, my sweet! What are intellectuals anyhow? Ball-less wonders! Half priests. Castrated capons of the mind . . ."

"*¡Papa, por favor!*" Diego said.

"*Sin favor, hijo.* Without favor. This was in Mieres, understand? A mining town, only a little way from Oviedo. There was this district manager of the mines—*un Vasco. Un Basque.* Called by one of those exceedingly barbaric Basque names: Zugazabastagui—"

"Now, Papa!" Diego said.

"So help me, he really was called that. All the names of the Basques are of a barbarousness and of an unpronounceability total . . ."

He stopped; filled his glass; drank it down at a gulp.

"If you keep *that* up," Diego said sadly, "you're going to forget what you're trying to say . . ."

"*¡Ojala!*" Jaime whispered. "That I *could* forget it, *hijo.* That *le petit bon Dieu* of *les Français,* or the great, roaring angry *Dios de los Españoles,* or even *el Ala* of the *Moros,* or the Virgin —*la pequeña y misericordiosa* Mother of God—would permit me to forget it. But I cannot. Would God that I could—"

"Go on, Papa," Diego said.

"Now *el jefe* Zugazabastagui wasn't a bad *type.* He was reasonably fair, reasonably just. But he had one great defect which is fatal when one must deal with Spaniards, particularly with Spaniards of the lower classes—he was not *campechano.* Do you know what this word means?"

"No." Diego said.

"*¡Ai yai, que pena!*" Jaime groaned. "What luck most black! I—who love them so—must endure to have a son who is in all ways a Frenchman!"

"You should have gone somewhere else. To Mexico, say. Then maybe my ways would suit you better. Come on Papa, what the devil does *campechano* mean?"

"You don't even *say* it right. *Cam pay chan noh. Cam pay chan noh!* Say it!"

"*Campechano.* But what does it mean?"

"About what '*un brave type*' means in French. The English do it better. What does *un brave type* mean in English, Lilyan? She *speaks* English, you know, *hijo*? She learned it underneath the whole North American Army. And the British."

"*Cochon!*" Lilyan said. "Swine!"

"It does not," Jaime said, and filled his glass again, "signify that. Neither *cochon* nor swine. Come on, Lilyan, what does *campechano* in Spanish, *un brave type en français,* mean in English?"

"A good fellow. Hardy. Hail, well met. A jolly good chap."

"Voilà! And Zugazabastagui was none of those. He was stiff, held himself above the miners, would not permit his daughters to associate with their children. Which, in Mieres, meant they could associate with nobody. And since they were *niñas bonitas*—very pretty girls—"

"Ah!" Lilyan said.

"All the young men of the town were in love with, or at least desired to couch themselves with them."

"Even *you?*" Lilyan asked, incredulously.

"Even I. Except that I wished to *marry* one of them. María Luisa, the youngest one. I might even have accomplished it, since, as the school master, I was considered a cut above the miners by Zugazabastagui. The trouble was that I was too poor. But perhaps he would have found a way to put me in a minor official post with the direction of the mines. And María Luisa did not dislike me, I am sure. . . . But those miners had always resented the ambiguity of my position: a miner's *son*, who had obtained studies, was a teacher, had no carbon beneath his nails, spoke Spanish like an educated man, better, in fact, than the village priest—"

"So?" Diego said.

"And I, being a coward—"

"Now, Papa!"

"*Un corbade. Un lache.* A coward. *¡Sí, hijo!* I tried to appease them. I tried *not* to hold myself too far above them. I drank with them, gambled with them, even—rarely—went to the *putas* with them—"

"*Ça, alors!*" Lilyan said.

"I would have been better off to have imitated Zugazabastagui. To have held myself stiffly apart. Then they would have killed me as they did him. And I would be dead now, and at peace."

"But I—where would I be?" Diego said.

"*¿Quien sabe?* Who knows? Somebody else's son. . . . A rich man's, maybe. The Baron Rothschild's, *por ejemplo . . .*"

"*Il est juif,*" Lilyan pointed out.

"So are nearly all Spaniards," Jaime said, "when they are not Moors. That morning, they came and got me. To accompany them. To assist at the blowing up of the church—"

"Papa, this of blowing up churches—" Diego said.

"Was true. And in Barcelona, in nineteen-nine, they danced in the streets with the disinterred bodies of long-dead nuns. Our people, especially when *exaltado,* are of a barbarousness unimaginable, *hijo.* So, being, as I have told you, a very great coward, I went. In fact, I had to—just this one last glass, *hijo,* and after that no more. Do you mind?"

"You're in your own house, Papa." Diego said shortly.

"I thank you," Jaime said, and downed the glass. "I think they suspected me of religious tendencies. They were wrong. In those days I was a freethinker. I believed in nothing. So I assisted impassively as they blew up the church. As a spectacle, it was fine. They were very good at blowing up things, those miners, you understand? This was, of course, the first week of October nineteen thirty-four, after the start of the uprising in Asturias, but before the Legionnaires and the Moors sent by Franco, and commanded by Colonel Yagüe had arrived—"

He picked up the bottle. It was empty. He stared at it thoughtfully, put it down again.

"No more, Papa!" Diego said.

"Eh? Oh, all right. No more. Where was I? Oh yes, after they had blown up the church, using such an excess of dynamite that bells from the tower actually fell into one of the outlying streets of Oviedo itself, I was told, they retired to the tavern to drink. Taking me with them, of course. Then after we were all very drunk, and the wine had made me, as it usually does, sad, one of them saw the tears trickling down my face, and sang out:

" 'Look at the poor maestro! He is crying! Do you know why he is crying? Because that high-toned María Luisa will not give him a little *coño*!'

"And the rest of them: 'We'll fix that! Let's go get a little *coño* Zugazabastagui for the maestro! C'mon boys, let's donate the Maestro a piece of perfumed Zugazabastagui tail!' "

"Papa——" Diego whispered.

"I—I—couldn't stop them, *hijo*! They attacked the fine house of los Zugazabastagui. Blew in the door with dynamite —dragged me up the stairs and threw me into the bedroom of María Luisa. They themselves entered the rooms of Juanita and Mercedes and la Señora de Zugazabastagui—and abused them. After knocking in the head of Zugazabastagui with a bar of iron. I tried to talk some sense into María Luisa. 'Pretend to scream!' I whispered. 'I will not harm thee. Thou knowest that—' But she was staring at me with mad eyes and then she did scream and scream and I pushed her down on the bed and pulled up her skirts—to make it appear that I was abusing her in case they came in—and she screamed and screamed and screamed and clawed my face bloody with her nails. I had not the desire, you know, *hijo*. I had a coldness in me—a horror. My flesh had failed me . . ."

"Ha!" Lilyan said.

"Somehow she got from under me. Then she was standing by the *comoda* and she had those long scissors in her hand. I thought she was going to kill me—and I was glad, *hijo*! With the shame I had in me then, death would have been a mercy. Then I *saw* what she meant to do. She raised those long scissors high. Pointed at her own sweet breasts. One of them was out of her dress by then and I stood there staring at how white it was and how firm and the pinkness of its nipple and how it stood up and then she said: '*¡Tú! Thou!*' Nothing more. No other word. But making of it a curse to curdle the milk in the breasts of my mother. And then she brought that scissors whistling down. I leaped for her, of course. But being an intellectual and doing, like all intellectuals, the things that truly have importance, that count for something in this life, very badly indeed, I was too late. She died very quickly and cleanly and at once. I was sitting there on the bed holding her in my arms, with her blood all over everything, all over me, and I was not even crying—when the others came. That—sobered them. Then they were sorry. And that, *hijo mío,* was the worst day in my life. Except, perhaps, one other—"

"And that one was?" Diego whispered.

"The day that the Legionnaires and the Moors of Yagüe took the town."

"Tell me about that," Diego said, not that he wanted to hear it, but because he thought it might strike a balance, ease a little what he saw in his father's eyes.

"No," Jaime said. "It serves for nothing, this piling up of horrors, on one side or the other. As Salvador de Madariaga has written truly: 'When the ardent sun of Spain dries up the land —not particularly rich in water at that—the parched earth splits open. The well-meaning foreigner, set ablaze himself by Spanish passion, says, "The earth here on the right . . ." or else, "The earth here on the left—is responsible."

" 'But there is but one earth.' "

"Papa—" Diego said.

"One Spain. They and we," Jaime whispered. " *¡Igualmente bestias!* Equally beasts. Cowards. Saints. Heroes. Men. Go home, son. It is very late. Thy mother will be worried."

"All right, Papa," Diego said, and bent to kiss him. Then he saw that Jaime was crying. "Papa!" he said.

"It is nothing," Jaime said. "A weakness, no? *¡Vete, Diego!* You hear me, son: Go home!"

But he didn't go home. Instead he took the métro all the way up to the place de l'Étoile. Then he walked three quarters of the way around the place until he came to the avenue Foch. He walked all the way up the avenue Foch until he came to the end of it at the place de la Petite Dauphine.

Then crossing that really splendid avenue, he walked down it again in the direction of l'Étoile once more, but on the *trottoir* of the other side. At both times, going up the avenue and coming back down it again, he examined the windows of all the grand and imposing houses slowly and with great care. Especially those windows that were lighted.

"She's up there," he told himself. "*La Chatita*—the little pug-nosed one. With *son visage de macaque*—her monkey face and her nigger lips and her flower eyes. Ana María. Yes, Ana María. *Sí, Ana María. Mais oui, Annemarie. Non! Ça ne va pas.* In French, it doesn't work. I should like to see her. Right now. *De suite. Immédiatement. Comme elle est moche!* How ugly she is! *¡Más fea que pegando un padre!* Uglier than beating a priest! *¡Sí Fea. Laide. Moche.* Ugly. So ugly that I ride the métro from

Bastille to Étoile and walk *una barbaridad* of a distance on the bare chance that I might see her. Her, Ana María. *Mi pequeña condesa Roja.* Not *your* little Red anything, fool! Nor anything of yours of any other color. Forget her. She's a member of the corrupt and degenerate *noblesse d'Espagne. Je m'en fiche!* Hair whacked off like a boy's. *What* boy's? No boy wears his hair that short nowadays. Skin like *lo de una mora.* A Moor's. Lips —God! I could kiss them. I could really kiss them. I could kiss them until she closed those eyes of one color of *pensées*—pansies, and—

He stood there under the street lights, shaking his mop of blond hair; trying to clear his head. This was not useful, and he knew it. This was anything but useful. This was *une bêtise, una tontería,* a stupidity. This could make what he had to do very difficult. This could make it impossible. He had to stop this. He had to stop it now.

"I'll go down to l'Étoile and pick up a *poule!*" he told himself furiously. But he wouldn't. He knew he wouldn't. What was in him now no whore could cure. No woman could cure. Except maybe Ana María, herself. Or—make it worse, he thought, and moved off down the street.

From where she stood, just inside the window of her bedroom on the third floor of one of those grand and imposing houses, Ana María saw him go. She let her breath out very slowly. Measured it out upon the dead still air. She reached for the cord of the floor lamp beside the window. Jerked her hand away from it as if from living flame. Stood there watching him slouching away, his thin, gawky, awkward poor boy's figure growing smaller, diminishing, blending with the shadows between the street lights, reappearing ever smaller, as he passed under the next lamp, shrinking, going on, until she wasn't sure she could see him anymore.

"God!" she said, and whirled away from the window. Ran to her bed. threw herself face down across it, crying, weeping, sobbing: "*¡Tú! ¡Tú! ¡O, Tú!* Thou! This is a baseness. A lowness. *¡Una obscenidad!* He's—*¡un asesino!* An assassin. A murderer. A cowardly murderer who killed—Enrique. And thou. Oh thou. Thou—whore. *Putain! ¡Puta de todas las putas!* Thing of bad milk! Oh God, I—"

She put down her face, ground it into the sheets, crying. Pounded the bed with doubled fists. Stopped that, finally, knowing it was no good. Got up. Went to the window. Looked at the street lights. At the shadows between them.

"*Comme il est beau! ¡Que guapo es!* How handsome he is!" But saying that, thinking it, didn't arrange anything either, so she turned very slowly and went back to bed.

Exactly one hour later, she jacknifed upright and reached for the telephone. Dialed that number in machine-gun bursts of rasps and rings and tinkles. Gasped into the mouthpiece: "*Allo! Allo! Allo!*" Then: "*¡Hola, Pili! ¿Esta tu Madre? ¿Se puede poner ella?*"

Waited.

"*Hola, Ana María,*" the voice of Matilde Ximenez said.

She sounded strange. 'She's been crying,' Ana María thought. But Matilde's voice didn't sound hushed, humid, tear-choked. It sounded controlled. As if—"Nonsense!" Ana María told herself. "You're letting your *conciencia de burguesa* take over. Keep this up, and you'll be going to confession. 'Bless me, Father, for I have sinned! I accuse myself of—adultery. How many times since my last confession? Oh, two hundred and fifty-three times, *padre*! As for my penance, couldn't you give a good customer like me wholesale rates?' "

Aloud, she said: "Matilde—about that boy—"

"*¿Sí, Ana María?*" Matilde said.

"I—I am not convinced of his innocence. It could have been—an act. Perhaps he was looking for—another victim among us . . ."

"*¿Y tú? ¿Estas buscando otra víctima, tú, tambien, Ana María?*" Matilde said softly. "Did my poor Enrique mean so little to you that you seek to replace him before he is cold in his grave?"

"Oh!" Ana María said. "Matilde, I—"

"Don't talk. Do not give me—explanations. Nor excuses. Save them for—God. You do believe in God, don't you?"

"Yes," Ana María said. "Matilde, listen! I—"

"No. Your voice causes a sickness in me. But I shall ask one favor of you, Ana María—"

"Yes, Matilde?" Ana María said.

"Leave that boy alone. He is a good boy, ¿entiendes? Decent. Poor. But fine. He could do without being—corrupted. Especially without *your* variety of corruption . . ."

"I see," Ana María whispered. "And if I were to tell you that I *know,* or at least am practically sure—he killed Enrique?"

There was a silence.

"Then I forgive him," Matilde said softly, "because he didn't kill anything much. Only what you had left, Ana María. And that was—shall we say?—a good deal less—than a man?"

"Oh, no!" Ana María said. "This I shall not permit! I cannot! Say what thou wilt of me—think even worse; but do not say these things of—Enrique! *¡Por favor, Matilde!* Hear me! Listen to me! Please, please, please! Matilde, Enrique left me —months ago. He said—he said, *¡O Dios mío!*"

"What, Ana María?" Matilde said.

"That to exchange thee for me was an attempt to put a— a lecherous little she-ape in the place of an angel," Ana María said slowly, "and hence a bad bargain. That what was between him and me had—no future. That I was to forget him. To find —or make—my own life. He had thee—his pledged word. His daughters, his hostages to fortune. That's from Shakespeare, isn't it? While I—"

"And thou. What dost thou have?" Matilde said.

"He said, youth. A certain—grace. I say——"

"What, Ana María?"

"*¡Nada!* Nothing! Now—nothing. And then—nothing. Today—nothing. Tomorrow—nothing. The coming week— nothing. Next month, next year—nothing. All the rest of my life—nothing. Until eternity—nothing. And, after that——"

"*¿Y despues?*" Matilde whispered, hearing how she was crying, how that "*¡Nada, nada, nada!*" "Nothing, nothing, nothing!" tore her throat so that the sound of it grated over the wires, bearing with it so heavy a freight of despair, so physical an anguish that their sheer force confused, confounded the senses, causing, by some quirk of mental suggestion, Matilde to smell, or to momentarily believe she did—the thick, hot stench of blood. "And—afterwards, Ana María?" she said.

"*Despues—el infierno.* Afterwards—hell," Ana María said.

Matilde didn't say anything. The silence hummed. Crackled. Sparked.

"No," Ana María whispered. "*Not*—afterwards. Now, Matilde. Now. For thou hast robbed me of what is necessary for supporting it. *¡Adios!*"

"No!" Matilde said sharply. "Thou art not to do something foolish, child!"

"Foolish?" Ana María said, laughing and crying at the same time. "But when have I done anything that was *not* foolish, *mi Señora* widow of the man I loved? It was a *payasada*, a clownishness, of me to be born! It was moronic of me to breathe air! A folly to grow! An idiocy to live! And to love—to love! That was insanity! So do not tell me that—dying will be foolish. I do not believe you. It appears to me that it will be the *only* sensible thing I have *ever* done . . ."

"Ana María," Matilde said, to distract her, to break through that mad intensity of hers, "that—boy. *Ese chico.* You want to take vengeance upon him, because you believe—?"

"Vengeance? *¡Otra idiotez!* And I know nothing. Believe nothing. When I called you—two million years ago now, wasn't it? I thought I wanted to see him again. Who knows why? Not God, Himself, I suspect! To talk to him? *Tal vez, quizá. Peut-être.* Perhaps. To hold his hand? Look into his eyes? They are blue —*¿sabes?* As blue as the sky above *las rías bajas de Galicia.* To kiss him? *¡Sí! ¿Porque no?* To go to bed with him? Very likely, being *me, ¿verdad?* To make a baby? *Un niño.* A little boy baby so tiny and soft and sweet whom I could call—Enrique. *Enrique, Dos. Segundo.* Junior. You *would* permit me that, wouldn't you, Matilde?"

"*¡Eres loca!* Thou art mad!" Matilde said.

"Yes, I am mad. But I am growing saner by the minute. And since my madness consists of breathing, the cure for it is very simple, no?"

"*Niña,*" Matilde said, "do not be a fool."

"You are saying that I am not to be *me.* Likewise for that, the cure is very simple. In fact, it is the same one."

"No," Matilde said, "I cannot have thee upon my conscience. There is another cure. Perhaps it is even—right. And just. And pleasing in the sight of God. There is, so far as I know, no impediment to it——"

"And that cure is?" Ana María said.

"Go to church. This very Sunday. To the Church of Sainte Roquette in the street of the same name. Near la place de la Bastille. The name of the priest is Père Dubois. Confessing your sins to him might help. But just going will be enough. And —Ana María—"

"Yes—Matilde?" Ana María said.

"You may. Call him Enrique, I mean. Thy first-born son, since I shall never have a little Enrique of my own. *¿Que mal da?* What harm can it do? Call him that. And I will be his *madrina*—his godmother. *¿De acuerdo?*"

"Oh!" Ana María gasped. "Oh, now thou hast killed me! Now thou hast destroyed me! To act with—*nobleza,* while I— have been to thee—a thing of utter lowness, *una cualquiera, una fulana, una*—"

"Thou hast been merely a fool. A *young* fool, which is not grave. Go to church, child. To *that* church. Promise me?"

"Oh!" Ana María whispered. Then: "*Sí,* Matilde. Yes. How can I deny thee anything, now? Yes, I promise thee. I will go . . ."

"Ernesto," Diego said to his father, as they walked toward the church that Sunday morning, "says that an intelligent man will leave nothing to chance. That there is only one kind of luck: bad. And that, therefore, one must eliminate luck from any activity of a serious nature. . . ."

"Does he now?" Jaime snorted. "Here we have intellectual arrogance taken to its ultimate extreme! And he has, of course, told you how this miracle is to be accomplished? The methods you are to use to eliminate luck, chance, blind accidentality from the affairs of men?"

"Well—" Diego began, then hesitated. One had to be careful about starting a debate with Papa. All right, the old man's mind worked in odd ways, shooting off upon oblique tangents, ringing in arguments of rank sentimentality, of notorious illogicality, irrationality, even. But when you tried to refute them, you'd experience the sinking feeling of a novice chess player up against a grand master. He was always crowding you into plays that turned out to be fool's mates—because it was his seeming illogic and not your logic that was closer to the stuff of life, to the essential nature of that mad, self-tormented, clownish creature that calls itself—man.

"Well—by foreseeing all the possible contingencies—" Diego plunged in—"and safeguarding oneself against them. Of course that's not completely possible, but—"

Jaime shook his head.

"Diego, *hijo,*" he said sorrowfully, "*por favor,* leave out that 'completely'! It is not possible at all. We are the sports of chance. The toys of blind accidentality. We live in a world that has neither rhyme nor reason. In which what we do, say, think, are, have no influence upon what happens to us. Influence? They have no discernible relation! Which is why, perhaps, we need God."

"But—" Diego said, "is he—there?"

"How should I know? I speak not of his existence, but of our need for him. If you are not a monster like Ernesto, but a human being, you begin to learn life's lessons. The chief of which is that a man, any man at all, alone is—nothing—*polvo, ceniza, nada.* Dust, ashes, nothing. You and I, *hijo,* to arrive at la iglesia de Santa Roquette, have to cross the place of the Bastille. What guarantee, what assurance have we that we will get to the other side—alive?"

"Well—" Diego said, "statistically, even considering the number of mortal accidents of traffic . . ."

"*¡Statisticamente mierda!*" Jaime said. "Today, in Paris, a certain number of strollers will be killed by automobiles. I care not how many there are, or how few, or what the law of probabilities says. What guarantee have we that you, or I, or both of us, will not be among them? Tell me that, *hijo!*"

Diego thought about that. Said, "None, Papa."

Jaime bowed his head. Looked up again. Smiled at his son. That smile was infinitely sweet, infinitely sad.

"Do you know how many millions of people live in Paris?" he said.

"Something like seven, or eight millions, I believe. Why, Papa?"

"In 1948, there were fewer. Say one, or two millions less. Doesn't matter. The day I got here from Russia—hungry, bearded, louse infested, smelling to high heaven, I passed through a fine street. Knocked on a door to ask a crust of bread to still the growling of my belly. A maid servant answered it. *Una doncella. Une bonne.* A thin blond woman with burning eyes. Tired looking. Stringy. Jumpy as an overridden horse. With no looks at all. I said: '*Est-ce que vous pouvez me donner un bout de pain, mademoiselle? J'ai faim. Je n'ai mangé rien depuis—*'

"And she said: 'Speak Spanish, will you! You are. I can hear it!' "

"Yes. Thy mother. Of all the hundreds of thousands of servant girls in Paris. Of all the thousands of streets I could have passed through. Of all the millions of doors upon which I could have knocked. And here you are, telling me that it is possible to eliminate luck, accident, chance!"

"Papa—" Diego said.

"Diego, my son, *now,* at this very instant, this exact second, things are happening that will forever change thy life. Happening to people you don't even know, upon whom your eyes have never gazed. People thousands of kilometers away from here, perhaps. Totally unaware of your very existence. And they, because of you, will live—or die. And you, because of them. Come, take my arm. This traffic frightens me . . ."

Diego stared at his father.

"It doesn't frighten me. *You* do that, Papa!" he said, and took the old man's arm.

Then, at that exact instant, in Madrid, capital of Spain, the woman called Amparo knocked on the door of the Minister. Pushed it open without waiting for an answer. Said:

"A phone call for you, sir. On number four. You'd better take it. It's—the President of the Government. And he doesn't sound happy, sir."

"*¡Maldita séa!*" the Minister said, and picked up the phone. Listened. Said: "Yes. Why yes, of course I'll hold the line . . ."

He smiled at Amparo. Beckoned to her. She came up to his desk. He reached out and took her arm, pulled it. Trembling, she came around the desk and stood beside him. He put his arm around her waist, rested his head against her left breast.

"Oh, Fredi, no!" she said. "The door—"

"Is not locked. And anyone could—" He spoke briskly into the mouthpiece of the telephone: "*¡Buenas dias, su Excelencia! ¿A cual buena fortuna debo yo el honor de—*"

"Oh, come off it, Fredi!" the President said. "I called your house. Consuelo told me you'd gone down to your office. On Sunday! That's overdoing zeal, my boy. What in the name of everything unholy made you—"

"Some loose ends, sir. It came to me that to really implement the provisions of the tax law on personal income, we'd—"

"Fredi," the President said, "there's trouble. That confounded newspaper again. Brewing up a new mini crisis. And *you're* the target this time. So lunch at my house today, my boy. You know where it is—in Somasaguas. And bring Consuelo and the kids. Window dressing—a purely social afternoon, you understand? After lunch you and I will take a stroll around the grounds—away from the lovely shell-pink ears of our dutiful and loving wives—"

"Which will be vibrating hard enough to make them take off like a pair of birds!" Federico Sales Ortega, the Minister, groaned. "And after we come back from our stroll, what will you tell *yours,* sir?"

"A pious lie—as always. That we are discussing weighty technical matters. Too weighty and too boring to interest her, especially since they involve no danger to my tenure of office, or to our much too luxurious style of living—the only two remotely political themes that interest my darling Luisa at all. Will Consuelo also swallow that one?"

"Yes," Federico said. "She won't really believe it; but she'll accept it—coming from you, sir. She has, unfortunately, become quite convinced that my mouth and the Holy Catechism are two different things . . ."

"I know," the President said shortly. "That is one of things we have to discuss, Fredi. This time you've been even more—indiscreet—than usual. So—come early. Say two o'clock sharp. Can you do that?"

"Yes, sir," Federico said slowly. "I can. Two it is, sir. And sir, if I've caused *you* any difficulty—I—"

"*¡Jesus del Gran Poder!*" the President said. "Don't talk about it over the phone, you idiot! Just *be* there. *¡Hasta luego, Fredi!*"

"*Hasta luego, Señor Presidente,*" the minister said.

He looked up at Amparo. Her eyes were very wide, deep, and black in the smooth, almost too perfect oval of her face. Her mouth had tightened up on her. He could see that the cords of her neck were rigid with strain.

"I am very sorry, *mi vida,*" the Minister said, "but our day together is, as of now, spoiled. A thing of bad luck, merely. But do not preoccupy thyself. There will be very many other days."

"Will there?" Amparo whispered. And suddenly the tears were there in a sudden flooding, a rush, a spill. "Oh, Fredi, I'm so afraid!"

"Of what, *niña?*" Federico said.

"Of—of losing you," she got out. "Fredi, he *knows!* His voice—that oh so wonderful voice of a grand orator—carries, even over the phone. He said that you'd been—indiscreet— and that means—"

"Merely that that old buzzard of the long nose who thinks he runs Spain sub rosa from the office of that filthy rightist political rag of his probably found out about *your* background. That's all. Not necessarily that we *most* discreetly and damned infrequently share the same bed. That his Excellency, the Minister, sleeps with his lovely secretary would be no weapon against one in this benighted country. *Amparita mía,* you ought to know *that!* What minister, head of the council of directors, prominent businessman and what have you in Spain does not? Only those who are impotent, or whose wives wear the trousers to the extent that they, not *los caballeros en cuestion* choose said secretaries. We prominent citizens have to, or the institution of marriage, as marriage is conceived of in Spain, would not even be possible, considering how Spanish upper-class girls are brought up. But *lo nuestro*—our thing—wouldn't even seriously interest that old scandal-monger for the simple reason that he couldn't print it anyhow. The censor wouldn't let him. But of your family——?

"That they were *Rojas.* That my father was—shot. That they shaved off the hair of my mother, forced her to drink a liter of castor oil, made her scrub latrines. That both of my uncles were shot, too. That I am a *solterona*—an old maid of thirty-three—because I was all my mother had, since I was born six months after my father's death—before the firing squads, up against the civil cemetery wall. And if thou wert not a fool, Fredi, thou wouldst take a young, pretty secretary of twenty-two or -three, say, and——"

"I am a man, Amparo. I have need of—a woman; not a baby girl. I have need of thee. Who art something barbarous! And glorious at the same time. Before thee, I didn't even know what love was! Why——"

"In spite of thy beautiful and aristocratic Maria del Buen Consuelo and that army of children she has given you?" Amparo said.

"The classic Spanish mistake," Federico said. "That we confuse love with procreation. That our girls are trained to be wives and mothers—never lovers. I lost Consuelo to a rival—to the ultimate, invincible rival—the day my eldest son was born. The love of Spanish mothers for their sons is actually incestuous—in every sense but the physical one. And it is the root of all our troubles! The English are trained to have their second thoughts first. We are trained—by the most ferociously maternal women on the face of the earth—that the world is ours by divine right! Hence a difference of opinion outrages us. A man who disagrees with handsome, wise, important me is a criminal who deserves being shot! Oh God, if we could only learn a little humility! If we could only bring ourselves to accept adverse criticism, to recognize that because *we* think, believe, do a thing, it is not necessarily right! A million dead, and thirty-odd years and we still haven't found out that the greatest political statement of all time was Voltaire's—"

"Which was?" Amparo whispered.

" 'I disapprove of what you say, but I will defend to the death your right to say it!' " Federico said. "Amparo, I am sorry! I love thee—"

"Do you, Fredi?" Amparo said.

"Too much!" he groaned. "If I had a peseta for every time I've decided to count the world well lost, leave Consuelo, the children, my imposing career, chuck it all for thee, I'd be richer than Juan March. But since I am also a coward——"

She bent then swiftly and kissed him, flattening that hateful word against his speaking mouth.

By that time, Diego Fernandez and his father were entering the Church of Sainte Roquette.

In the doorway Jaime paused.

"My son," he said, "are you aware that we have been followed? All the way from the place de la Bastille to here? Perhaps even before that?"

Diego sighed.

"Yes, Papa, I am aware of it," he said.

"They do it very badly, don't they? *Une traction avant* of almost ministerial class—"

"A DS twenty-three Pallas," Diego said. "Black. The same kind of car that the President of the Republic uses. With the back seat curtained off to hide its occupant—a privilege of high officialdom. They might as well have put a flashing roof light on it, and a police siren. Which makes me wonder—"

"Wonder what?" Jaime said.

"The Sûreté is not usually that clumsy. Or that stupid . . ."

"*Hijo,*" Jaime said. "You're in trouble, aren't you?"

"Yes, Papa. But trouble of my own making, which is neither political—nor grave."

Jaime gripped his son's arm hard.

"Tell me!" he said.

Diego smiled, very slowly.

"A case of bourgeois prejudices—and my own stupidity, Papa. You see, I knew that Vice Consul who was killed . . ."

"You *knew* him! How, *hijo?*"

"Worked on his car. Most natural thing in the world. He lived in the Sixteenth, you know. And he owned a five-oh-four. So that he would bring it to the garage where I work was normal enough, since we specialize in Peugeots. And also that

I, hearing him murder the French language, would volunteer to aid him in Spanish. We became quite friendly. Every time his *bolide* needed work, he would ask for me. So, out of a sentimental impulse, I went to his funeral. A mistake, Papa. A garage mechanic with grease under his fingernails doesn't usually assist at the *pompes funèbres* of *un caballero español.* And most especially not at those of a *murdered* Spanish gentleman!"

"So they—*les flics*—?"

"Are investigating me. But since all they can find out is that I told them the truth, strict, absolute, and whole, they ought to give it up, soon. By the way—*that's* one of them. That man across the street. All to the good. That he sees a dutiful, well-washed son, and with a fresh haircut at that, attending mass with *son papa,* I mean . . ."

Jaime glared at Diego.

"So *that's* why you did it? You ice-cold little bastard!" he said.

"Now, Papa," Diego said, and grinned at him, "you know better than that. That I could be a bastard is an utter impossibility considering the fact that although my mother is, being Spanish, and hence an extremist, far redder than Camaradas Stalin and Mao put together, she also is—being Spanish!—possessed of morals that would put Isabela la Catolica to shame. And, as for my being ice-cold, a number of *filles très gentilles* would dispute that one—somewhat warmly, shall we say? Now come on. We'd better get busy at saving my so-called soul."

"*¡Sin vergüenza!*" Jaime said. But he allowed Diego to lead him into the church, all the same.

"Fredi," the President of the Government said, "are you sleeping with your secretary?"

Federico looked around the grounds. Since the President's house was in Somasaguas, next door to the Club de Campo, they were extensive. A full *hectario*—two full acres—ten thousand square meters—at the least.

"Nice place you've got here, sir!" he said.

"I'm sorry, Fredi," the President said, "but it *is* my business. I was responsible for your being appointed, remember?"

"Do you want my resignation, sir? I assure you it will be on your desk by——"

"No! Damn you, Fredi, listen! You and Carlos are the best young men I've got. And—Enrique was. I was planning to bring him back from Paris, just before——"

"They killed him! Those miserable, murderous *Vasco* idiots! Who actually believe they have the wherewithal to transform their province into a nation! If they had any notion of economics, they would know——"

"That Switzerland couldn't exist," the President said drily. "Luxembourg, Monaco. And yet they all do exist—and fairly well, most of them, with a far less solid economic base than *Vasconia* actually has. So don't underestimate the Basques, Fredi. Their province is better equipped for nationhood than Portugal ever was—though that our Lusitanian friends can continue to exist as a sovereign state without their African colonies seems to me doubtful. Enrique was your friend. Your views on most issues I seem to recall, were practically identical . . ."

"Strike out that 'practically,' sir. They were identical. We worked them out together. Enrique was the most brilliant chap I ever met! Why——"

"And you were much alike in *other* ways," the President said drily. "I don't mind telling you that the real reason I was going to call him back—regretfully and prematurely, of course, from Paris was——"

"His affair with Ana María Casaribiera y Borbón. His much-too-well-publicized affair. That wouldn't have been necessary, sir. He broke with her last January. He wrote me a letter to that effect. The longest letter I've ever had from him. And the saddest . . ."

"Did you know her?" the President said. "Wait, I don't want to indulge in idle gossip; but that little girl has caused us, the government, more damned trouble than the ETA and all the rest of our semi-exiled political dissenters put together. Her life-style, if you can call it that, is a permanent blot on the good name of Spanish womanhood. If her *parentesco* didn't reach so high, I'd find out some way of putting her under restraint——"

"Which is precisely what should be done with her," Federico said grimly. "For my money, she's as mad as a hatter!"

"So you *did*—do know her?" the President said.

"Say *did.* During last year when, as his invited guest, I spent the entire summer with Enrique in Paris. Or rather, Connie and I spent the summer with Enrique and Matilde, to make the matter perfectly clear. During that summer, I saw quite a lot of Ana María. A bit more than I should have liked to . . ."

"I take it then, that *you* at least were not swept off your feet by her so very well advertised charms? A point I've never been able to understand. I've never seen her, but from her photo she——"

"Appears to be an ugly, skinny little thing, with lips as thick as an African's, and oddly pale eyes? Did you ever see a color photo of her, sir?"

"No, Fredi, why?"

"You'd have to. Nobody would ever call her beautiful, or even pretty; but she is the single most exciting female creature I have met in all my life. The most exotic. And the most erotic. Five minutes in her company, and you'd forget how she looks —hell, not even five minutes, two!—and she has become something better than beautiful, something so exquisite, heart-stopping, mind-blowing, to borrow a vulgar American phrase!— that you find yourself not only wanting to make off with her, but to *keep* her. Forever. And, truthfully, the reason I *hated* the times I spent with her was that near her I was always burnt up with desire, and with *the* most abysmally base male rut-dog sexual jealousy you ever saw, because all she did was to talk about Enrique, whom, apparently, she adored. Or weep bitterly on my available shoulder because she was becoming increasingly aware that she would never be able to take him away from Matilde. And that voice of hers! Like a deep-toned bronze gong, or the echoes of one, anyhow, that someone has struck —ever so softly!—in some pagan temple, somewhere very far away. I'd recognize it anywhere. Even over a telephone. Why—"

"Restrain your enthusiasm for the little lady, Fredi! Though it does make me understand the, well, psychological origins of the devil of a mess you're in right now. Oh, damn women, anyhow! Every time I get together a first-class team, like *this* one, of which you and Enrique were to be my starring players, some ruddy woman appears, and—— But that's natural enough, I suppose. Brilliant men, worthwhile men, always seem to have a fine excess of virility—an extra something that acts as a lodestone, swerving the needles of a woman's deepest instincts abruptly toward your north—"

"I'd say, rather, towards our *south,* sir, if you'll permit me the implied indelicacy. Well, sir?"

"Well, back to square one, as the military say: Fredi, are you having an affair—specifically a sexual affair with María del Buen Amparo Leal-Solana, I believe her name is? And I demand an answer, you young fool!"

"Forty-six is hardly young, sir . . ."

"In Spain, it is infancy. Answer my question, Fredi!"

Federico stood there. Looked down at the President's well-tonsured lawn. Looked up again.

"Guilty—as charged, sir," he said slowly. "And as I said before, my resignation——"

"Shut up, Fredi, and listen! You've got to get rid of her. Right now. Tomorrow. Fire her, you fool! Find some pretext. There always is one, you know. Say that Consuelo has found out—"

"She *has,*" Federico said sadly.

"All the better! And that she—all bathed in righteous tears

—came to *my* wife, threatening to ask for a legal separation, unless . . ."

"She's capable of it," Federico said. "Only it hasn't occurred to her yet . . ."

"But it will. *¡Jesus del Gran Poder, Fredi!* This grows graver all the time! You know perfectly well I couldn't care less how many *chicas'* lacy *bragas* you remove, but keep the *chicas* in question out of your *office,* will you? Especially when, as in this case——"

"Their fathers were filthy Reds, as were Amparo's. That's what you mean isn't it, sir?"

"So!" the President said. "You *knew!*"

"Naturally. Amparo told me the day she came in for her first interview, sir. She said she *always* made the facts clear before accepting any job, because it was easier not to get the place at once than it was to lose it some months later when said facts were brought in on a tray, with *aires triumfalistas* by those morons from the Direccion General de Seguridad's Political Section . . ."

"And knowing *that,* you hired her!"

"Yes, sir. But only after having some of my own people, who are *not* morons, sir—check her out thoroughly. She belongs to no political group. She is devoutly religious. In which regard our—relations—have cost her considerable pain; and more shame than I like to think about. She's stopped going to confession. Says she can no longer face the priest of her church . . ."

"And you think that she couldn't have been planted in your office to—"

Federico smiled.

"Good heavens, sir!" he said. "If you were going to plant a *chica* in someone's office, would you choose one of demonstrably Marxist background? Whose father was *shot*? And who is additionally all of thirty-three years old?"

"No," the President said. "But your figures don't add up. If her father was shot—presumably by *us,* by our side—she couldn't be only thirty-three. She'd have to be older. Considerably older."

"He was shot in 1941, sir. After we, with our habitual Christian mildness, and willingness to forgive, had lured him back from exile in France with promises of amnesty. We were *still* shooting people as late as 1946, sir. After that we realized that our procedures only served to remind the world of a historical fact we want forgotten—our connection with our ex-pals of the concentration camps, gas ovens, *et al* —and began to display discretion. Amparo, it seems, was conceived late in 1940, while her father was momentarily at liberty . . ."

The President stared at the young Minister.

"Whose side *are* you on, Fredi?" he said.

"Spain's," Federico said. "And so, sir, are you. For a short time ago, when our Caudillo was apparently at death's door, two emissaries visited Santiago Carillo, head of el Partido Comunista in Paris. It was widely rumored at the time that one of them was from la Casa Real itself. And the other, sir? Need I say it?"

The President went on staring at Federico.

"Fredi," he said slowly. "You *love* this girl, don't you? Enough to threaten me this way in order to—"

"I am not threatening, sir. I would defend that secret with my life. Because you—your government—is the best hope our poor martyred country has. You know as well as I do that the danger does not—or at least not immediately—lie on the Left. The Left in Spain, as in Portugal, is composed of relatively intelligent men. Even the Communist Party—now that Russia rules the world—is beginning to display signs of moderation. Our native, outlawed Socialist Party——"

"To which you belong," the President said drily.

"To which I and a great many patriotic Spaniards belong, sir, is another hope for the future. A fact which you realized, and counted upon when you engineered my appointment! Even this *engañar bobos* of a law——"

"The Law of Political Associations?" the President said. "But why a 'fool killers' law, my boy?"

"Because it *is*. You know it is! Political associations are to be permitted *within the framework of our national movement.* Translated into *sense,* what does that mean? That a man can be anything he wants to be as long as what he wants to be is a Falangist!"

"Fredi," the President said, "I got that law through the Cortes. And you know *me*—"

"Yes, sir. Which is why I don't understand—"

"Laws can be changed, my boy. Modified. Expanded. Was it not better to get some kind of a law through that later on, with luck, can be made into something that matters?"

"I see," Federico said. "Then I *must* get rid of poor Amparo? She's an excellent secretary, sir. By far the best I've ever had . . ."

"Not to mention her abilities as a bedmate," the President said drily.

"Which are more than excellent. They're stupendous. They keep me alive, sir. Functioning. Contribute in a small way to Spain's future, by giving me—hope. . . ."

"Are you *that* depressed, Fredi?"

"Good Lord, sir! Aren't you? We're a fief of the U.S. Navy and Air Force. We've sold our land, our souls, for foreign money. Our most beautiful landscapes have been bricked over. When you get to our coasts, you can't see the ocean for the skyscrapers—mostly foreign owned, and built so that hordes of French hairdressers, English doormen, and German beerhall waitresses can come down here and be snotty to us, as we bend humbly for their tips! Our one solvent truck manufacturer was squeezed out by Chrysler motors. Ford moves in on us; General Motors is said to be contemplating buying out Authi. ITT is already here. And when ITT shows up, can the CIA be far behind? Look what happened in Chile! Parke-Davis. Rank-Xerox. IBM. *And Readers Digest!* And our tourist business, which originally saved us—not because our government has, in its entire history, done one remotely intelligent thing, and you know as well as I do it hasn't, but because God gave us sun and sea and pure air and orange blossoms, and because Europe grew rich enough to need a place to play in, as long as the prices remained dirt cheap, as ours *were*—is in the hands of foreign tour operators who squeeze us 'til we scream——"

"Go on, Fredi," the President said. "Your wildly indiscreet way of saying what I often think helps me. By keeping me from having to say it—*¡tal vez!*"

"We send off our best, our most ambitious, our most talented workers to become the niggers of Europe, virtually slaves, doing the dirty jobs the lordly Europeans refuse to do. And when things turn sour—as they have now, despite our serving our Arab friends as a willing substitute for toilet paper—"

"Fredi!" the President said.

"All right. Perhaps that *is* too strong. I'll modify my statement! And now, having made our hereditary anti-Semitism, which was one of the factors that cost us the rulership of the world, another substitute—for an intelligent foreign policy this time—we find ourselves faced with the necessity of providing jobs for our poor exported niggers as they come flooding back. In a country where there are no jobs. With the list of bankruptcies growing every day. With inflation through the sky, and strikes all over. And yet, with problems like these, sir, you take time out to make my affair with a poor, tired, thirty-three-year-old woman—a matter of state! Is it, sir? Is it, really?"

"It is, because it provides our enemies with a lever which could topple my government, Fredi. I flatter myself with the thought that not even you want *that!* Or perhaps I'm wrong. Do you?"

"And have *los Immobilistas* and the rabid Right take over? To ruin Spain beyond repair by dragging us back into the past by main force? We've been ruled by an anachronism for thirty-six years now. What would people who think even *he's* too liberal do to us?"

"So?" the President said quietly.

"So Amparo goes. You'll give me two weeks to find her something else?"

"No, two hours. And *you* mustn't find her a job. Don't worry, she'll have a first-class one, day after tommorrow. In Barcelona.

"In Barcelona!"

"Perhaps too close. Maybe I'd better make her an embassy secretary—in Beirut, for instance."

"Good God, sir!"

"Fredi—think. Getting her out of your office is not enough. You have to get her out of your life. Or else the same leverage applies. Anything that even smells like a leak appears in a foreign leftish publication and—"

"I see," Federico whispered. "Let's go back now, sir. To your bar, anyhow. I propose to put down a good stiff one. Some of your bonded Scotch. Believe me, I need it."

"And I. Come along then," the President said.

All through the services Diego had that feeling. There was a warmth between his shoulder blades, a burning. He moved uneasily as he knelt there beside his father. But when he glanced over his shoulder, he could see no reason for that burning sensation. For one thing, the church was packed. Since the economy of the Republic had gone straight to hell due to the 400-percent rise in the price of crude oil, people were worried enough to take religion seriously again.

Then, at the very end of the service he saw her: a small female figure draped in black, her face covered with a widow's veil. So heavily covered that he couldn't see her eyes. But he knew. Absolutely and surely and totally he knew. The ache in him knew. The hurting, the wanting, knew. The gut-blazing, breath-stopping need.

At the sound of the last sonorous "Amen" from the pulpit, he was out of his pew, dashing down the aisle towards her. But as fast as he came, she was faster still. A doe-thing moving, all night-misted, black-chiffoned grace.

Out of the back pew. Out the door. Across the *trottoir* to where that imposing Citroën waited, arrogantly parked in double file. But as fast as she was, he caught up with her just as she bent and swooped to enter the back seat through the door the chauffeur was holding open for her.

Diego's hand shot out, clamped over her shoulder, yanked her backward so hard she fell against him heavily. He could smell that perfume again. That damnable perfume.

"Why?" he got out. "*Pourquoi,* Ana María?

Her gloved hand blurred sight, moving. Exploded open palmed against his face.

"Let me go, you filthy murdering swine!" she said.

The chauffeur, who was the type form of what the French call a gorilla, by which they mean not the gentle and largely inoffensive greatest of all the apes, but a professional body guard, trained in judo, karate, all the martial arts, started towards Diego. Easily, swiftly, smoothly. Diego hadn't a chance, and he knew it. But something, his atavistic Spanish pride, perhaps, held him there. He fell into a crouch. He had, after all, some training too. But not enough. He knew that very well.

Her voice cleared the noon air like a knife.

"No! It's—a mistake, André. Don't hurt this boy. He's—not who I thought he was. I don't believe he really knows who I am, either. Do you, *garçon?*"

"If mademoiselle would be so kind as to lift her veil," Diego said.

Her hand came up. Slowly her face was born again out of the dark.

"*Ojos de flor,*" he murmured, "*cara de mona, labios de negra.*"

"What did you say, *gar?*" the chauffeur said.

"Nothing. *Rien.* That I have never seen mademoiselle before. That I was mistaken. That I thought she was someone else . . ."

"Are you sure of that?" another voice said.

Diego turned. Stared into the face of the Sûreté man. The

same detective who had questioned him outside the Spanish church.

"Vous êtes bien sûr de cela?" the agent repeated.

"M'sieur l'agent," her voice came over sweet, soft, tremulous, tender. "We—belong—to different worlds. *Mes parents*—do not approve. You comprehend this, do you not? It is—so very hard for us to meet. Sometimes religious services—even funerals—must serve us as excuse. You, yourself, are still very young. Surely you can understand . . ."

The Sûreté man stood there. Everything checked. The boy had a perfect military record. The *garagiste* vouched for him. The priest. And he was a *beau gar* for a fact. While this skinny little monkey-faced creature wasn't every man's cup of tea. It checked. It checked too *sacré* well. It woke unease in him. Touched a nerve deep in his policeman's soul.

But now wasn't the time to pursue it. Better put a tail on the boy for the rest of the day. Check where he went. Whom he met. Because this little high-spiced bit of Spanish she-flesh was an untouchable. He already knew that. And—she could be telling the truth. He had your Frenchman's deep appreciation for a well-conducted *affaire,* no matter how incongruous. Besides, it fitted the known facts as well as any other theory did. The kid wasn't even of Basque descent, which ruled out the ETA. There was nothing to connect this oddly Nordic-looking towhead with the Vice Consul's death except his appearance at the Spanish diplomat's funeral. And the girl had obviously come here to this workers' quarter, to this dingy, run-down church run by a *prêtre ouvrier,* looking for the *gosse.* He hadn't gone up to Passy. . . .

It was enough to give a man a bellyache. It all added up, and came out wrong. If there were only one more detail, one piece that didn't fit, or even that completed the puzzle, he'd——

He leaned forward, suddenly.

Cette robe! That dress. Its cut was odd. No woman, no girl of *haut monde et bon ton,* would ever wear a dress so badly cut, so baggy, ill fitting, loose—except—

He looked at her face, her eyes. Smiled at her sadly with real pity. Poor little thing. She was going to have it rough, now. A garage mechanic *et cette trop gentille, si petite dame. Dommage.* He knew how these cases ended nine times out of ten. With the girl in the Seine. Floating. Amid the oil slicks, the green slime and the muck. Accusing the gray skies with sightless eyes. Or in some filthy outlaw clinic where they'd scar, mar, ruin this slim body forever. Leave even uglier *cicatrices* on her heart, her soul . . .

He bent close, putting his broad back between her and the boy.

"Et vos parents, mademoiselle," he whispered. *"Est-ce qu'ils savent, eux?"*

"No!" she husked. "Of course they don't know! *Et il non plus, lui!* I haven't told him. I was hoping that today, I—we—"

"Tell him," the Sûreté man said. *"Et—bonne chance, mademoiselle!* The case against *votre ami* is—closed. Dropped. I shall so recommend it to my superiors. The two of you have trouble enough, it seems to me—"

She stared at him, whispered: *"Vous êtes trop bon, monsieur."*

He stood back. Said to Diego: *"Ça va. Vous avez vraiment de la chance, vous!"*

Ana María leaned forward. Said, speaking Spanish, fast, quietly, without expression, so that even those wide, warm, wonderful lips his imagination could taste seemed almost not to move: "Go home. Stay there. Beside the phone, you miserable cretin! Don't move a meter away from it until you're called—which will be sometime tonight! You have understood what I have said?"

"Sí, camarada; lo he comprendido," Diego said.

"Don't call me comrade!" she rasped. "Now—kiss me!"

Diego stared at her.

"*¡Payaso!*" she said, almost crying from pure exasperation now. " *¡Bobo! ¡Tonto! ¡Cretino! ¡Idiota!* Clown, moron, fool, cretin, idiot! *Kiss* me! And make it look good, damn you!"

He bent. Kissed her. Shyly. Clumsily. Timidly. Tried to draw back. But those long, slim fingers were locked behind his neck, moving through his thick blond hair. Those lips of scalding wine and blood and the pulp of figs were opening under his, moving, moving, while she played maddening braille games with a tonguetip designed to stop his heart, his breath, his mind. Wreck all three. Destroy them.

She drew back at last, letting those long fingers slide slowly along his face, his jaw, before pulling free. Branded him forever with the feel of them. Smiled at him with those lips of a *negresse,* her flower eyes aglow with—what? Tenderness? Mockery? Love? Hatred? Joy? Rage? He didn't know, couldn't decide between all the opposites he saw there.

"You will pay for that kiss, *mi Diego,*" she said softly, slowly, sweetly, "pay for it with your miserable murder's life . . ." Then switching easily into her almost too perfect French: *"Adieu, mon amour! À demain! André, allez-y! Il faut que je rentre!"*

Diego stood there, watching the black shark-shaped car sliding soundlessly into the traffic, moving away. Felt a hand on his arm. Turned. Stared into his father's deeply troubled eyes.

"Diego—" Jaime said, "who was—*that?*"

"Oh—just a girl I know," Diego said.

"You know—well enough to kiss her in public—a girl like that. Dressed like that. With a car like that. A chauffeur—"

"Like that. Yes, Papa. And an apartment on the avenue Foch. And more millions than you and I could ever count, even if we started counting right now, and kept it up for the rest of our poor, miserable, working slobs' lives. Daughter of a grandee of Spain. With *un título de nobleza* on top of all that. Which, come to think of it, is—rather sad, isn't it?"

He heard what got into his father's voice then; felt, even, the immense weight of sorrow in it.

"No, not sad, *hijo*," the old man whispered. "*Sad* is the wrong word . . ."

Diego turned. Stared at his father.

"I would call it—tragic," Jaime Fernández said.

When Diego stopped the "special" before the door of that miserable, dirty rundown hotel—called La Bergère Alsacienne, he noted automatically with one part of his mind—she was already on the sidewalk, waiting for him, with her luggage —and his—piled around her. The luggage was tactically correct, his professional eye told him at a glance: it was cheap, badly made, not even new. One valise had its lock broken and was tied together with a rope, which was overdoing things a little, he thought!

At that hour of the morning it was still almost dark, and the street was hazed over with the lung-eroding smog from the exhausts of the trucks rumbling through it on their way to make their deliveries to the stores, restaurants, hotels, supermarkets, and apartment buildings before the traffic became absolutely impossible instead of the merely appalling it already was now, so Diego couldn't see her very well. For one thing she was sitting on one of the suitcases, doubled over with her elbows resting on her knees, and her chin cradled between her two hands. She looked so absurdly sad and lost and forlorn that what hit him, seeing her there, like that, actually hurt. He wasn't used to that kind of a feeling. It clawed so deep it frightened him.

Then the hall porter of the hotel came rushing out, 'To collect his tip, the bastard,' Diego thought without real anger. 'Though, for all I know, she probably had to lug all those bags down herself. Probably, *merde!* Surely, in a fleabag like this one . . .' and she stood up. Came slowly, heavily towards that ancient wreck of a car.

Diego sat there, nailed to the seat of the Peugeot. He couldn't move. He really couldn't move. He would never be able to move again. Dead men can't, anymore, can they? Only, he told himself, they don't hurt like this. Or feel this sick. Or—

She bent to the car window. Said—What? What did she say? He could see her lips move, but he couldn't hear her. He couldn't hear anything for the sodden, leaden, funereal, slow beating of his heart. Not even the rumble of truck motors, the blast and blare of horns, the snarl, the whine of shifting gears, brake shriek, police whistles—nothing. Sound didn't exist. Nothing existed except her little round belly, the size of a child's football, that was straining against the waistband of her skirt.

She said again: "Give him a tip, hon; I haven't any change." Or rather that was what she meant. What she actually said in the complicated language of the complicated French was more like: "Give him a for drinking, my cabbage, for I haven't any little monies . . ."

Diego got out of the car, thus proving that he wasn't quite dead, or that his body wasn't. 'Or that I have become a Zombie . . .' he thought, and came around to where she stood beside the hall porter.

At once she caught him by the arms, and going up on tiptoe, kissed his mouth. Hers was cold. It tasted salt. Her breath was unpleasant. It smelled of—of vomit, maybe.

He said, in control of himself now, in control of his rage, his hurt, his sickness: "Are you all right? Did you sleep well, my little angel?"

She grinned at him mockingly, said: "Of course. *Both* of us did. But around three thirty this morning he started to kick, and woke me up. Takes after *you,* my love! Lots of donkey in him!"

Diego didn't answer that. He didn't because all the answers he could think of to it he couldn't say before the hall porter, and because none of them made the slightest difference anyhow, now. Instead he opened the trunk and put two of the valises into it; then he held the back door of the 204 open while the hall porter put the other two into the back seat. After that he tipped the hall porter extravagantly, receiving for his pains the same grumbling *"Merci beaucoup, m'sieur,"* that he would have got for half as much, or twice as much, for, as he knew very well by then, it is a matter of honor with Parisian porters, bellhops, taxi drivers, *et al,* never to admit satisfaction with any tip whatsoever, even though it is made up of what's left in Fort Knox, combined with the gold reserves of the Bank of France.

He helped Ana María into her seat, as tenderly, as carefully as though she were a figurine blown of the finest, thinnest wine goblet crystal, displaying to the hall porter's totally unappreciative eyes a letter-perfect representation of a worried young husband taking exquisite care of his pregnant wife. But once he was behind the wheel, he remembered suddenly the feel and taste of her mouth on his as she kissed him outside the church yesterday morning, and the fury in him, the gut-corroding rage, poured acid and bile along his veins.

He left rubber on the pavement taking off. That vastly over-powered car—a 504 motor with electronically timed fuel injection exists on another level of sheer brute force altogether from the docile, four-cylinder, single-carburetor mill with which the old 204 had originally been equipped—shot forward like a rifle bullet. An instant later he had to slam brakes to keep from burying the front end of the Peugeot in the tailgate of a truck. Those immense, finned and air-cooled disc brakes took hold at once. Both times, taking off, and stopping dead, he almost snapped Ana María's slender neck.

She turned, glared at him, said, her voice low, torn and shaken with icy fury: "You've killed his father, but I should thank you to let my son live, Diego. Drive carefully, will you —you murderous swine?"

He was trembling on the inside. Every nerve he had had come loose and was crawling. His knuckles, on the steering wheel, were snowy. He hoped she wouldn't notice anything. He prayed she wouldn't. He didn't know to whom or to what he was praying; but he prayed, anyhow. It took him three attempts to get her name out.

"Ana María—" he said.

She whirled upon him.

"Don't talk to me," she said. "Don't—ever—talk—to me. Don't you dare. You hear me, Diego Fernández?"

"Yes," he said. Closed his mouth. Snaked that hybrid monster of a *Deux cent quatre-Cinq cent quatre* between two trucks with maybe a millimeter to spare on either side, poured it through an amber caution light, leaving most of the traffic caught by the red, and piled up behind.

"Killing us both won't arrange anything," Ana María said. "Except to abort the mission. Not even that. Ernesto will send someone else. So slow down, will you? Besides I don't feel like turning on the charm for the *flics this* early in the morning."

"Nor you," he said forcing the words out between locked and grinding teeth.

"Nor me what?" she said.

"Don't talk. Not to me, anyhow. Shut up and let me drive, will you?"

He could feel those eyes burning his face. He half turned and saw that her big, thick lips had twisted into a curiously enigmatic smile.

"D'accord," she murmured. Turned her back to him.

Curled up in her seat with her legs under her body. Went calmly to sleep. Or pretended to.

But less than an hour later she straightened up, said: "Stop at the next gasoline station, will you?"

"I thought we weren't going to talk to each other," he said. The sound and the feel of his rage, his hurt, came through his voice, and she heard it. She smiled again. Gloatingly. With triumphant malice.

'*Merde, alors!*' he thought. 'I'm playing right into her hands!'

"We aren't—beyond the minimum essentials. Communication when absolutely necessary. No conversation. So stop this heap at the next *poste d'essence.* If you want, I'll even say 'please.' "

"Why?" he said. "We've still got three quarters of a tank of gasoline."

"And I a bladder four quarters full, camarada. I have to urinate. Pregnant women have to very often. Our passengers take up all the room."

"All right," he said shortly. Then: "Did—Ernesto know that you—that you—"

"That I was knocked up, caught, *embarazada*—there's your Spanish mentality for you! What's embarrassing about being pregnant?"

"In your case, the lack of a husband," Diego said.

"Which is your fault, not mine," she said coldly, and now it was his turn to hear the anger underneath her voice, like the second harmonic on a radio, or the fourth. Faint, but there. It and something else. Contempt, maybe. Yes, surely contempt. The one offense that no man with even one drop of Spanish blood in his veins is even remotely equipped to hear. But his French upbringing saved him now.

He said evenly: "I don't believe that. I got to know him pretty well, remember. He would never have left his wife for you. Never."

She stared at him, and those oddly pale eyes of hers went paler still.

"What makes you think that?" she said.

"I don't think. I *know*. You might start by considering the fact that I have seen his wife. And that I have also seen—am seeing—you. Or didn't you have any mirrors in that apartment of yours on l'avenue Maréchal Foch?"

To his utter astonishment, her eyes hazed over suddenly, went light-glazed, glittering, blind, so that pity tore him. Shame. He opened his mouth to say—

But she cut him off with a gesture of her hand. Her self-control was superb. More than superb. It was regal.

"Low blow," she said quietly. "You're a dirty fighter, aren't you? And—it's unbecoming in a man. Feline, somehow. Even—female. Unmanly. But then, what could one expect—of a cowardly murderer?"

He shrugged.

"What you think of me doesn't matter two sous worth of *merde,*" he said calmly, "since I know—and every person who has ever spent two whole days with me, say, also knows—it isn't so. So why should what *I* think, my opinion of your looks matter to you?"

"It doesn't!" she said sharply. "I thought you were quoting—*him*!"

"No. We didn't discuss you. Or his wife, either, for that matter. Even though during his—captivity—we talked a lot. He was very advanced. But deep down he was Spanish. *Very* Spanish——"

"So?" she said.

"Spanish men don't leave their wives for—whores. Especially not beautiful wives for ugly, skinny little whores."

She flinched visibly, as though he had slapped her physically across the face. But when she spoke, her voice was perfectly controlled.

"Don't try to—to tear me down, Diego," she said. "You

can't. For to do that you'd have to be able to reach me. Which requires being what you're not—and what *he* was. A man—"

He shrugged again. It was a very Gallic shrug. He did it very well. It was one of the things that caused people—even his father—to believe he was ice cold.

"Oh I say!" she said. "There's a gasoline station ahead . . ."

"I see it," he said, and slowed the car.

She said: "Let's go back to our original agreement. Let's not talk—unless what either of us has to say concerns our mission. We've got to—endure each other—for several days yet. So let's not make it any harder than it already is . . ."

"All right," Diego said, "but what I started to ask you before you went off on that tangent *does* concern it: Did Ernesto *know* you were pregnant when he sent you along?"

"Yes. That's *why* he sent me. A tribute to his knowledge of Spanish character. We're coming home, my dearest husband, so that our first child can be born in *la Patria!* Instead of prying into our bags for contraband, subversive literature, machine guns, bombs et al, the *aduaneros* are going to fall all over each other helping us, says Camarada 'Rubles.' He's right. They will."

"Ernesto's getting soft. Too many precautions. Or—*merde alors!*—you don't mean to tell me that there actually *are* guns and stuff in those bags?"

"Of course not," she said coolly. "Ernesto's no fool. Well, here we are. Stop the car, will you?"

While she was in the rest room, he topped off the tank, checked the oil, the water, the tires. But she took a long time. Too long. He was beginning to worry, to think she had got sick, maybe, when he saw her coming back towards the car. And the way he felt about her still, hopelessly, helplessly, in spite of everything, got into his eyes and betrayed him. She saw that look. Stopped dead. Stared at him. Those incredibly pale eyes of hers—incongruous in a face as essentially African as hers was —darkened visibly, went smoky with—what? Worry? Trouble?

Doubt? He didn't, couldn't know. Then she recovered, came on.

This time he didn't get out to help her. He leaned across the seat, opened the door from the inside. She got in easily enough. Said, as they moved off: "Why were you looking at me in that fashion, Diego? While I was coming back, I mean?"

He shrugged.

"Since I don't know *how* I was looking at you, how should I know?" he said. "Besides, I thought we weren't going to talk. . . ."

"I—I think we'd better, a little," she said, and a new thing got into her voice now, a curiously negative thing—a retreat from conviction, maybe; an admission that other interpretations of his acts and his motives could at least exist—"because it would be just too terrible if——"

"If what?" he said.

"If I were wrong about you," she said. "Though wrong or right, it's too late now. . . . Are you—religious, Diego?"

"No," he said shortly. "It's all superstitious *merde.* Why?"

"A pity. Because I'm not either. And one of us ought to be capable of prayer. To go where we're going—without even an *Ave María* or a *Padre Nuestro* could be a little too much . . ."

"And where are we going?" he said. "I thought we were going to Spain."

"We are," she said. "But after that to—hell. By way of Spain, of course."

He shot a glance at her little round belly.

"You've made a good start anyhow," he said. He tried to keep the bitterness out of his voice, but he couldn't manage it. He couldn't manage it at all.

He could feel her eyes upon the side of his face.

"You damned Spaniard!" she said, very, very quietly.

"*¡Y tanta honra!*" Diego said. "Honored to be one!"

"I know. Honored to be—by a mere biological accident— a member of that race which produces—in wholesale lots!—the most reactionary male chauvinists on the face of earth, whatever your politics. And— *¡salvo excepciones rarísimas como mi Enrique!* —*the* worst lovers in Europe. Bar none."

"And how would you know *that,* may I ask?" he said.

"Well, you might say that I've been—slightly generous. No, *very* generous, to be quite honest about it. I've spread happiness around. All over."

He took his eyes off the road; glared at her.

"Please watch your driving!" she said sharply. He knew without looking at her that she was smiling, that those eyes that were the color of the palest shade that pansies ever get to be, short of actual white, were alight with mockery, with mischief, with unholy glee.

"So I see," he said. "One time too many, wouldn't you say?"

"Not one time too many. One time on purpose. Trying like mad to *make* this happen. So I could have what I wanted most in life—"

"Ha!" he snorted. "You don't mean to tell me—"

"That I'm pregnant because I wanted to be? Precisely that, camarada. I persuaded Enrique—with ludicrous ease, since, being Spanish, he was quite as selfish a beast as all the rest of you are— to stop using contraceptives early in the game on the score that I had access to a reliable *contrabandista* who was smuggling in the Pill from Switzerland by the carload, and making himself carloads of money in the process. That was true. But what neither he nor I realized at the time was the degree of abysmal idiocy that any woman in love is capable of. Even a *soi-disant* enlightened, liberated, modern woman like me. . . . There came a day—" her voice choked up on her, went humid, hushed, dark—"when I simply stopped taking *la pilule.* Deliberately. *Comme ça! Voilà tout. . . .*"

Diego looked at her again. She looked like grim death. Her eyes were deep sunken, blue rimmed. Her curiously Negroid lips were bluish, too. Her cheeks were inhollowed, had an almost greenish cast. Her skin looked—unhealthy. Pity caught him by the big gut and squeezed.

"Why?" he said. "Because you—you loved him?"

"Yes, because I loved him. But more because I'd found out—realized—I could never have him. Not on the only basis I wanted him by then," she said, "which was permanently. I wanted him in a house, with ten kids at the very least, coming home to *me* every night. Belonging to *me*. Not sharing him with any *maldita* woman born! Me—liberated, enlightened, free me! —wanted that . . ."

"So this—" he said, "was to be your vengeance? Your exhibition of the fury of the woman scorned?"

"No. Neither. In the first place, *she* would never have known it. I meant to go away. In the second, I *wasn't* scorned. Enrique would have kept me forever. . . ."

"As long as you were content to remain *sa 'tite ami—sa maîtresse, sa drôle de poupée, sa gamine, sa—*"

"*Sa putain*—his unpaid, useful little whore—as you also pointed out to me. Only I was *not* content. I'd fallen into the tender trap. Men can keep sex meaningless, maybe. But women can't. For us, it either becomes meaningful or nauseating. Which means we either fall hopelessly in love with our lovers —or we leave them. That's why the feminism I've spent my life fighting for, that got me run out of Spain, exiled by my own family, *can't* work. You see, I know myself much better now. I am *not* cool, remote, controlled. I am not even European. Africa begins at the Pyrenees, doesn't? *¡Soy española!*"

"*¿Y tanta honra?*" Diego mocked her. "Honored to be, of course?"

"*¡Y tanta desgracia! Tanta pena.* I am as primitive a woman as any *gitana* from some *aldea* in Andalucía. *¡Una Africana con sangre mora en mis venas!* Yes—Moorish blood, Moorish grief, Moorish pain! I wanted to pay her back—Matilde, I mean—but with *subtileza*, because she didn't even have to know about my baby—that *I* knew was enough!—for all the bitter tears she made me shed. *¡Todas las lagrimas de celos y de rabia!* I, who was supposed to be civilized, European, free. And then—God knows how!—she found out. And behaved—nobly to me. Crushed me beneath *una sierra nevada,* a snowy mountain range of purest shame. So now I have to die——"

"*¡Ana María!*" he said.

" *¡Sí! ¡Sí! ¡Tengo que morir!* Why do you think I accepted this mission? This totally suicidal mission? That I may die—usefully. Doing something for my poor oppressed people. Something for—Spain. Bah! Sounds false, doesn't it? Grandiloquent. Fake. Only I mean it. Why not take leave of my bad, false, fake, promiscuous, dirty life—in a good way? Make its meaningless, meaningful by—my dying?"

Again he jerked his thumb sidewise in the general direction of her belly.

"And—him? Thy son—or thy daughter? Would you also——?"

She said softly, slowly, clearly: "Why not? What kind of a life can my baby have? I am not a shop girl, you know. Wherever I go in Europe I am still *la hija de los Condes de Casaribiera, y—¡una madre soltera!* An unmarried mother! And my son—the poor little bastard!—must bear my name. Kinder to spare him *that,* no?"

He stared at her, whispered: "*¡Eres loca! ¡Eres loca de remate!*" "Thou art mad! Stark, raving mad!"

Ana María smiled at him.

"Yes, Diego, dearest. Yes, dear little husband, I am mad. And thou?" she said.

They stopped that night in Limoges. He had decided upon that because, coming down from Paris, Limoges was the last city where he could make up his mind about how—by which route —he wanted to enter Spain, because Limoges is almost equidistant from Hendaye on the Atlantic and Perpignan on the Mediterranean. But if they crossed the frontier at Hendaye they'd end up in San Sebastian on the west coast of Spain, while if they crossed it below Perpignan at le Perthus or Port Bou, they'd end up in Barcelona. Which made very little difference as far as distances from Madrid were concerned; what he had to worry over—with absolutely nothing to go on—was at which crossing the Guardia Civiles, *aduaneros et al,* were likely to be the more watchful, vigilant, suspicious, have, as he put it, *"la más mala leche . . ."* an untranslatable phrase that meant, more or less, would be the worse sons of bitches, which, as far as he, or any Spaniard in any opposition group was concerned, they *all* were . . .

He also decided, with a certain bravado, to stop at Le Grand Hôtel Moderne on the boulevard Victor Hugo in Limoges, because he already knew from previous missions that its restaurant, Le Tortillard, really wasn't too bad. He'd even toyed with the idea of stopping at the Frantel Royal Limousin, the one really first-class hotel in Limoges; but at the last minute he lost his nerve on the score that they wouldn't be warmly welcomed if they came driving up to the Frantel in a wreck like that 204. On the other hand, none of the hotels of the class where working people stopped had restaurants at all, and dragging Ana María and her little passenger out to look for supper seemed to him too much.

But, as he drew the car up before the Grand Hotel, he felt her eyes performing their now familiar alchemy of burning holes in his cheek. He turned, looked at her; said: "Say it!"

But she shook her head. "I don't think it's necessary—is it, Diego?" she said quietly.

"If you mean that it's not necessary to ask me not to attempt to—well—take advantage of you when I've got you upstairs in our bridal chamber, you're right," he said acridly. "The idea of screwing pregnant women doesn't appeal to me. I'm not sure that the idea of laying *you* would appeal to me under any circumstances. Though, truthfully, it might. Without your—passenger—you could be kind of cute. Skinny little monkeys like you quite often are . . ."

"Thank you," she said solemnly.

"*¡No hay de que!*" he said. "Though I must admit I don't know what the devil you're thanking me *for.*"

"For the compliment. You've built up my morale no end," she said. "Now, come on!"

When they were upstairs in the old-fashioned, high-ceilinged, quite comfortable room, he took out a coin and said: "Let's flip for who gets the bathroom first. Which do you want, Ana María, *cara o cruz?* But even if you win, I hope you won't stay in there *all* night. . . ."

"No!" she said tiredly. "You first, Diego. I mean to have a long hot bath. And a shower would probably suit you just as well, wouldn't it?"

"Yes," he said. "But I do have to shave, and change clothes—which won't leave you too much time to get ready for supper. They close the dining room at ten o'clock here and——"

"Diego—let's call room service, please? I—I don't want to go down there. I hate people—staring at me—and speculating and making calculations inside their heads. Besides—even though we're still in France, it's better that we're not seen too much. Someone might recognize *me.* My picture's been in too many magazines now. The wrong kind. The sort that serve up to their readers a play-by-play account of who's sleeping with whom. Especially when the 'whom' in question legally belongs to someone else. One kind soul paid me the compliment—in print—of declaring that I was ahead of Deneuve in those peculiar sweepstakes—and catching up with Bardot—fast."

"Which, of course, pleased you immensely?" he said.

She sat down on one of the twin beds.

"No," she said sadly. "It didn't. I'd give anything to be *une petite bourgeoise* right now. So I could find my baby—a father. *Un petit gar* who'd come home to our little walk-up flat—in the *Cinquième Arrondissement,* say—every night. Sure he was going to find me there instead of out helling around. And d'you know what—he *would.* Every night. Happy to be there. To be— wanted, needed, protected—safe . . .''

He took a deep breath. Said: "Even if the *gar* were—a garage mechanic—with grease under his fingernails?"

Her head came up. The pale lavender of her gaze rested upon his face. Glowed. Then it hardened. Turned sapphire. Very still and cold.

"Grease, I have no objections to. But—blood is a little too much," she said.

She stayed in the bathroom a little aeon, a small, nerve-cracking edge. But when she came out, she looked much better. Her skin, without make-up, glowed like burnished bronze. She had on a cotton print nightgown and a quilted bathrobe. Seeing her like that he guessed she was close to four months gone. Or five, maybe.

He held out the chair for her to sit at the table that the room service waiter had set up. Then he sat opposite her, watching her eat. But he didn't eat. He couldn't. Less than ever now. After a couple of minutes, she noticed that.

"Diego," she said. "What's wrong?"

"Nerves," he said. "My guts are knotted up on me. I haven't been able to keep anything down since—last Wednesday."

"The day—you killed him," she whispered.

"Yes. The day—I killed him," he said.

"And—you—you—came to his funeral. And you—you—cried! Diego—this is all wrong! It doesn't make sense! Why——"

"What does?" he said wearily. "Eat your dinner, Ana María!"

But now she couldn't either. They sat there staring at each other across the table.

"Nothing—adds up," she said. "I—loved him. In spite of the fact that he—didn't love me. I was—a convenience. Accepted at the price tag I'd pinned upon my self. Gratis. Free tail.

And he—Enrique—made me see hell, trying to persuade me to have an abortion, to murder—the child that we had made. To sacrifice its—life to hide our sins. Our cheap little lying sneaking clandestine sins!''

"Ana María—" he said, or groaned—or both.

"Or so that—Matilde wouldn't find out—and leave him. So that—it all boiled down to this—he wouldn't get stuck with me! With ugly, skinny, monkey-faced me. With my big mouth and——"

"Tus labios de negrita," Diego said. *"Tus ojos de flor. De la flor llamada pensamientos—"*

She stared at him.

"Diego!" she got out. "What *are* you saying?"

"Me? *Nada.* Nothing. Get on with it, Ana María."

"I loved him. And then—he was making me hate him with his weakness and his selfishness. But the Party—*my* Party, the great and glorious Partido Comunista Español—to which I belong—"

"Why?" he said. "Why do you, Ana María?"

"I told myself that it was the only organization that could save Spain from the effects of thirty-five years of intellectual and moral dry rot. That to cure what we're dying of by asphyxia, by stultification, atrophy, want of will, surgery was necessary. That maybe a Red dictatorship, an Iberian Gulag would be sufficiently worse than the wooden-headed brainless paternalism of the Franco state to make the Spanish people revolt and free themselves. Because the worst thing about Franquismo is that it hasn't been bad enough. Just to the degree to keep us in political infantilism, but not—in the last few years anyhow—sufficiently cruel to make us angry enough to rise to our responsibilities and learn finally to govern ourselves. To become grown up, responsible Europeans. As the Portuguese are getting to be now . . ."

"Interesting," Diego said. "Your parents, of course, don't agree?"

"My parents don't agree with the sight of me!" she spat. "I induce nausea in them—instantly. I have a huge allowance which is conditioned upon my staying the hell out of Spain! Or upon managing to behave myself and not disgrace them for the two weeks that they allow me to come home—for form's sake —every year!"

"And now—you arrive with your little bundle. *Tu pequeño bulto*—unblessed by church or state. What then, Ana María?"

"That's where you're wrong. I don't *arrive.* I have no intention of—killing my father, by giving him a heart attack, or a stroke. Nor of breaking my mother's heart—again. Worse, this time, than I've ever broken it before . . ."

"Then what will you do?"

"Don't know. Go to the pueblo—to Casaribiera, maybe. My parents don't live there anymore. Too ruddy backward. Primitive. I could hide out there, I suppose, until my baby's born. My old nannie would take me in—at the price of telling me what she thinks of me, and my behavior, morning, noon, and night. At that I should still be lucky—to be my father's daughter, I mean. At least the villagers won't stone me. That's what they'd do—and without a second thought—to any other girl from there who came home in my state. . . ."

"Ana María, I don't believe——"

"Casaribiera is unbelievably primitive, camarada. During the Civil War, one of the girls of the pueblo came back home from a convent the Reds had closed. Since it was too dangerous to travel in her nun's robe, she had to buy an ordinary dress. And she couldn't do that either, because they were rioting and burning churches and shooting people in the place where she was. So she stole one in the excitement. Only it turned out to be a beaded dress, with fringes. Low cut in the front, and the back. And when she turned up in the *pueblo* in that outfit, her father, her brothers, her uncles, and all the other backward oafish louts of the village stoned her to death. In the public square. On the theory, dear Diego, that she'd been a whore because she was dressed like one."

"*¡Dios mío!*" Diego said.

"That's a funny oath for a Communist," Ana María said.

"I see how—you could turn against—your own," he said.

"I'm not against anyone. I'm for Spain," Ana María said. "You Reds took fully twenty-five of my relatives for the *paseo*. Left them as *besugos en el Club del Campo . . .*"

"*Besugos?*" Diego said.

"Dead *fish*. That's Madrileño humor for you. Now it's my turn: Why did *you* join the Party?"

"No—you first. Only the *real* reason, Ana María!"

"I'm not sure I know it. Say I was a born rebel. And I soon realized that the Spanish woman is centuries behind other Europeans as far as her human rights are concerned. Say I wanted to wreck my world, recreate it nearer to my heart's desire, build it anew with liberty and justice for all. For dogs, *gitanos, quinquis* —and women—in that precise descending order! And since the most obvious way I could implement my personal rebellion against constituted authority was by having flagrant, visible, and public affairs, I did that . . ."

He shook his head slowly. Said: "You're not convincing me, Ana María. No one *ever* does things for such nicely worked out theoretical reasons. Dialectics is the science of justifying human errors, *after* they have been made . . ."

Ana María stared at him. Smiled.

"*¡Bueno!* And you're right. Say, at about age thirteen I discovered I had—a body. A maddeningly troublesome little body with all sorts of itches and twitches and tingles. Equipped with a perfectly horrendous and most unmaidenly set of carnal desires! I honestly wanted to kiss every boy I met. And that, my dear Diego, only because I hadn't yet discovered what *else* one could do with boys . . ."

"And?" he said gently.

"Certain of my cousins—handsome devils every one of them!—could touch my *hand* and things would happen inside me. Terrifying, awful, maddening, delightful things. Before I was fifteen, I had discovered what boys are *for . . .*"

"So?" he said.

"I soon found out I was a misfit. A Spanish *señorita de alta cuna* isn't supposed to have a body, y'know. Only a womb—which her husband keeps eternally filled while she lies there perfect-ly *still,* and prays to the Virgin for him to get his incomprehensible and repugnant attentions over with. Having married, become *una señora,* she discovers love—but only for her children. Her husband she tolerates, and quite often grows fond of. But *love* in my sense, she usually *dies* without having experienced, as poor Matilde will, likely."

"I think you're wrong, you know," he said, "at least in part. I lived in Madrid two years, once. And there *were* girls, of quite respectable families even, who——"

"Had bodies of their own, honest passions, and knew it? Of course! Not even church and state can alter the basics of human nature that far. But what they can do to those girls is to make them lie and sneak and hide—and feel guilty and dirty. Which is what they couldn't do to me. A good many Spanish girls these days sleep around. But they don't flaunt it. I *did.* I was living my life, having fun, quite innocent fun—for if you know anything, Diego, you know *good* sex is the most innocent activity there is—naked, gay, playful, and I didn't care who knew it. Which turned out to be *everybody,* since boys will boast of their conquests, even though truth to tell it was I who did the seducing most of the time. . . ."

"So it reached your father's ears . . ."

"And he tried to persuade me to remove my disgraceful self from his path by repenting my sins and entering a convent. I told him I thoroughly enjoyed said sins and meant to go on committing them as long as I was able. So he shut me up in the tower room on bread and water. I refused even that—until they found me unconscious on the floor and rushed me to the hospital."

She paused, smiled to herself, clearly savoring the memory.

"While in the hospital I had still another affair with a

young doctor. And told Papa about it. He had the doctor fired, wrecked his career. . . . When I came out, I staged the absolutely most horrendous piece of bad melodrama you ever heard of . . .''

"Which was?" Diego said. He was getting that feeling again, but he didn't care very much now. She was outrageous, and mad as a hatter, but she was—somebody. She was herself and that self was really something. No brakes, of course. Out of control. Wild, crazy. With the whole randy mess, the unmitigated female disaster that she was, housed in a body a little more shapely than a fence post, but not much. Wearing a face that some African idol worshipper had carved out of teak. With —flower eyes. And—nigger lips; and a dead man's bastard brat in her belly. And he—loved her. Which was a damned fool thing, but there it was. He loved her so much it hurt. But he wasn't ashamed of that feeling anymore.

"I walked into a family dinner party—there were about thirty people there, for, of course, we're kin to *everybody,* y'know—with my father's revolver in my hand. Held it out to him butt first. Poor Papa! You should have seen his face! I don't think he's ever fired a shot in anger in his life. Unlike most Spanish noblemen, he doesn't even hunt, the poor old dear! He said: 'And what am I supposed to do with *this,* Ana María?'

" 'Take it,' I said, 'and kill me. All at once instead of by millimeters—since you won't let me live!' But he couldn't take it. So I turned it on myself. I think I said: 'Good-bye everybody,' or something else equally bright. But the safety was on, and since I knew absolutely nothing about guns either, I couldn't get that awful, heavy, oily, messy thing to shoot. Three of my aunties fainted outright. Half a dozen of my uncles and cousins grabbed me. I was dragged away and locked up again while the whole *maldita* family held a conference over *what* was to be done about poor, mad nymphomaniacal Ana María!"

"That's nonsense. There aren't any such things. Nymphomaniacs, I mean . . .''

She grinned at him. Made an impish face.

"Oh yes there are! That's what *normal* women are called by repressive bourgeois society."

"You may be right there," he said. "Go on, Ana María."

"I was packed off to France—supposedly to study, which I surprised them by doing, I've a doctorate you know—but actually to go to hell by the quickest route. Only I was—more resistant than they thought. For five years now I've been both *la bête noire et l'enfant terrible* of every Spanish ambassador and consul in Paris. Every time the phone rings they clap hand to forehead and groan: 'Oh God! What has Ana María done now?' "

He smiled at her, said: "None of which explains your joining the Party . . ."

"Yes it does. To implement my ardent feminism I was willing to destroy *my* world. And what better weapon lay to hand? Besides—I knew people that Dolores Ibarruni, La Pasionaria, saved from the Red firing squads by her personal intervention. I also knew a woman, a friend of my mother's, whose father, an admiral, was executed by the Reds. And when the judge who had condemned him to death was captured by the Nationalists, she, being a Catholic, and what is even rarer, a Christian, tried to save the man who had cost her father his life. She appealed to General Franco—or tried to. She got nowhere, for already our Caudillo had given the order he never thereafter wavered from—that no plea for clemency was ever to reach him until after the execution had already been carried out . . ."

Diego said quietly, "You can't argue from a humanitarian point of view, Ana. For every atrocity on one side can be matched—or topped—by another atrocity from the other . . ."

"I know that. But the Reds never claimed that their revolution was a crusade for *God* and for Spain. The followers of God —or of tender, merciful Jesus—should not, as good Catholic people did in *la Coruña*—my mother's hometown; she's *Gallega,* y'know—shoot not only the loyalist, or so-called Red, civil governor, but also, after first performing a rough and ready abortion on his pregnant wife, lower her alive into her grave on a stretcher and shoot her there. D'you know how I know that? Because my mother took care of one of the stretcher bearers, who went mad at that sight, for the rest of his life . . ."

"Still——" Diego said.

"Still I do not argue I have chosen the better side, Diego! But surely the necessary one under today's conditions. Everywhere in the world the men of the Left—or at least of the more moderate Left—are simply more intelligent than those of the Right. We have been governed by pure political idiocy—for what else can you call setting up the *Falange Española Tradicionalista y de los Jons?* Which, Dr. Madariaga points out in a recent work, is exactly equivalent to the President of the United States setting up the Republican, Democratic, Socialist League of the Daughters of the American Revolution so he wouldn't have to bother his head about politics anymore! Our system consists of letting troublesome issues gather dust on Our Leader's desk until time itself solves them, or they simply fade away! With *every* first-class brain, *every* authentic talent in exile —forced, or voluntary, it matters not! With a censorship that insures that our novelists, playwrights, and poets produce gutless *merde* while the *Hispano Americanos* are making of our native tongue a glory—"

"Still," Diego said quietly, "what would our side have done had *we* won? Produced a Gulag Archipelago in Spain? Built a Wall of Berlin across the foothills of the Pyrenees?"

She stared at him, whispered: "Perhaps—yes. And turn—angels into murderers. Hear me out! I loved a man—a brave, charming, brilliant man—who used me as—a convenience. And the Party—had him kidnapped, just as I was learning to hate him a little—with a hatred that might have saved me! Put him under the guard of a boy—a beautiful, beautiful blond boy with a face like a Luca della Robbia angel—"

"Now look, Ana María!"

"You are, and you know it! And—*este muchacho guapísimo, con cara angelica*—murdered him. Apparently in cold blood—"

He stared at her, said: "Let's not talk about *that*, Ana María. . . ."

"*De acuerdo.* Tell me—the story of your life. How eyes that look like the skies above *las rías bajas de Galicia* can contemplate —death. How that soft and kissable cupid's bow of a mouth can twist into an assassin's snarl. Or start further back. Why did you join the Party, Diego? How did you rise so swiftly from the ranks? School—Czechoslovakia—demolition expert! Marxist dialectics at the clandestine Party schools. Political Science at the University of Paris—all while pretending to be a lowly garage mechanic with grease under your fingernails . . ."

"You know too damned much!" he said.

She leaned forward across the table and her mouth was nearly touching his.

"Then kill me—and silence me," she said. "You're good at that, aren't you?"

"No," he said sadly, "I'm not good at it. Or else I should be able to keep food in my stomach now. I drifted into activist operations, Ana, because, being young and stupid, they seemed glamorous to me. And once you're in, there's only one way out —the day they find you floating with a bullet through the back of your head. . . ."

She said quickly: "You could stay in Spain, hide, find work! Live——"

"I couldn't and you know it. Any more than Trotsky was safe in Mexico City. Or John Kennedy in Dallas. Or Ché in Bolivia once he'd outlived his usefulness. Or anyone, anywhere whom the Party has marked to die . . ."

"So you mean to go on being an assassin?" she said coldly.

He shrugged.

"And you—an assassin's assistant? As guilty as he—being an accessory before and after the fact?" he said quietly.

"That's what *you* think," she said. "Come, let's push this table out into the hall. I'm going to bed."

But during the night he woke up to hear her crying. Crying very softly in the separate twin bed a meter away. He switched on the light, said: "Ana! What's wrong?

"Nothing!" she sniffed. "My damned back aches and I can't sleep and——"

He got out of his bed. Came over to hers. Sat down on the edge of it. Began to massage her back for her. At once he felt the straps.

"What the devil's this?" he said.

"A support. A sort of a corset, really," she said. "My stomach muscles are weak. My doctor gave me this—to prevent an accidental miscarriage. Go on rubbing my back, Diego . . . it feels so good when you do that . . ."

"But," he said, "this damned thing gets in the way. Couldn't you take it off?"

"No," she said. "I only do that when I take a bath. And even then I have to move like a sleepwalker. No abrupt motions. Go ahead—please. Above and below the straps. Pass over them lightly . . ."

He massaged her back for ten minutes. Maybe fifteen.

"That's enough, Diego," she murmured. "Your hands are —sweet. And you didn't kill Enrique! You couldn't have! You don't have the hands of a murderer!"

Diego looked at her. Sighed.

"You're wrong. I killed him, all right," he said.

The next night, they got to Perpignan. By that time, she'd got all his mother's stories out of him, and all his father's, too. As they drove up to the Grand Hotel on the Quai Sadi-Carnôt, she was strangely silent, mute, rapt. He dropped her and their luggage off, then drove the Peugeot to the parking garage at the other side of the canal on the Quai Vauban. When he got back to the Grand, walking, she was just coming out of the hotel's telephone booth.

He stared at her. Said: "Whom did you call?"

She said, without hesitation: "Pili—in Paris. You know, Enrique's daughter—and my friend. I've asked her to close my place. Put it in the hands of the rental agents. You see—I'm not going back. Not ever."

He sighed.

"You're being rash," he said. "And, anyhow, I'm sorry. I was hoping that when this was over—and *that*—" he pointed to her belly—"we could see each other. Get to know each other —better. Even—maybe—become—friends."

"Why not—lovers?" she said mockingly. "Besides we are going to see a great deal of each other from here on in. Perhaps too much—like *los Amantes de Teruel* maybe. Hand in hand, forever. Because you see, *mi querido Diego,* you aren't going back either. Not *ever.*"

He stared at her. Shrugged. There was no understanding her, and he knew it. He took her arm and they went up to the desk together.

F redi," Amparo said to the Minister, "I've been granted a stay of execution. Two weeks to set my affairs in order before flying to Beirut . . ."

"I know," Federico Sales Ortega said. He was the youngest Minister in the Government, but now he felt as though he were the oldest. And that he was getting older by the minute. No, by the second. With his life bleeding out of him, draining away.

"Could—we—does the possibility even exist—of our spending those two weeks together?" Amparo whispered. "All of them? Every instant of the day—and night?"

Wearily Federico shook his head.

"No," he said, "the possibility does not even exist, and you know it, Amparo . . ."

She looked down at the floor. Looked up again. The tears were there on her face now, bright, hot, glittering, unashamed.

She said: "A man—followed me here. Who was he? One of—*hers?* Or one of the President's?"

Federico sighed.

"One of Consuelo's, I sadly fear," he said. "The President —wouldn't. I've—obeyed orders. So have you. He doesn't even expect me not to see you while you're still here. He merely asks that we be—discreet . . ."

"Oh God!" Amparo said.

"Don't worry about Consuelo's private detectives. All they can do is confirm what she already knows. And since, beyond providing her with motives for hysterical scenes, that will change absolutely nothing at all in this medieval country where divorce doesn't even exist—"

"I'd settle for a legal separation," Amparo said wistfully. "Wouldn't you, Fredi?"

"God, yes! Because that would automatically kick me out of the Government. And you and I could simply live together openly as a good many couples in Spain already do since our laws are based on religion and not on sense . . ."

"Fredi—if you were to ask *her* for the separation; what would happen then?"

"Absolutely nothing. She's got me, and she knows it. That's precisely why she isn't going to act upon any information that her detectives bring her. Legally—and, truthfully, in most other ways, except to bore me stiff!—her conduct has been above reproach. I am the guilty party. So I must suffer the punishment for my sins, which in this case consists of being held as a captive husband by the woman I don't love, while tamely letting the one I do slip out of my life."

"And I," Amparo said, "for the sins of my father. Because our entirely commonplace sin—of adultery—couldn't do that, could it, Fredi? I'm being blasted out of your office not for being your—willing and delighted!—mistress, but for being the daughter—of a Red. For bearing in my veins the blood of a man who was—shot. Who slid down the wall of the civil cemetery like a grotesque broken doll—while his life soaked out of him, turned the dirt—into mud. Brownish-black sticky mud. Have you ever seen an execution, Fredi?"

"God, no!" Federico said.

"I have. My mother used to take me to see them. You see, your good, kind, Christian—or *¡por lo menos!*—Catholic—regime went on shooting people until I was six or seven years old. Even after that, probably. No, certainly—they shot Julian Grimau in 1963, didn't they? And, by then I was twenty-two years old. No one knows how many people they shot—more, I suspect, *after* the War than during it. . . ."

"How," Federico said, "did your mother know *when* there was going to be an execution?"

"I don't know. But she *did*. Always. And took me to see them. Explained to me very carefully what was going on. We couldn't get very close, of course; but there's a little rise above the cemetery wall and there——"

"Kind of her," Federico said, drily.

"Kind? Say—mad. To do that to a child, I mean. Insane. Sick. But she did it. To instill—hate in me. To inspire me to vengeance . . ."

"And did she—succeed?" Federico whispered.

"Yes. And no. She made me hate—injustice. Cruelty. Stupidity. But it never occurred to her that those—characteristics —were no exclusive monopoly of one side—or the other. That they were—Spanish—"

"Or even—human?" Federico said.

"Or even human. As our German allies proved at Dachau, Auschwitz, Mannheim, Treblinka. As our British friends proved over Dresden. Our present allies—or should I say—Our Masters?—the Americans, demonstrated at Nagasaki. Hiroshima. My Lai. Song My. Still——"

"Still, what?" Federico said.

"It's a thing one doesn't forget. One minute—there's—a *man*. With—breath in him, Fredi. Something that we call—life. More than—just a force, somehow, wouldn't you say? A—a quality, too. Made up of hopes. Yes, yes, illusory; but does that matter? Dreams—false, to be sure; but *dreams, amor mio!* Immortal longings, totally unrealizable, of course; but—having a certain grandeur about them, no? That the poor little featherless bipeds crawling across a cinderspeck on the far edge of an incomprehensible Universe expanding—or exploding—out and away from it in every direction at at least the speed of light —a concept I got from *you*—"

"To avoid being contaminated with the disease called life, probably," Federico said. "Go on, Amparo—"

"That such poor creatures could *dare* conceive—believing them's another matter! Believing them scrapes the edge of a rather monstrous arrogance!—such a concept *is* grand. And here we have—a man. Tied to a stake before a wall. One minute sensing all that, hoping all that, feeling all that. And even— believing some of it, maybe. The next—"

"The next?" Federico said.

"Meat. Carrion. That doesn't even *look* human anymore. Pouring—blood. Sprawled out in grotesque positions that nothing *human* can ever attain. With the little black flies buzzing above it—above that *thing.* That awful, awful *thing*—"

"That a minute before—or less—had dreams, and hope and—immortal—longings in it—" Federico whispered.

"*¡Sí!* Yes. And—love—and tenderness. And—"

Federico stood up.

"Come on!" he said.

"Come on—where?" Amparo murmured.

"Don't know. Anywhere as long as it's away from here! And I don't care who sees us!" Federico Sales Ortega said.

Which was, of course, one of the two things Ernesto "Rubles" Ramirez hadn't taken into consideration; could not, in fact, by his very nature take into consideration. And the other was that Ana María surprised Diego—again.

"Let's go downstairs tonight," she said. "Have dinner in the restaurant. It's quite a good one, Diego. Besides it's—dark —and cozy. And—romantic. Tonight I feel romantic. In spite of my big belly. Or is it forbidden for women with big bellies to feel romantic?"

"I guess not," Diego said. "In fact, if they *didn't* feel romantic occasionally, they'd never get big bellies, would they?"

She looked at him. Her pale eyes were very soft and clear.

"I wish—he were—*yours,*" she whispered. "That would solve so many problems, wouldn't it?"

"Yes," Diego said. "And I suppose I could *make* him mine —legally, anyhow, couldn't I? Only—"

"Only I wouldn't let you," she said tartly. "I'd never burden you—or any other man for that matter!—with the consequences of my sins—"

"That's not where the burden lies in this case, Ana María," he said quietly.

"Then where does it?" she said.

"With—or upon—the consequences—of my own," he said.

She stared at him, and her lips made a soft, round, silent "O!" in the midst of her thin, inhollowed face.

"Don't you know that if he were anyone else's—anyone's at all—I should have already offered you that way out?" he said bitterly. "I have no bourgeois prejudices! But suppose—he looks like *him*—like your Enrique? I should have to spend the remainder of my life, staring into a replica of a face I murdered. Shattered. Splattered his blood and brains all over—"

"No!" she got out. "Don't say it! Oh, Diego—no!"

"All right," he said. "Sorry."

"Diego—don't let's spoil—tonight—please? Let's be— very careful of each other. It may be—our last night—together. And I don't want it spoiled. Oh, I don't! I don't!"

"All right. We won't spoil it. We'll celebrate instead. Only —what will we be celebrating, Ana María?"

"Don't know. Our funerals, maybe . . ."

"You've a very rare sense of humor," he said. "*Très rare.*

Muy raro. All right, the bathroom's yours. Go get prettied up. . . ."

When she came out, she was radiant. She had on the same black silk dress she had worn to church last Sunday. It was so loose that her pregnancy scarcely showed at all.

But her eyes were—queer. She seemed to be hovering on the very brink of tears. But she smiled at him, tenderly, and, going up on tiptoe, kissed his mouth.

"What was that for?" he said.

"*Por nada.* For nothing. A sample, maybe—"

"A sample of what?"

"Of my wares. Of the goods I usually *give* away. Thus defining their exact value. That *was* what you said, wasn't it?"

"Now Ana María!" he groaned.

"All right. I'll be good. Now, come on."

The first thing she said when they were seated at their table was: "Diego—order champagne . . ."

He groaned at her. Said: *"D'accord."* Signaled the wine steward.

The champagne helped. He actually got a little food down and kept it there. The more so because she kept cutting everything on her plate up into tiny pieces and pushing them into his mouth on the end of her fork. All around them, the other diners watched that performance and smiled at them. They looked so young. They seemed so devoted. And they had all of their lives before them.

After their desserts, Diego had a cognac and Ana María, a Cointreau. Which, on top of the magnum of champagne they had drunk, was maybe a drop or two too much. When they got up from the table, the floor slid out from beneath them. It took them a few seconds, and some deft footwork, to straighten the restaurant up again; to snap the walls into perfect right angles to a level floor, swing the ceiling horizontal and parallel above it. The blurs all around them grew into faces, grinning at them with a peculiarly Gallic savor, pleasantly sure of what would happen next.

"Good!" Diego said, as they groaned upstairs in the tiny, ancient lift. "I'll sleep like a log tonight!"

"No, you won't!" Ana María said.

"Just try and stop me!" he said blissfully.

She dived into the bathroom, giggling: "I'm going to have *another* bath. And get rid some of this champagne! Don't you go to sleep, Diego! Don't you dare!"

But he did go to sleep. In fact, no sooner had he got into his pajamas and tossed the covers back, than the bed rose up and hit him in the face.

Then—sometime later—he heard her voice. It was very low. But curiously harsh, somehow. Dark toned. Vibrant.

"Diego—" she said.

He opened one weary blue eye. Saw a blur standing a little way off. Then very slowly the blur cleared. Turned into her. Into Ana María. His other eye popped open. He jackknifed up. Sat there in the bed, staring at her.

She had on a nightgown made of open-meshed black net. A mist of darkness that concealed almost nothing. In fact, it would have concealed nothing at all if it hadn't had three lone sprays of embroidered black flowers strategically placed to camouflage areas, zones of her that, even small as she was, they did a far better job of calling attention to than hiding. As they had been designed to do, he realized. Deliberately.

And because that piece of gross provocation she wore accomplished its evident purpose, his eyes, with that built-in reflex that male glands, like a host of Palovian alchemists, condition into the psyche of every man, wandered all over her slender form. She was, he saw again, much too thin. She wasn't really very appealing sexually, or she wouldn't have been, except for the fact that he loved her. She was a skinny little thing with her thighs set too wide apart and tiny breasts and—

Then his brains, specifically that part of them that housed his memory, caught up with his eyes.

"*¡Niño Jesus!*" he all but screamed.

Because, below her navel, quite visible through that net,

down to the tiny tuft of jet black pubic hair that the embroidered roses didn't quite hide, her belly was as flat as table. She wasn't pregnant. She wasn't at all.

He stared at her reproachfully, sorrowfully. Saw that she was hiding something, holding it behind her.

"*Et—ton fils?*" he whispered. "*¿Tu hijo?* Your—son?"

"*Le—voilà!*" she said. "Here he is!" And brought that—thing—out from behind her.

It was a sort of pouch made, he could see, of a child's big rubber ball. It had a zipper in the top of it. Rings sewed to its sides through which those straps had been run. Under her clothes, its shape, and even its feel, had been perfect. He would never have guessed. No man ever would.

"Ana María!" he said. "Why on earth—"

"It's an invention of Ernesto's," she said calmly. "Always works. One can smuggle absolutely anything—as long as it's small enough—through the most suspicious customs men on earth in it. No one ever suspects. You almost did, though. Thought you had me—when you were kind enough to rub my aching back last night, and felt those *maldita* straps. That's the only drawback it has—gives one a fiendish backache if one has to wear it too long . . ."

"And you wore it all this time—why, Ana María?" he said.

"I wanted—to discourage you," she said. "To make sure you'd keep your hands off me. Not that I'm anything much. I've —no physical vanity. You know that, by now. But most men will sleep with a female alligator if she's—available. So . . ."

"So now you've taken it off."

"Yes. Tomorrow morning I'll put it back on again. It—gets to be awfully tiresome, y'know . . ."

"And that's why you took it off? And put on this peek-a-boo nightgown?"

"No," she said. "I took it off because I—I want to make love to you. Or with you. Or however you say it. I want to—very badly, Diego. D'you mind?"

He went on looking at her. Said: "Why?"

"*¡Oh, maldita séa!*" she exploded. "Does there have to be a reason? I just *want* to, that's all. Isn't that reason enough?"

"No," he said. "No, Ana María, it isn't."

"Ohhhh!" she wailed. "What d'you want of me, Diego? That I—I *beg* you? I won't. That's too—humiliating—even for *¡una pobre y sucia zorrita como yo!* Instead, I'll go downstairs. Take a walk. Loiter on street corners. Pick up the first man who passes by. *Gratis.* Free. Prove I'm what you think I am! Only there's no name for women like me, is there? But less—than even a whore. Although you gave me too much credit by calling me one. For whores get paid for their services—don't they?"

"Ana—stop it!" he said. "You're wrong, you know. I don't want you to beg me. But I don't want you to *use* me, either. If I'm just—somebody—you'll take on when you feel in the mood, merely because I happen to be around, forget it. Besides, *my* services aren't gratis. In fact to you, anyhow, my price is high. Too high, maybe. You couldn't pay it, I'll bet. Or you wouldn't be willing to . . ."

She stared at him, whispered: "Try me, Diego. See how much I'll offer. You might be—surprised . . ."

He shrugged; said evenly: "An offer's one thing. But the —wherewithal, Ana? To pay my—stud fee—call it? Really pay it?"

Her eyes were huge, now. Paler than ever. But they were also something else: Hurt. Troubled. Sick, his mind suggested.

She said, very, very slowly, pushing the words out like fledgling birds, tremblingly on little spurts of breath: "You know my family's rich—if that's what you mean—only—"

"Only *merde!*" he said. "That's *not* what I mean and you know it!"

"Then what *do* you mean, Diego?" she wailed. "I—I don't understand you!"

"I know. I'm asking you the highest price there is; the one you haven't even got what it takes to pay, likely. That you say, meaning it: 'I love you, Diego.' And that's rough, Ana María. Because it involves turning that 'Forsaking all others' into something more than words. Something—grave. No more fun and games. That little flat in the *Cinquième Arrondissement* you mentioned. And you in it every *sacré* night when I come home. My woman. Mine. *Mi hembra*—pledging me your life, because I'm a primitive *bestia* of a Spaniard who'll break every single bone in your body, starting from your narrow little ass and working both north and south, the *first* time you even look sidewise at another *type.* I stopped being a civilized European —stopped it for good—the exact instant I first laid eyes on you. So all you can get out of me is something you don't even want: A *Spanish* husband, damn you! *Señor y dueño de mi propia casa, y—¡más aun!—de mi propia mujer.* Lord and master of my own house, and even more than that of my own woman! You have well understood this which I have said, Ana María?"

She crossed very slowly to where he sat. Stood there before him, crying a little; already crying. Sank to her knees.

"See—" she whispered. "I'm—on my knees, Diego. How else shall I shame myself, humble myself, *mi dueño y señor?* Shall I kiss your feet?"

"No!" he said harshly. "I don't want—"

"And I'm begging you to—to take me. To take—my poor, narrow-tailed little body. Because that's the only way I know to —to say 'I love you.' Not because you asked me to say it, but because I do. I have since that day you knelt in the church at Enrique's funeral—and cried. Proved that Spaniard or not, filled with these idiotic concepts of *machismo* or not, you were —a human being. A suffering, hurting, lonely human being— conditions I could relate to, despite your face of a della Robbia angel! *¡Tan guapo y tan digna de lastima!* So handsome—and yet so pitiful. I wanted to hate you, and I couldn't. I still can't, don't. I just love you—that's all . . ."

"And I, you," he said.

"No! No! You don't have to say that! You don't have to

lie to me. Just—ease me a little. Stop me—from hurting so!"

"Ana," he said, "one night I walked all the way up the avenue Foch, and all the way back down it, looking in every window, trying to guess which one was yours—"

"I know," she whispered. "I saw you. I wanted to call out to you. I didn't dare. But I wanted to. Wanted *you* so bad I almost went out of my mind!"

"And the next Sunday, when you kissed me before *l'église de Sainte Roquette,* you said I'd pay for that kiss with my life. Do you know what? I was perfectly willing to. I still am. It's—worth it. To me, anyhow—"

"Oh no! Don't say that! Not now! Oh no, Diego, please!"

"Then, the next morning, I—almost did. Pay for it that way, I mean. When you got up off that valise and started towards the car and I saw your belly parading *la grand curva de la felicidad* before thee, I almost died. Some of me—did die, *Anita mía*—the *Spanish* part. The essential part, maybe. *Mi hombría.* My manhood. Screaming."

"Once," she whispered, taking up that contrapuntal duet of muted voices in a darkened room, "I almost—believed—almost allowed myself to believe or— *¡por lo menos!*—to hope—that you loved me. When I came back from the *cuatro de señoras en la gasolinera,* and saw you looking at me. With naked eyes. As though you were—hurting."

"I *was,*" he said grimly.

"As I am hurting now. Diego—"

"Yes, Ana María?"

"Kiss me? And—do things to me. Anything you want to. Anything that comes to your mind. And I will do anything you want me to. *Anything,* Diego!"

"No," he said, "just—love me, Ana. Just be my love. My bride. My wife. The wife you're going to be—as soon as we get back from Spain—and all this is over and—"

"Oh Diego, Diego, Diego, thou tender fool!" she said. And kissed him. Pushed free of his arms. Stepped back.

Caught the hem of that gown, and clawed it upward, making a brief, lovely Veronica of swirling net and broideries, and silk and lace. Emerged out of its darkness to become a slender reed, almost uncurving, lance straight, delicate, hollowed, night shadowed where she divided, golden all over, wild cherry tipped, now trembling, trembling under his grave blue gaze, then doubling, contorting, incurving, covering, or trying to, breasts and pelvis, with hands, arms, legs; moaning: "Do not look at me, *mi Diego!* I am too ugly! *¡Un palo!* A stick! With nothing to please a man! *¡Oh Diego, Diego—tengo miedo, miedo!* I am so afraid! I have never been afraid before, but now I am, because this will be with thee, with *thee!* And also I have a shame unsupportable, and even a coldness and—"

He put out his arms to her.

"Come, Ana," he said, "come—be my love—"

With a wild skip and scamper she hurled herself into his arms and lay there curled up against him, soaking his pajama top with bitter tears.

"Thou canst not love me!" she wept. "Thou canst not! I am ugly and *una esqueleta*—a skeleton—all bones—and, additionally, I am a bad, cheap promiscuous woman—*less* than a whore even and—"

He bent and kissed her mouth. Her eyes flared all the colors of a predawn sky. Palely. Then she closed them, slowly, slowly. Her fingers came up and toyed with the top button of his pajamas. Stopped. Trembled there.

He smiled at her. Said: "Go ahead. For I am as much thine as thou'rt mine, and I ask no more of thee than I almost promise. Thou wilt be the only woman in my life, Ana. And the last one."

"Oh, Diego!" she moaned; and tried to strangle him and devour him and crush him all at one and the same time, which made getting out of those pajamas much more difficult; but he managed it, finally.

And then—he couldn't. He really couldn't. His male flesh

failed him. She looked so small and fragile and doelike and helpless. She woke a crippling kind of tenderness in him, an emasculating pity. He was too aware of—*who* she was. That this was—Ana María, achingly beloved, in spite of everything. A—person. A human being, quirky, odd, awful, mad as a hatter, complicated, complex, frightening and—lovable. That *he* loved her, adored her, worshipped her to an extent, degree, depth, completeness that included every fiber of his being, every breath he'd ever draw, every hope, dream, joy, pain he'd ever know until they laid him forever underground. With her beside him, maybe.

So to him now, she wasn't, couldn't be just a warm, usefully female little body. She was too much more than that.

Far, far more than a casual piece of tail, than a hairy, hot wet little slit to be plunged into, roaring, fierce, wild, until—

'I spill my life in her,' he thought, 'make with her another life—'

Then he felt, and, raising his own, saw her eyes. The hurt in them, the shame were, without any doubt whatsoever *the* most unbearable things he had witnessed in all his life.

"Thou seest?" she moaned. "Thou canst not love me! Thou canst not, Diego! I awake a repugnance in thee! Or my body does! My ugliness! Oh, let me go! Let me go!"

But he bent and kissed her. Her mouth. Her throat. The dark cherry colored nipples of her tiny breasts. She clung to him, crying.

And then, quite suddenly, he could. He broke through the stranglehold his nerves had on his senses, broke through it all at once in a shattering surge of feeling, uncontrolled and uncontrollable, and, rearing up, arching his body like a bow, slammed down upon her, piercing—and violating—her narrow loins with one brutal, mindless thrust that ended the matter in half a heartbeat, helplessly bursting within her, hopelessly exploding, scaldingly jetting into her soft fleshly passage, flooding her all too receptive womb with the thickened juices of all his private disasters: his loneliness, terror, pain, the long horror of his existence, his blinding, aching need—for union and continuation, both—which is a hell of a thing to do to a woman under any circumstances, and lacking, as it did now, even the saving grace of sharing, of mutuality, became unpardonable.

Which he realized, sensed, knew. He lay there, trembling, gasping for breath, sick to his guts, or to his soul, or both, with shame. Raised his face from where he had buried it between her shoulder and her neck. Looked into those pale, pansy-colored eyes.

"Ana, I—I'm sorry!" he all but wept.

"You damned Spaniard!" she spat. "Bulls in a china shop, every one of you! Apes not even trying to play a violin! *The worst lovers in Europe, bar none!*"

"Ana!" he wailed.

"Diego!" she mocked. "Oh, why do I *always* have to fall in love with *cretinos?* With baby boys who don't even know *how?*"

She paused, peered into his eyes. Grinned at him, mischieviously. Went on: "You aren't going to *cry,* are you? So help me, I'll belt you one if you do! All right! All right! Calm down. It doesn't matter. I'm not going anywhere. And you aren't either, *Diegito mío!* Which means I've got all night to teach you just what this is all about. So—relax. Rest. Lie back down, *niñito,* and allow thy *mamacita* to attend to thee. To thee, my tiny, *dulce,* baby boy! My boy baby—my sweet little helpless boy baby who needs to be kissed—like this—here and here and over here and down here—and all over!"

"Ana!" he gasped, shocked to the core of the stern, essentially puritanical Iberian soul his mother had instilled in him or inflicted up him, or both: *"¡Por el amor de Dios!"*

"No. Not for God's love. For thine!" she laughed, and bit him in several outrageous places, sharp little nibbling bites that stung and tingled; then she straightened up and chewed playfully upon his left ear. "Don't you like being made love to? I'm good at it, y'know. Let's see, what form of celestial music shall I play to insure a rapid resurrection? The trumpet of the angel? Let me see—let me see—Ah! Sweet! D'you like—this?"

"Ana!" he cried.

"Ah—so? One blast and the dead awakens! But Diego—dear Diego—let us not kill him quite so fast this time, no?"

And it was all right. Just barely. But all right. For her, too. And it got better all night long. By morning it was wonderful.

Until they couldn't anymore. Not either one of them. They lay in each other's arms, sweat soaked and three quarters dead and fairly swooning from sheer tenderness, and Ana María was still kissing him every place she could reach and sobbing aloud and saying: "No. Let us not cross the frontier today but stay here without getting up for a week a month a year! Let us go back to Paris together and I will be thy woman and I shall murder Ernesto so that he can never harm thee! Abort the filthy mission for I was wrong. Thou didst not kill Enrique, thou couldst not have done a thing like that and even if thou didst I love thee and—"

And he sadly: "I killed him all right. Ana—tell me something. In the church—you had on that black dress. A dress from the *prémaman.* At his funeral. *Before* you knew me. Ernesto guessed I would go that funeral—and gave you a message for me. But you had no reason to put on that—thing—then. None at all."

She looked up. Tightened her arms about his neck. Drew him down so that his head was resting on one of her small, firm breasts.

"I was—mad then, Diego," she said quietly. *"Loca de remate. Folle*—insane. You see—Enrique—left me last January—"

"What!" Diego said.

"And, after he had broken with me, I found out I was pregnant. Called him and told him. Got him back that way. He made me see hell—trying to make me get an abortion, leave Paris, go back to Spain. Anything—to insure, or regain his own peace of mind. Then late in February I—I lost my child. Or maybe I never was pregnant in the first place. When one gets that desperate, the mind plays tricks on the body, sometimes. A woman's mind does, anyhow. Quite frequently, in fact. Then —I *think*—because I don't really remember anything about that time—I must have remembered Ernesto's—invention. And I had one of the obscene things at home, because I'd run microfilmed directives into Spain last year, as a dear little pregnant wife rejoining her nonexistent husband in Gijon, I think it was. So I started wearing it. To—torment him. To torment myself. By the time—he died—I really wasn't very clear about what was real and what wasn't. I used to vomit in the mornings. Every morning. My ankles swelled up. My belly, too. Even without that thing I could look quite remarkably knocked up. And since I really wasn't sleeping with anyone, I couldn't have been, now could I—?"

"It's all right," he said. "It's going to be all right for us now. Everything is. Just you wait."

"Yes," she whispered, "but I do wish you hadn't killed him. Not for him, Diego, but for you! For you! To kill like that —in cold blood—does something to a man. In a raid—a gun battle with los Guardia Civiles—it's different. A man who kills defending his life, his cause, even his woman is—much! Shooting *back,* not just shooting—"

"Ana—" he said, "*Anita mía, chatita de mi alma*—it wasn't like that. It wasn't like that at all. I *didn't* kill him in cold blood. In fact, *I* didn't kill him at all. A potato omelette did . . ."

"A potato omelette? *¿Una tortilla española?* Thou art— mad, too, Diego! Madder than I am!"

"No. *Escuchame, niña.* Listen to me, girl. We talked. Much. Hours and hours of talking. He—got to me. Unsettled my ideas. Shook my beliefs . . ."

"He *could*," she whispered. "Enrique was a marvelous talker. Go on. Diego . . ."

"We became friends. *Amigos.* Almost brothers. I grew *very* fond of him."

"True. Everyone did—always," she murmured.

"So one day I said to him: 'To hell with the Party! Nothing is served by jeopardizing a man like thee. I am going to let thee go!'"

She stared at Diego. Her pale eyes had eclipsed her tiny face.

"And he said, 'Won't you get in trouble?' And I, 'Yes—very likely.' And he: 'Come then, let us arrange it—make it look good . . .'"

"And?" Ana María got out, her voice a ripple beneath a pool called silence.

"We arranged a story that I had to take the leg irons off him because they had chafed his ankles and he was bleeding. A story which was almost true. Then he was to hit me. Hard enough to bruise my face so that it would show . . ."

"And—he—he *did* that?"

"Yes. But first we wrecked the place between us to show how fierce had been our struggle before he bested me, knocked me unconscious. And the potato omlette he was supposed to eat for lunch fell on the floor . . ."

"And?" Ana María said again. Or at least her lips shaped the word. Not that he could hear it.

"When he hit me—as arranged—he punched me so hard that I reeled, stepped into it. *¡En ese mil veces maldita tortilla española!*—slipped, fell back up against the shelf I'd laid my little machine gun on. The shock knocked it to the floor—and it went off. One bullet, just one, *Ana de mi alma*—went through his head. But that one was enough. What a nine millimeter parabellum slug does to the human skull is—horrible. I stood there looking at him. At what was left of him. And I started to shake. To vomit. To cry. I cried like a *niño. Un bébé.* A—Ana!"

For she had turned over face downward and had buried her face in that sweat-soaked pillow and was screaming into it like a mad woman and pounding the bed with both her fists and twisting all her small, much too thin, naked body as though she were being tortured to death, as she maybe even was.

"Now," he said sadly, "now I have lost thee, haven't I? For thou wilt never love another as thou hast loved him, truly. And of a verity that he died of my clumsiness and my stupidity is even worse than my murdering him would have been—is this not so?"

She whirled; faced him; lunged for him like a wild thing; clawed him into her arms.

"No and no and no and no!" she stormed. "Thou hast it wrong—all wrong! I screamed like that because I have betrayed thee, Diego! And for nothing! For a crime thou didst not do! The day we left Paris I called La Dirección General de Seguridad in Madrid and gave them the description and the *matrícula* of our car! Last night I called both Port Bou and le Perthus and told them it was *this* frontier we would cross, gave them additionally a perfect description of us both! In my kangaroo pouch I have *dos pistolas*—one for thee, and one for me! We were going to have to make a stand this morning, *amor mío*! We were going to have to die!"

He stared at her. Even his lips were white.

"But—*together*. Because I could not help loving thee, and thought thee a cowardly murderer, and the combination of the two, too shameful!"

"But this of—of couching thyself with me—why that, then, Ana María?" he said.

"Thou wert to—to die. And I—also. And to the condemned they grant always a hearty meal and a visit from his woman if he has a woman. So I said: 'I have taken away his life. The least I can do is to give him a little pleasure. I will let him screw me.'" She used the ugly, explicit word *joder,* which is every bit as rough in Spanish as "fuck" is in English, and the sound of it got him wild. He tore free of her, slapped her across the mouth. Slapped her so hard that her big, thick lips broke like ripe plums and showered blood all down her chin. Then she was kneeling on the bed before him and had taken the hand he had slapped her with and was kissing it with great, wet, bloody kisses and shaking and crying until he drew her to him, whispered: *"¡No importa, Ana María, te quiero! Y si tengo que morir sería una felicidad contigo y una muerte buena. So—"* "It doesn't matter, Ana María, I love thee. And if I have to die with thee it will be a happiness. And a good death. So—"

"So . . ." she smiled at him through her tears shaking still, still crying, "I also was—am condemned, *mi* Diego, and that was *my* last hearty meal and also *my* pleasure! More mine than thine, for I wore thee out!"

He pushed his big hand through her close-cropped gamine's hair. Grinned at her. Said: "Get up from there! Go take a bath. But a shower, not the tub, for we have no time. For of a verity thy smell is of the grandmother of all the whores, and mine of the oldest billy goat among thy customers! You hear me, woman! Go!"

"But—but," she whispered, "where are we going? Where *can* we go now? If we go back to Paris, Ernesto will order thy death—and maybe even mine, though that matters not . . ."

"Not to Paris. To the airport. We'll ditch the heap before we get there. Wreck it. Make it look like an accident. Set it afire even. Then an Air Inter plane to Nice . . ."

"And from there?" she whispered. "In another plane?"

"To Málaga. Barcelona and Madrid are no good. But no one will be looking for us in Málaga. There we'll rent a little car. With Spanish plates. A little Seat one-thirty-three, say. Drive up to Madrid, enter it amid all that traffic . . ."

Ana María stared at him.

"And we—carry out—the mission?"

"Yes," he said. "We have to. Which will give us—a breathing spell. We return to Paris—convince Ernesto that our pictures are plastered all over Spain. That our cover is blown for good. Ask to be transferred to Agitprop—Agitation and Propaganda. Political action. . . . And in time . . ."

"In time—what, Diego?" she said.

"America. Where it is easy to—disappear. Where maybe

even Ernesto cannot quickly find us. Long enough to have him write us off as being of too little importance to hunt us down. . . ."

"Will he?" she whispered. "Has he—ever?"

"So far, no. But there has to be a first time, hasn't there? For everything. Now, come on!" Diego said.

8

*E*rnesto," the man in the black fedora said, "I don't like your methods. I find them—disquieting. Audacity is one thing. Taking—well—insane risks is another. We can't afford public failure, you know . . ."

Ernesto looked at the man in the black fedora. The eyes hid behind dark glasses even though it was night, and seeing through them must have constituted a problem. And the hands were encased in tight, black leather gloves, although at this time of year—

'Sheer theatricality,' he thought with cold contempt. 'Straight out of Hollywood. "The spy who came in from the cold." The Third Man, lacking only the zither. With this kind of cheap—and dangerous—histrionics, is it any wonder that we so often fail?'

"Have you ever known anything *I* set up not to work?" he said.

"No. I grant you that. But with each—action, you've grown—bolder. Everything you do—is always more spectacular than the effort immediately preceding it was. So, when you *do* fail—as you *must,* one day, being human, and the laws of probability being what they are—"

"My failure will be a success," Ernesto said, "achieving ends even greater than those the original project called for . . ."

The man in the black fedora glared at Ernesto. Even through the thick glasses the glitter of his pupils showed.

"Megalomania has been the destruction of many another Chief Operative, camarada," he said.

"True," Ernesto said, "but to a far less extent than a want of imagination has, Comrade General."

"All right," the man in the black fedora said. "Explain this one to me. I take it that—your objective is not—either the Chief of State, or his Prime Minister? Or as they call that office in Spain, the President of the Government?"

"Of course not. Why should we kill our friends?"

"Friends!" the Comrade General said.

"Friends," Ernesto said, "or at least useful to us. Tell me, Comrade General—would you rather take over—or, more accurately, attempt to take over—a government headed by liberal moderates, busily handing out concessions to the workers, students, intellectuals, and other discontented elements with both hands—or a government headed by rightist political blockheads whose concepts of statesmanship consist of clamping the lid firmly down on *any* type of even apparent liberty, and reposing their buttocks—of Isabela la Catolica—as the Spanish wags put it!—atop said lid to keep it in place?"

"Hmmmmm. I see. So that was why you opposed the liquidation of the Admiral?"

"Of course. A man of such monumental, magisterial stupidity was all but invaluable to us. But *our* blockheads insisted upon aiding those Basque idiots in that one. Wait. Listen to me a moment, Comrade General! The time is ripe now—and getting riper. If we do not blow all our chances, we cannot fail. The Prime Minister—the President of the Government—is a man of *great* intelligence. A most worthy foe. Even so we cannot afford to decorate him with a martyr's crown. He is tired. Very tired. And being intelligent he knows that his identification with the Franco regime sharply limits his possibilities for effective action in the post-Franco era. *No one* tarred with that brush is likely to survive. The whole country, right and left, has had a bellyful of the lot of them . . ."

"So?" the Comrade General said.

"So he is training a crack crew of replacements. Most of them socialists, or at least technocrats, apolitical public servants of the highest order. His grasp of what is necessary to save the country, to prevent chaos—and hence block *us*—for in private you'll permit me the weary observation that without chaos we *never* get anywhere, won't you?—is impressive. So, Comrade General, I submit that to attack—except publicly, making the required noises which win the applause of cretins—the very neanderthal rightist troglodytes whose crashing, thunderous stupidity— *'¡Abajo la inteligencia! Viva la muerte!'* will insure our final victory—is, shall we say, something less than bright?"

"Again I grant you your point. But that is not the source of my disquietude, Comrade Ernesto. Your methods are what worry me. You send a couple of children—"

"Ah! But *what* children, Comrade General! The best. The very best."

"Best for what? To make all the stupid mistakes that young hotheads always do?"

"Of course. Even *that.* Put it this way, Comrade General. There is absolutely no mistake that they *can* make that will not benefit us in one way or another. Have you ever heard the story of the two Japanese businessmen in the Tokyo railroad station?"

"No," the man in the black fedora said.

"They met there by accident, those two oh so subtle Oriental gentlemen. And one of them says to the other: 'Where are you going?' 'To Osaka,' the other replies. Whereupon the first wags his finger in the other's face and chuckles: 'Oh, you clever fellow! You only told me you were going to Osaka to make me think you were going to Kobe! But I have investigated and I know you are *really* going to Osaka!' "

"So?" the Comrade General said. "Makes no sense to me."

"On the contrary, it makes beautiful sense, Comrade General! The Party gives me a directive. An objective to carry out. Which I obey—after I have arranged two or three *other* objectives far more important than those dullards in Agitprop could *ever* conceive of, to which our efforts can be diverted if their usually quite moronic original objective proves too dangerous or impossible or—better still, the very failure of the original objective will automatically cause to succeed. You see?"

"I see you're a devious man, camarada," the Comrade General said.

Ernesto shrugged.

"Devious—perhaps. But never stupid," he said calmly. "Please listen. Take my children, as you call them. The boy sustained two weeks of the cleverest kind of persuasion at the hands of the very best of their socialist technocrats. Allowed him to believe that his so very subtle—no, even intelligent—arguments had convinced him. Then killed him when he attempted to escape . . ."

"The Vice Consul?" the Comrade General said.

"The Vice Consul. So now you have this boy of mine. Mine in the sense that I trained him. That I *know* I can trust him. An idealist. A true believer. But he has—other qualities. Or defects depending upon your point of view. Other—limitations say. So I use both his virtues and his defects, his qualities and his limitations, for the greater good of the Party. For instance, I've told you he is a true believer. So, among the things that he believes—and will confess to if captured and tortured sufficiently—is that his objective is the Prime Minister, the President of the Government. He believes this most sincerely, because I have taken a great deal of pain to plant that idea into his charmingly idealistic young head without ever specifically telling him so in concrete terms, explicit words. So if he fails —and I don't think he will, because his domination of his nerves is admirable—the only information they *can* get out of him will be entirely misleading. On the other hand, if he succeeds, we will have eliminated one of the few men in Spain who is a real danger to . . ."

"And the girl?" the man in the black fedora said.

"A marvel. A perfect marvel. Daughter of the Counts of Casaribiera. Related to *both* the warring Bourbon branches of the royal house. *Very* bright. A feminist. A rebel. But one who supports us out of ardent conviction. In fact, the mere revelation that a girl of her background, of her social stratum could belong to the Party, would be, if it is ever made public, a major victory for us. The only thing *I* fear is that if they do capture her, they'll probably turn her loose and keep their mouths shut —which would be, actually, the intelligent thing for them to do. Because the scandal attendant upon a public trial of *la petite* Ana María would be major, and contribute greatly to the breakdown of the Government's trust in a powerful segment—I refer, of course, to the Monarchists—of the people who currently support it."

"That being so," the Comrade General said drily, "and I can see how it could be, they'll attempt to discredit her. And they can. She's given them ammunition enough to use against her, camarada. Her private life is not only deplorable, it's not even private. She has been a public scandal ever since she came here to Paris . . ."

Ernesto smiled.

"One can see you do not know the Spanish, Comrade General," he said.

"I have never claimed to. They are all incomprehensible, not to mention mad in various tiresome ways."

"Say anachronistic ways, Comrade General."

"I do not follow you, camarada!"

"They have a quaint old-fashioned belief in national honor. They honestly believe that they are not as other men are. That their women—are more womanly. Chaster, purer, more decent."

"Are they?" the Comrade General said.

"Since women are remarkably adaptable little creatures who, in every society, tend to take upon themselves the protective coloring of the image that their particular society has of them, I rather think they are. The experience of my youth in that country was that they were quite tiresomely difficult to seduce; and that, having seduced them, the whole thing was never worth the bother, because every mother's daughter of them was appallingly inept at making love. They have to be for the very simple reason that when, for generation after generation, the whole female half of a nation's population has been taught to despise the instrument—in this case, the human body —and hate the process—simple normal sex—by their Father Confessors, those curious emotional castrates and/or secret homosexuals that any man *has* to be to even want to become a priest of a religion that demands celibacy of him, that result is inevitable, or very nearly. Of course some Spanish girls are blessed with enough African warmth to overcome the problem finally, if one has the time and the patience to wait for them to arrive at a state that for any other European woman would be mere normality. Having neither, I soon decided that any French barmaid was worth the lot of them!

"But we digress, don't we? The point is, Comrade General, that given the Spaniards' conception of themselves, they won't use that particular weapon against our Ana María. They won't, because they can't."

"And why can't they?" the Comrade General said.

"Because the very admission that a highborn Spanish maiden could be capable of such behavior is, to their way of thinking, even *more* damaging to their national pride than her belonging to the Party would be. They'll try to dismiss her as *una tonta util*—a useful dupe of ours. To the peculiar Spanish concepts of honor, that is far, far more acceptable than calling her the little bitch she unfortunately also is, would be. Besides which, she knows too ruddy much about too bloody many of them, anyhow. So—"

"So in the resulting display of soiled aristocratic bed linen, the results will be—much do I fear it, camarada!—that the main objective will be forgotten. That Sales Ortega—"

"Will die. He must. He's the President's hand-picked successor. I had the occasion to study him because during the whole of last summer he was the invited guest of the *late* Vice Consul, Don Enrique Ximenez Calvo, here in Paris. And even more usefully, to study his *wife*. Incidentally, the very best, the most accurate—venomously accurate as far as the wife, Doña Consuelo, was concerned—notes on *el matrimonio Sales Ortega/Marin Serrador* were brought me by our dear little Ana María, herself . . ."

"And?" the Comrade General said.

"They confirmed the impressions of our people in Madrid. Even went beyond them. María del Buen Consuelo Marin Serrador de Ximenez is your typical haute bourgeois Spanish woman. In short, *une idiote*. A highly decorative idiot, but still an idiot. And what was rather better for my purpose, a *dull* idiot in addition."

"While Sales Ortega?" the Comrade General said.

"Is a brilliant, imaginative man. So brilliant and so imaginative that he fell—with ludicrous ease—straight into my Japanese trap."

"Your Japanese trap?" the Comrade General said.

"Yes. I planted a girl in his office. Not very pretty. Not even very young. Amparo's thirty-three. From a *Republican* family. Her father was shot by the Franquistas—"

"In short, all *wrong* from the viewpoint of conventional espionage?" the Comrade General said.

"Exactly! And hence perfect for *our* purposes. What class

of bed-bait would one ordinarily *not* place in a Spanish minister's office? A brunette, because Spaniards are wild over *suecas* —Swedes—as they call all blondes. A woman of thirty-three, because most Spaniards of forty or fifty are still playing with doll babies young enough to be their granddaughters. From a *Red* family because no man in his right mind would use a girl from such a background as bait. Which is *why* he believed her sincerity at once when she timidly and tearfully confessed her origins to him, as I had instructed her to do. So we arrive at Osaka, by way of Kobe—"

"What was to guarantee he'd pay her the slightest attention?" the Comrade General said.

"Amparo, herself. She invented charm, and still holds the original patent on it. She has at least ten times more sex appeal than any of the faded peroxided whores that people pay fortunes to see in the cinema here. *Subtle* sex appeal. And she has a mind. Vast culture. She can talk his language. And she's got him. Operatives of mine report that he's literally eating out of her hand—"

"And she will—"

"Ask him to take her to lunch at a certain midtown restaurant. A popular, public place. Excuse herself to go powder her dainty nose. By which time my pretty blond boy and his monkey-faced little aristocratic accomplice will have delivered a small package to said restaurant. After which the boy, I hope, escapes. He's good. I have high hopes for him."

"But the girl?"

"I'd rather like for them to capture her. As I said before she will prove to be close to the most embarrassing captive they've ever taken. If the daughter of the Counts of Casaribiera turns out to be a Red, *whom* will they dare trust thereafter?"

"I see. And I withdraw my objections. For the time being, anyhow," the Comrade General said.

"We *could* take a plane," Diego said to Ana María. "Fly straight into Barrajas. It would be perfectly safe. We don't have to pass through passport control any more, now—"

Ana María stood there before the window of their room in La Pension Derby, in the Place Quiepo de Llano, in Málaga. At an oblique angle she could see the Mediterranean. It was very blue. Above it, the gulls wheeled, crying.

"You know, I'd almost forgotten how blue it is," she said.

"How blue *what* is?" Diego said.

"The sea. *Mare Nostrum. Our* sea. Come look at it, Diego."

"Ana María!" said Diego. "Can't you understand? We've got to get to Madrid as quickly as possible, and—"

"No," she said. "I can't understand. You'll never make me understand that we *have* to go to Madrid, have to kill people, instead of—just staying *here,* say. In this beautiful place. You could find work. You really are a good mechanic, aren't you? And Papa would send me money—especially after I'd told him that I—that we—had got married. That I was going to be a good *pequeña burguesa* housewife and make him just loads and heaps of grandchildren and—"

"He wouldn't approve, Ana," Diego said sadly. "I don't have a coat of arms. I don't even know the names of my great-grandfathers . . ."

"He wouldn't like it," Ana María whispered, "but he *would* approve, Diego. In comparison to what my life was, before I met you, I mean, my marrying a nice, decent working boy and settling down would appear to him a vast improvement. Especially after I tell him we plan to—emigrate—to South America. To Brazil—*why* Brazil, Diego?"

"Big enough to get lost in. And there're opportunities there. And the government's fairly stable. They're not killing people day and night there the way they are nearly everywhere else in South America—"

She turned, faced him. Her eyes were very big. Pale—luminous. Or—illuminated. From within, maybe. Set afire by all the things that were happening to her inside herself. At the center of her being.

"Diego—you're *not* a killer. You don't *like* killing people.

So what we *ought* to do is to go out to the airport right now and buy tickets for São Paulo. We don't have to go to Madrid! We don't! We don't! We don't!"

"We'd get to São Paulo almost without a centavo," he said slowly. "As tourists—with a limited permission to stay in the country. And before even that limited permission were halfway up—a couple of faceless men—"

"Faceless?" Ana Maria said.

"In the sense that the kind of faces they do have would fit almost anybody, because they have no distinguishing features, Ana; not a single one. The nondescript kind of mugs that make it impossible for a witness to be sure that the *types* in the police lineup actually *were* the men he saw doing what he saw them do. The faceless men that Ernesto always uses. In Brazil, they'd be dark. With *bigotes*—mustaches, some of them. Others, without. Average height, because people remember both dwarfs and giants. Mixed breeds: Portuguese, Indian, Negro. Like forty million other Brazilians. And they'd ride by in a car. A stolen car, with an altered license plate. And you and I would be sitting at a sidewalk café when they came. Or walking hand in hand. And they'd poke those Mauser machine pistols through a window rolled only a little way down. Those long-barreled Mausers, equipped with silencers. In the kind of traffic São Paulo's got, nobody would even hear the shots. People would think we were having fits. Until they saw the blood . . ."

"So—to save our lives we've got to—to kill someone else?" she whispered.

"Perhaps. Though I hope not," Diego said. "I'm going to see if I can't avoid it. First we'll try to find a place that's got a pay phone in it—and that's only a few meters from our target. What's that place called, Ana?"

Ana María picked up the big magnifying glass of the type that stamp collectors use. Turned on the table lamp. Unrolled the strip of microfilm against its parchment shade. Studied the microfilm frame by eight-millimeter frame . . .

"You should know it by heart by now!" Diego said crossly. "We've got to burn those damned instructions, you know!"

She didn't answer him. She went on studying the film.

"La Marisqueria Principe," she said, "in la Calle de Esparteros. Just before you get to la Calle Mayor."

"Jesus!" Diego said.

"I *told* you that this was a suicide mission, Diego!" she said. "I told you! He *wants* us dead. For reasons of his own he wants—"

She stopped. Her pale eyes widened.

"No," she whispered, "that's *not* what he wants. Not entirely, anyhow. He wants you—to kill—whoever the prospective victim is—"

"The President of the Government," Diego said.

"No! What the devil would the President *ever* be doing in an ordinary shellfish bar? He *couldn't,* Diego! His own security men wouldn't *let* him. And besides there's this—girl—we're supposed to contact. This Amparo. She's to *bring* the victim there. What does that tell you?"

"That she's his *querida.* His mistress."

"Right. His—mistress. Thrown into his path—like so much tasty *meat*—by Ernesto. To—buy a man's *death,* with her body. To use what we did last night—"

"And *this* morning," Diego said, and grinned at her.

"And this morning. And are going to every blessed night and morning, and as many afternoons as we can manage—"

"*¡Ten piedad!*" Diego groaned. "Have pity, will you?"

"For all the rest of our lives. To use *that*—as an instrument of murder. All that—"

"That *what?*" he said, teasing her.

"*Tenura.* Tenderness. That—miracle. That blinding, crippling, shattering instant—*¡de asesina dulcura!*—of murderous sweetness!—when I stop being *me*—ugly, skinny, big-mouthed, disgusting me. Become *you,* sort of. Or part of you, anyhow."

"The better part," he said.

"No! No! But not the worse part, either. Just *you*—and therefore—perfect."

"I don't think you're getting this right, Ana María," he said solemnly. "Maybe we *both* change—into someone else—"

"Yes. But only *one* someone, not two, Diego! The only time between the instant that the doctor smacks our little wet, messy, slimy, bloody behinds to make us bawl—and thereby live! for what is life but crying?—and the moment they nail us into our wooden pajamas and shovel us underground, when we aren't—separate and alone. The sole interval—so short, so short!—we really and truly aren't afraid. When we're actually happy. Happy without doubts or reservations. When we—defeat *Death, amor mío!* Or at least push it back—another lifetime. Prolong ourselves—renewed—and—and—combined. Oh, Diego, Diego! How lovely! You and me combined into one, little, soft, warm, sweet, gurgling—"

"Little bastard who pisses and pukes, and shits all over himself, yells all night long and—"

"Diego, I'm going to *hit* you!" she howled.

"I'm only teasing, Ana. I want him, too—this son that only *cretinos* like us would even try to make under the infernal circumstances we find ourselves in. And if he does yell all night, I'll get up and walk him."

"We'll take turns. But what *can* she be like, this Amparo? To do that? You said once that I was less than a whore, but she—"

"Is more. Enormously more. I think she must be like my Tía Juana—"

"Your *aunt?* And what's she like?"

"Mad. She's in the *manico mio de leganes.* Near Madrid. Only she's calm now. Apathetic. At first—she would throw up if a man tried to touch her. After the Moors and the Legionnaires got through with her. In Asturias. In nineteen thirty-four. She's my mother's sister, y'know. She was visiting Mama —and Mama's first husband—when the miners' revolt broke out. Then later on, she went through a stage where she tried to kill every man who came close to her. But now, they say, she's calm. I haven't seen her in years, of course . . .''

"And you think that this—Amparo is—"

"Mad? No. Because she evidently functions on a level high enough for Ernesto to trust her. Say—damaged. To the extent that getting even seems to be her only *raison d'être.* Hate's a powerful fuel, Ana. Stronger than love, sometimes.''

"But—to do *that.* To use herself—as *ceba*—bait. Her body —as—''

"A weapon of warfare. An instrument of murder. Yes. Didn't you ever study abnormal psychology? It's a Party requisite, above certain hierarchical levels . . .''

"Did *you?*'' Ana María said.

"Yes. In Czechoslovakia. Under a German psychiatrist. *The* most brilliant man I've ever known. Put it this way: Any goal strong enough to become obsessional depersonalizes. So her body probably doesn't seem very real to her. Apart from the fact that she's probably frigid—as all whores are, or soon get to be—screwing this *type* to get him into her power probably gives her superiority feelings, mental satisfactions of a purely malicious keenness you couldn't even imagine, *chata,* and—''

"Don't call me *'chata'*! I'll admit I've got a pug nose, but I *hate* that name. Well, if her mental satisfactions can come anywhere close to matching my physical ones, why— No. That's not right, either. Or at least not entirely.''

"You've lost me again,'' he said.

"That's because you're a mere *man.* What I mean is that for a woman, a *real* woman, a true one—her satisfactions *have* to be mental or maybe even spiritual, or they never even *get* to be physical. In other words, a woman *can't* separate the two things and doesn't even want to . . .''

"Greek,'' he said. "Ancient, Attic, and pure!''

"I know. A man—*¡Que bestias sois!*—can go up to the Étoile

or down to the Madeleine and pick up a *poule.* You know what would happen if I got into bed with a man—however handsome —whom I didn't even *know?* To me, I mean, because quite a lot would happen to him—*¡el animal!*—to me—nothing. Absolutely nothing. And it wouldn't matter how *expert,* how skillful he was. Make it *worse,* likely. All that *technique*—ugh! There's —depersonalization for you!"

"You know," Diego said quietly, "I doubt that. I don't think you're telling the truth now. Not the whole truth, anyhow."

"And you're right. I—*might*—respond. If he were handsome enough. And gay—and silly—and romantic—and I liked him. I might. A little. In fact, I've had a fairish amount of that kind of—of—meaningless fun. But the trouble is that it *usually* doesn't work at all, and when it does, it works only a little and leaves a girl all—hung up—"

"And *hard* up," he said drily.

"And hard up. *Le mot juste, n'est-ce pas?* So that she's likely to do something extravagantly and excessively foolish, and go through some really rotten times as a result. But for my body to *do* what it did with Enrique—what it does with you—"

He said, even more quietly: "Thank you for throwing in that sop to my pride . . ."

"Oh, damn you, Diego! I'm twenty-six years old! There was no reason on earth for me to put on a medieval chastity belt and sit around in it waiting for *you* to show up! I loved Enrique. I *love* you. And don't ask me to even try to judge which of the two of you I *loved*—love—more. I don't know. You're—day and night. Or you *were.* And you have *all* the advantages. You —love me. Or at least I hope you do. And you're—alive. Oh, no! Oh, no, *amor mío!* I'm not reproaching you for *that.* It has nothing to do with us, any longer. All I'm saying is: For me to respond to a man the *way* I respond to you—to cripple myself like that, murder myself like that—I have to love him. Therefore, it has happened to me just *twice.* In all my life—twice. In

spite of all my—whoring around, as you so delicately put it!—
I have only—gone mad, broken my heart, shattered my mind,
lost consciousness physically, maybe even died a little—with
two men. Enrique—and you. And he's—dead. And you're—
here . . . Only I think that a political murder—or any other kind
of a murder for that matter!—is one hell of a basis to start our
lives together on. That it will—ruin us, even if we get away with
it. Poison what we've got right now . . ."

"I agree," Diego said sadly. Then: "Ana, you're right! It
can't be the President, can it? No President *could* keep a mistress these days, could he? What with the media watching every
move he makes and—and his never being able to be alone with
her because of security regulations—*merde,* he has a hard time
being alone with his own *wife* without some gorilla hiding
under the bed to make sure he doesn't do it to her too hard and
give himself a heart attack! And la Calle de Esparteros! Hell,
they'd cordon off the whole *maldita* street with carloads of
uniformed apes, if he ever decided to drop into that *marisqueria*
to eat a *langosta*! So who—"

"Someone *less* than the President," Ana Maria said slowly.
"*Far* less. Someone who *can* keep a mistress. Whose life is not
watched, controlled. Hence someone not very important—"

"Then why the devil would Ernesto—?"

"Want to kill him? I don't know. But I can guess. Say—
it's because the way Ernesto's mind works. Like a chess player's.
Always forty moves ahead of his opponents like the grand
master he is. So he has seen that this one will get to be important. Perhaps after the Caudillo dies. Very, very important
likely. Therefore he has planted this Amparo in his life. In his
bed. But forget that part, Diego. We're not concerned about
who the white king is; Or the black queen—Amparo. Nor the
bishops, rooks, knights. What we've got to take care of right
now is a couple of lowly pawns—"

"Pawns?" Diego said.

"Yes, you and me. Why did Ernesto choose *us* for this

mission, *caro?* We're all *wrong,* y'know."

"Wrong how?" Diego said.

"The Party is not ETA. It has *never* been guilty of the sort of abysmally stupid tactical mistakes that those Basque imbeciles make *all* the time. And ordinarily to send in a couple like you and me is precisely what the Party wouldn't do and what ETA *would.* . . ."

"Why not?" Diego said.

"Because, unlike the Party, ETA uses *young* operatives constantly. Nearly always in fact. And they're always blowing their cover, getting caught, killed . . ."

"And we, you and I, fall into the category of young, inexpert operatives?" Diego said.

"As far as the Party is concerned, yes, my love. You're twenty-four. I'm twenty-six. Too young, both of us, by rigid Party standards, for any mission of this importance. The Party sends only veterans for a job like this. Who *never* blow their cover. Are *never* caught . . ."

"Never, Ana?"

"Never. The poor fools you read about in the papers are from splinter groupuscules, only. *Maoistas, Trotskistas, Fidelistas, Montoneros, Tupamaros.* But *real* party people, Diego?"

"I see. And you're right."

"I know I am. So since Camarada Ernesto is always out to kill six or seven birds with one stone, he sends you to assassinate Señor Don Personage-Not-Yet-Of-Importance. He sends you because you made a stupid mistake and accidentally blew off the top of poor Enrique's head and thereby convinced him you're an ice-cold killer. You're good at the gestures, I'll give you that. I'll bet you studied every ancient Humphrey Bogart film in La Bibliothèque du Cinema, now didn't you?"

"*And* those of George Raft," Diego said.

"You even had *me* convinced until I got to know you better. You're nobody's *dur,* thank God! But you're also young, unimportant—and expendable. Say you do this job and escape. Good! You climb a couple of rungs up the Party ladder. You do this job and are captured, or killed. *Tant pis!* 'But, after all, we could *afford* to lose *ce gosse, camaradas*!' "

"And—*you?*" Diego whispered.

"I'm—to be taken. Oh, *merde alors,* Diego! Can't you *see?* What a show trial *that* would make! *¡La hija de los Condes de Casaribiera!* A cousin—somewhat removed—of Juanito, himself, the poor dimwitted dear! *Less* removed from Alfonso, Duke of Cadiz. And I, with my stupid self, concerned with my idiotic lovelife, fell right into this! Oh, Diego, Diego—don't you realize that no matter *how* we do this it's going to come out wrong for *us?* That we're sacrificial goats staked out to achieve the Party's ends at the cost of—"

"Of what?" he said.

"Not our lives. Not *my* life, anyhow. I'm worth more—alive. Disgracefully alive. Diego, promise me a thing . . ."

"What thing, Ana?"

"Those—pistolas. Don't let them—take *me* alive. *Cariño.* If you see they've got me, kill me. Try—not to—to muck me up like you did poor Enrique; but—let me have it. Please?"

He shook his head. Whispered: "I—couldn't. You *know* I couldn't, Ana. My hands would shake. I'd miss. Or hurt you in some terrible way that *wouldn't* kill you, outright. And then have to listen to you—crying. So, don't ask me—this, Ana. Don't!"

"All right. Then *I'll* do it, myself. Because since you, you *burro,* won't do the sensible thing and call the whole thing off, I—"

"You'll do nothing of the kind. In the first place, I'm not going to give you one of the pistols, so you can't."

"Then I'll go home. Visit Papa. Steal his. Or use his razor. Would you believe that in this day and age he still uses an old-fashioned straight razor, Diego? He *does.* Leaves his poor old face looking like *un Cristo crucificado* every time he shaves, but he will not use one of those *'malditos jugetes de niños'*—those damned children's toys—as he calls safety razors . . ."

"Ana, you stop it! Or so help me I'm going to take up wife beating as my favorite indoor sport. Ahead of time, at that."

"Your *second* favorite, I hope?" she said. "Diego—let's call it off. Escape. Go to—"

"Where, Ana? Where on *earth,* that Ernesto's hired guns couldn't find us? *Anita mía, chatita de mi alma*—listen to me. We pull this one off. I station you across the street in a place that has a pay phone. The minute you see me come out of—of—la Marisquería Príncipe, isn't it? you phone them and warn them to get everyone off the premises—"

"But if—they can't, Diego? If they panic? Start a stampede? Crush people underfoot? Hurl themselves through plate glass windows trying to break out?"

"Someone will be hurt—or killed. But not because we didn't at least *try* to save them. Speaking—coldly—for *us,* selfishly, it would look better if there *were* a victim or two. Then we could go back to Paris—and gradually disengage ourselves from the Party, the way Papa already has. If—we pretended—to be remorseful over the deaths of our victims—"

"Pretended? *¡Santa Madre de Dios!*" Ana María said.

"If we *showed* our remorse. Started going to mass regularly, say—Ernesto would write us off—as failures—as useless to the Party, and—"

"All right, Diego—where'll we meet, afterwards? You know we can't leave—that place together—and—"

"You go home. To your father's house. I'm going to take the car—our rented car—and head south. The one direction they won't expect an ETA terrorist to go. To Algeciras, where the police are too busy watching drug runners coming in to pay much attention to a *type* going out. I'll leave the car there. Take the ferry to Tangier. A plane directly to Paris, where *you* will join me in three weeks—"

"*Two* weeks. *One.* Two days!" Ana María said.

"Three weeks. After you're *sure* they're not watching you.

Look, *niña*; three weeks we can spare out of fifty years—"

"Can we?" she whispered. "Will we have fifty years, Diego? Will we have *any* years? Any years at all?"

"Don't talk that way!" he said sharply. "It's bad luck!"

"What—isn't?" she murmured. "All right; come on . . ."

Ismael, Federico Sales' chauffeur, turned the Minister's car —a Mercedes 450 SE—into the entrance of the Puerta de Hierro residential section.

'And even this—means something,' the young Minister thought. 'To come home every night—in a chauffeur-driven limousine. To a house—no, a *palacete*—a mansion—in Puerta de Hierro. Because if I hadn't married Consuclo, I couldn't afford a car that cost three million seven hundred and fifty thousand pesetas. And if *she* hadn't married me, she couldn't or at least wouldn't have dared live in Puerta de Hierro. Of course she could have bought a house—or more accurately have had *mi querido padre politico*—my so dearly beloved father-in-law— buy a house in Somasaguas. Or in La Florida. Or even in— Moraleja. Because all you need to live in any of those districts is money. While to live in Puerta de Hierro—or at least to be *accepted* in Puerta de Hierro to the extent of being occasionally invited for cocktails or lunch by your neighbors—you need— blood . . .'

He grinned at his own reflection in the rear-view mirror.

'Don't be a bloody snob, Fredi!' he told himself. Then, more slowly, 'Why not? Why do we automatically condemn snobbery? What aristocrat has ever done the world as much harm as grubby little beggars like Hitler, Mussolini, Stalin—or that sawed-off Corsican brigand, Napoleon Bonaparte? No- blesse *does* oblige, damn it all! My father-in-law is one of the richest men in Spain because he has not one drop of nobility— of spirit, the kind that counts!—in his veins, and feels obligation only to his money, to the fortune he has ground out of the sweat of the very class from which he sprang. And having clawed his way upward out of that mire, what does he do? He marries above him. A not so *petite bourgeoise,* and allows her to bring up his daughters—especially my Consuelo!—to be perfect, useless *pequeñaburguesa* dolls. Useless? *¡Santa Madre de Dios!* That's the understatement of the year. Of any year for that matter. I could forgive Connie her inability to boil water without burning it; but that I cannot so much as *talk* to her is unpardonable! What does my lovely, perfect wife *know*? Nothing. Another understatement. She knows a great deal *less* than nothing. Has she ever read a book—even a cheap, trashy novel—all the way through? I doubt it. What *can* she talk about? *¡Trapos y niños!* Clothes and babies! And I—I accepted this state of affairs, as do all of my class, until—I met Amparo. Met—a *woman.* Who can turn my bones to water. Scalding water. Steam. Can hollow me out from the roots of my hair to the nails of my tight-curled toes. Who can kiss my mouth and stop my heart. Touch me where she shouldn't with her divinely lecherous hands, and—so what am I talking—or rather thinking—about? The usual. Sex. So—sex. What's wrong with sex except that in this priest-ridden land we're taught to be afraid of it! Especially when, as in this case, it is far from the usual. Because *here,* the usual means stupid, sluttish whores, and dull, complacent wives. Say—glorious sex. Wonderful sex. Marvelous sex. *The* best— Yet—

'Yet, if it were only that, I shouldn't be actually planning to leave wife, children, position, this insanely backward land I love, and count them all well lost for love of her. But it's—the *afterwards* that enslaves me. That chains me forever. Lying there naked in my arms, her mouth brushing against my throat, talking to me, branding me with her—wisdom. With her understanding. Because she's the first woman I ever met who realizes there are no solutions to anything—least of all *political* solutions!—and that the best we can hope for is—someone to—to just be there—always and in *all* ways—and help us bear it. Which is what she does. So completely that I can no longer even contemplate being without her. Oh, God, I—'

The long, sleek, black, magnificent car with the ministerial flags on its fenders drew up before the patio of the house. Stopped. Ismael leaped out. Opened the door for *su Excelencia el Ministro* with a deep and reverent bow.

"Will you be—needing me later, Don Federico?" he said.

Fredi looked at his chauffeur. 'How much does he know?' he thought. 'Not suspect, because he probably suspects a great deal more than is actually going on—at least as far as both variety and quantity are concerned. The *quality* he couldn't even imagine. But how much does he *know*? Too ruddy much, likely!'

"No, Ismael, I won't be needing you," he said.

When he walked into the foyer, he saw his wife sitting on the immense sofa in the sunken living room. She looked so small and forlorn and lost that a great wave of pity washed over him.

'I can't do it,' he thought miserably. 'I simply can't. She's my *wife,* whatever her faults, her lacks; the mother of my children and—'

Then she turned and saw him. And her face went white. Her lips. Whiter than the rest of her face, really. He could see that she was trembling. Seething with almost uncontrollable fury. She stood up. Came towards him. Step by step, slowly. When she was close enough she whispered:

"*She* called you. *Here.* That woman. *Esa fulana. Esa cualquiera. Esa—*"

"Spare me the hard names. They just don't fit Amparo, and you have no imagination anyway. What did she want? Did she say?"

"To talk to you. Oh, she excused herself quite nicely, thank you! Swore it was—an emergency. Fredi, tell me—is she —is that woman—pregnant?"

He smiled, wearily.

"That wouldn't be an emergency," he said. "A long-term matter, rather. And one easily taken care of—between civilized people, anyhow. Anything else—?"

"Yes. She was—hysterical. Completely hysterical. You've

always thrown her marvelous self-control into my teeth; but this time she was crying so hard I could scarcely understand her. Fredi! *¡Por el amor de Dios!*"

But he had already brushed by her, racing for that phone.

He dialed swiftly, surely, without hesitation or pauses. Listened for the ring. Heard it. It went on and on and on.

"*¡Santa Madre de Dios!*" he whispered, staring into his wife's white and stricken face.

Then he heard Amparo's voice. It was—ragged. Torn. Uncontrolled pulsations of breath whistled through the rents in it.

"Fredi?" she said; and his name became a sob.

"What's wrong?" he said. "You called me. Why? What's happening, Amparo?"

"Nothing. I—I—Oh God,—forgive me. *Cariño mío*—I know I shouldn't—have—called your house; but—"

"But what?" he said sharply, all his nerves become antennae trying to capture the signals in her voice.

"Nothing. Really nothing. Believe me, Fredi—"

But he didn't. He couldn't. She was lying, and he knew it.

"What's *wrong*?" he said, italicizing the word by his very tone.

"Nothing," she repeated. "Nerves. I—I panicked, Fredi. I suddenly realized that—we have—only three more days. When that hit me—I must have gone into shock a little. Before I realized what I was doing, I had dialed your number—your *office* number, *cielo*. But that little electronic device that plays a tape recording into your phone when you're not there answered. You know: The one that says His Excellency, the Minister is absent; but if the matter is of importance one has three minutes to state it, and it will be automatically recorded for his attention . . ."

"And?" Fredi said.

"I hung up. Panicked some more. Worse than ever. Called —your *house*. Which was—unpardonable of me. Please forgive me, Fredi. Say *you* forgive me, for I—I cannot—forgive myself

—for that. And she—your *wife*—answered. Is she—is she—anywhere—nearby, now?"

"Yes," Fredi said.

"Oh God! Good night, Fredi. I will see you tomorrow, won't I?"

"Yes," he said. "Good night, Amparo." And put the phone down on its cradle.

"Fredi," Consuelo whispered. "All right. You win. And so does she. I—I'll give you your legal separation. Because this is —too much. I—I can't stand it anymore."

He stood there staring at her, thinking bleakly how little her—surrender—arranged. That his life had become circular, and was closing in upon him. That there were no viable solutions to anything at all in life, and especially not to this. Because his leaving Consuelo, or her leaving him, added up to exactly the same thing, his automatic resignation—and that only to anticipate, with some shreds of honor left intact, his being dismissed—from any post in Government where he'd be able to do his country any good in the rapidly approaching hour of his country's greatest need. That he'd put a private matter—'An erect cock and a pair of aching balls!' he told himself sardonically—before his manifest duty to man the breach against bloody revolution—from the Right or the Left, it mattered not! —sure to engulf Spain, when the eighty-odd-year-old Generalísimo, who had imposed thirty-eight years of petrification upon his martyred country and called it statesmanship, finally died.

More, it meant exile. And—poverty. An unworthy thought, but there it was. So maybe *los Amantes de Teruel* had it right; maybe dying, swiftly, romantically and together was the only thing that lovers—in a world that no longer tolerates love, substituting for it the mere physical manifestations of sex—could do.

He said: "We'll talk about it tomorrow. Come, let's go to bed."

Consuelo stiffened. Stared at him. A little speculatively, he thought.

"I—I'll sleep in one of the guestrooms, Fredi," she whispered, then added, after a pregnant pause, "if you like . . ."

He studied her face. Saw how easily he could arrange the whole thing. Except that, actually, he couldn't. It was beyond him to arrange it now.

He thought: 'And you call Amparo a whore.'

He said: "No. I will. I have to get up deuced early tomorrow, anyhow. But thank you—for your exquisite consideration, Connie, in any event. Now, come on . . . And turn out those damned lights, will you? We aren't getting any richer y'know . . ."

"All—right—Fredi—" she got out. She was crying. Very quietly. Almost without making a sound; but crying.

He ignored it. There was, he realized now, in sorrow, and in shame, nothing else to do.

"Oh, dear! Now I'm not angry anymore," Ana said. "D'you know why I was angry with you, *mi amor?*"

"No. In fact, I didn't even know you were. But just to set the record straight, why were you?" Diego said.

"Because you could contemplate quite calmly going off and leaving me. While the mere thought of having you out of sight—and out of *reach*—for a whole hour even, makes me so sad I want to die!"

"It doesn't make me happy as a lark, either," he said.

"But you *can* contemplate it! You can! Oh Diego, Diego! I'm *so* afraid!"

"Me, too," he said, and drew her down into his arms.

"Ohhhh!" she breathed; then: "Diego—could we *stay* together? Throughout it all? No matter what happens?"

"We'd double the risks. No, quadruple them. Look, Ana —we go to that seafood bar together. After—it happens—after the explosion, somebody is *sure* to remember *us*. A couple. *Una pareja*. So we—become singles again. Wait! There's more to it even than that. I want you to wear your kangaroo pouch, *over* an ordinary dress. And over everything that loose black silk dress tucked in so that everyone can see you're *muy embarazada* —as pregnant as old hell—"

"Diego—" she moaned.

"Listen to me, Anita. A lot depends upon us keeping our heads—even—our fifty years together, maybe. Then you go across the street, kissing me fondly before you go—making *sure* that people notice you—"

"And *you!*" she said. "Diego, for God's love—"

"They'll notice a long-haired hippy *type* with a mustache and a beard. Hair down to my shoulders. Light brown hair that won't make my blue eyes seem strange—"

"What about *mine?* Everybody *always* notices my eyes because they're so out of place in the kind of face I've got . . ."

He got up, went to his valise. Dug in it. Came out with not one, but several pairs of dark glasses. Gave her one pair. They were the type that have one-way mirrors for lenses. That is, the wearer could see out of them perfectly, but anyone looking at the wearer would see only his own face reflected in them, instead of the wearer's eyes.

"Try these on," he said.

Ana María tried on the sunglasses.

"How are they?" he asked.

"I can see all right, if that's what you mean," she said, "but—"

"But what?"

"They're too unusual, Diego. One almost never sees this type of sunglasses in Spain—and then only on foreigners. They'd attract practically as much attention to me as my light eyes in my face of a *negrita* always do . . ."

"I see. And you're right. These then?"

She tried another pair.

"Perfect," she said, "except that I can't see a *maldita thing* out of 'em. I'm as blind as a bat!"

"Wait. Papa'll fix," he said. He took out his pocket knife.

It was one of those Swiss-made knives that have half a dozen odd-shaped blades, corkscrews, a pair of scissors, and an awl. He opened the awl. Took out a cigarette lighter and heated the point of the awl until it glowed cherry red. Plunged it through the exact center of one of the lenses. It went through easily. The lens didn't crack.

"Cheap plastic," he said. "Now the other." He repeated the technique. Gave her the glasses again.

"All right," she said. "Now I can see. Not much, but enough. At least I won't fall over things."

"Good. Now listen, *niña*. I told you to go across the street, but that's *not* what you do first. I see from the floor plan that the toilets are downstairs just as they are in many Madrid bars—"

"So?" she whispered.

"You kiss me. Go downstairs. You'll be wearing that black dress, your kangaroo pouch, and a wig."

"*¿Y no mis bragas?*" she said. "And not my panties?"

"Of course your panties! This no time for joking, Ana!"

"I'm not joking. I'll only wet 'em anyhow. I'll be so scared."

"Ana, please! You'll be wearing a curly blond wig of the type that has dark and light swaths of hair alternating, the kind that lets everybody *know* it's a wig, but is so stylish and well fitting that people admire them. And these glasses. The black dress, the kangaroo pouch, and under that a short, light-colored dress. After you kiss me, you go downstairs to the ladies' toilet. I don't think they'll have a woman attendant in that kind of place, but if they do, you come back upstairs just as you are, cross the street to another bar, and change there—"

"But if there is no woman attendant?"

"You take off the wig, the black dress, and the pouch. Leave 'em hidden under the lavabo or behind the toilet. Then you come back up, walk right past me without paying me the slightest attention, and out the door. Go across the street to another bar. Have a drink. Ask the bartender for three or four telephone slugs—paying him for them in advance—and make two or three idle calls—you know people you can call, don't you?"

"Of course. What I don't know is if I'll be able to get a word out!"

"I'll give you a tranquilizer," he said.

"All right. And then?"

"You'll see me coming out. Then you phone them and warn them to get everybody the hell out of there. I'll duck around the nearest corner, rip off my fake beard, wig, and mustache, ram 'em down a sewer or into somebody's garbage can. Pass where you are. Give you the high sign. Then we both beat it—in opposite directions, and—"

But she was staring at him, her pale eyes enormous.

"Diego—" she said.

"Yes, Ana?"

"You—you're awfully—professional, aren't you?"

"I have blown up five places to date. Wrecked them completely."

"Oh!" she said.

"In the middle of the night. With no one in them. Iberia's offices in Paris. Turismo Español. The Spanish Consulate. The Emigrant Workers' Office. Those kinds of places. But, except for—your—Enrique—I have never killed anyone. And I don't mean to—ever again . . ."

She smiled at him then, a little sadly.

"Where're you going to get the wigs?" she said.

"I have them already. Bought mine in a theatrical outfitter's in Paris. *Yours* in Perpignan. Remember when I left you and the bags at the airport and went to get rid of the car?"

"*Do* I! I was on the point of heart failure by the time you got back . . ."

"That was one of the things that delayed me. But it occurred to me that buying that damned wig in Spain wouldn't be smart. Speaking of which, you'd better try it on. It may be too big or something—"

It wasn't. It fitted her almost perfectly.

"You've a good eye," she said.

"Dumb luck. I asked 'em for the smallest size they had. And this was it. Now, we'd better get some sleep. It's a long haul to Madrid, and—"

"Diego—" she said.

"Yes, Ana?"

"*Put* me to sleep, will you? Otherwise, I won't. I'm so nervous and—"

He grinned at her. Bent and kissed her. Said: "*D'accord. De acuerdo.* All right."

But her hands came up, pushing.

"No," she said, "don't. I *still* don't feel like it."

"*¡Ana, por el amor de Dios!*"

"You know *why* I don't, Diego?"

"No," he groaned. "Why, Ana?"

"Because *you* don't. Not really. I don't want compassion, Diego Fernández!"

"Hmmmm—how would a little *passion* suit you?"

"Just fine—if you don't fake it. Wait. Let's see if I can't *get* you interested. Lie down, will you!"

"That's difficult to do," he mocked. "Getting me interested, I mean. In fact, it's practically impossible. But I'm game, if you are . . ."

He sprawled backward across the bed; put out his arms to her.

But she stood there.

"Diego—" she whispered, "this—this may be our *last* night together. Ever thought of that?"

"No," he said. "And I won't. I refuse to think that, Ana. I refuse it flatly."

"Strange—" she got out. "I—I think it—all the time. I've —a feeling—that's the way it's going to be."

"¡Oigame, niña! ¡No me digas eso!"

"I do say it. We're—going to—to die, Diego. Both of us . . ."

"Ana María Casaribiera, you—"

"So—*you* do it. Make me die happy. Fuck me to death."

"Ana María!" he howled.

She laughed then, gaily. But her pale eyes were all but hazed over, he saw. Then her laughter stopped. Cut off abruptly. As though someone had flicked a switch. Her pansy-colored eyes went huge. Too brilliant. Vanished behind a hard, bright glitter. Melted. Became all flooding, brimming spill.

"Ana!" he said, reproachfully.

"Undress me, Diego," she whispered. "I want you to. I want to feel your hands—"

He sat up. She came to him. Stood there between his knees. He undressed her very slowly. His hands were trembling. But haste seemed to him—unseemly. A blasphemy against that moment. That curiously terrible moment. He had the feeling that if he turned his head quickly he'd see something he didn't want to. The thing that was already in her eyes. Death, waving his moldy graveclothes. Dancing obscenely in that silent room.

She put one hand behind his head. Crowded his face against her small, firm breasts.

"Kiss them," she whispered. "Feed upon them. Be *mi hijito, mi niñito,* the baby I'll never have. . . ."

"Niña!" he groaned.

"¡Por favor!" she said.

He kissed her there. Cherished her nipples gently with lips and tonguetip. A long time. Until her breath went ragged, raced.

"Bite them," she said. "Make them hurt!"

He drew back, stared at her.

"Please!" she said.

He nibbled at her gently.

"Harder!" she said. Drew her breath in sibilantly at the feel of his teeth. Peered down at him, smiling at him through a rain, a flood of tears.

"Now, I'll undress thee," she said. "Diego, I—I want to make love to thee. . . ."

"Of course," he said, "we're going to—"

"No. You don't understand. I want to make love to you. Let me be—the aggressor—tonight. It—it's important to me, Diego!"

He stared at her, said: "All right. But will you tell me—why?"

"You—may escape. It may be—only—my hope—that whispered that to my heart, *amor.* My love for you. But—if you do—I want you *never* to forget me. Even if you live to—a hundred, and—and bed fifty women per week, I want to make sure—"

"You can be sure *now,*" he said grimly.

"No, I'm not sure, but I will be, if—"

"If what?" he said.

"If you'll *let* me love you. However I want to."

"Ana—" he said, doubtfully.

"You see! You're already starting in to spoil it! *¿Diego, por favor?*"

"All right," he said, "anything you want."

"I want to rape you. To violate you. Have you ever been raped before?" She was grinning at him now, all mischief, but her tears didn't stop. Not entirely. They only slowed, dancing like raindrops, light jeweled, and trembling upon the tender quiver of her mouth.

"No," he said cheerfully. "But, then, a man can't be. It's a physiological and psychological impossibility. Unless he *wants* to, he collapses. And if he doesn't collapse, that means he wants to. And *if* he wants to, it isn't rape . . ."

She laughed then freely, gaily, threw the last of his clothes down on the rug. Then she, too, disappeared. He struggled to sit up; but her voice came over sharply: "No!"

He lay back down. Felt her huge, soft lips press hard against the instep of his right foot. They were scalding. Her tonguetip came through them and played there. He howled and thrashed with helpless laughter. He wasn't ordinarily ticklish; but the sensation was maddening. She stopped that at once, and began to kiss his toes, one by one. Slowly. With aching tenderness. Climbed up his leg, lips branding his flesh, inch by inch. She was right, he realized; he would *never* forget her.

He waited, wrapped in a curious sort of terror, as she approached his aching sex. He didn't want her to do that. He truly didn't want her to. He didn't mind if *other* women did it. He had even liked it upon occasion. But this was Ana María, whom he loved. He didn't want to degrade her. And he was too much his mother's son not to think of this as degradation. He stiffened, his body rigid as a stone.

"Diego—" she said softly, "why are you afraid?"

"Ana!" he all but wept. "I—"

"It's—part of you, isn't it?" she said. "And I love *all* of you. Oh, all right, all right! I'll make a detour!"

She put her mouth against his belly just below his navel. Bit him there, hard.

He cried out, from the pain of it.

"I'm a cannibal," she said solemnly, "especially when you frustrate all my favorite perversions, the way you did just now . . ."

"You surely *are!*" he said. "And—a sadist. And—I'm going to explode in a minute!"

"Do. Maybe that will calm you down enough to make this worth my while . . ."

Then she went on kissing him, all over. When she reached his mouth, she lingered, performing exquisite prodigies there. He had never been kissed like that before by anyone. Not even by—he realized with sudden wonder, acute disquietude—Ana María, herself. She had been restraining herself with him until now. Holding back. Why? Had she been afraid, or ashamed, to put on display the appalling completeness of her sexual skills? But now, no more. For now she finished her grand tour by working her way down the other side of him to the sole of his left foot. But, by then, he didn't feel ticklish anymore.

"Ana, for the love of God!" he groaned.

But she rolled entirely out of the bed, stood up, came up to his pillow. Standing, her little black pubic bush was on a level with his eyes.

"Kiss it!" she said. "Kiss my little thing."

"Ana!" he said, shocked to the bottom of his soul.

"I *want* you to," she said solemnly. "But not because I'm a *viciosa*. Of course, I *am una viciosa,* but that's not why."

"Then—why?" he croaked.

"Because—judging from your reactions a little while ago —it's something you've *never* done—for *anyone* else. Not for any *other* girl. Am I right?"

"Do you need to ask? Of course not!" he said.

"Then—for me. Because now it means something. Proof —that you love me. Love me enough to do *anything* for me. As I would, for you, if you'd let me. Come on, Diego; kiss it!"

He kissed her there. It wasn't unpleasant. But her reaction surprised him. She wrapped both arms about his head; writhed against him, opening, salt and scalding; shuddered; groaned as if in anguish, wept, sobbed, said in a husk whisper: "Ahhhh God!"

"Ana—" he murmured.

She bent, weeping, caught both his ears in her two hands. Glued her big, thick-lipped mouth to his, stopped his breath, his mind. Swung herself up and over him, knelt astride him. Put down her right hand and encircled his sex with her fingers, aiming it, positioning it carefully. Lowered herself upon it ever so slowly. Sat there upon him, fully impaled. Hissed at him: "Don't move!"

She was right, he knew; for him to move now would have

been to court immediate disaster. But he found himself once again hating both her knowledge and her skill, with a cold, sick crippling anger, which, curiously enough, helped matters, for it distracted his attention from what was going on. She sat there upon him engorging his rigid and penetrant maleness, her eyes shut, her mouth opened a little, the whole of her motionless as a statue until he began to get used—somewhat, anyhow—to the interior feel of her, to arm—within the pitifully small degree to which a man's will has control over such things—his tactile sense against that close to absolutely maddening slow, soft tremble, cling, and scald, so that some of his actually painful urgency left him. Which she felt, or sensed, for very slowly, she started to move, rotating her slender hips in, astonishingly, a fully thirty degrees of arc, gyrating them with an almost fluid smoothness of motion, stiffening her thighs to rise, relaxing them to slide hotly, wetly down upon him, riding him with matchless grace, providing, his scientifically trained mind suggested the image, a movable cylinder for his motionless piston, except that that metaphor too, he realized, was wrong, was false, for there was nothing machinelike, unharmonious, unlovely about anything she did.

But when he tried to join in this solemn, rapt, ritual ceremony—her self-immolation before Aphrodite's high altar, and upon his fleshly sword—she cried out: "Diego, you promised! Tonight's mine! *All* mine!"

He obeyed her. Stopped. Relaxed. Lay there, thinking: 'I don't care. Even if it took—a million *types* to—teach her all this, it's worth it. Anyhow—she's—mine! From now on—mine! No one else's. Mine. Always—mine. Forever mine. 'Til the day we die—mine—'

"Diego—" she said, her voice a long, slow scrape of flint on brass, endlessly ashudder.

"Yes, Ana?" he whispered, or groaned, or both.

"Now. Come in me. Now that I am ready and—and wide open—and we cannot miss. Give it—*all* to me. All the milk-

juice of thy life—that we—make—a—a new life—in thy image
—and—and *mine*—and maybe—even—God's—"

"Ana," he murmured, *"¡Anita mía! Ana de mi vida, de mi
alma, de mi amor—"*

A spasm shook her, racing upward from her loins to her
throat like a sudden, smashing wave.

"Diego!" she wailed, her voice surf-shredded, passion
foamed, "can't you see I cannot wait? Ohhhhhh—here I go!
Oh, Diego, Diego—please!"

He arched, thrusting. Burst. Jetted his life into the undu-
lant broil and thrash and heat of her. Became in that instant
stark-naked god. Immortal. Beyond death. Outside of destiny.

And she went mad. Thrashed, writhed, ground down upon
him, jerking like a demented spastic, her scant flesh quivering
upon her slender bones as though it had an independent life of
its own, her teeth clamped into her lower lip to keep locked in
her throat her anguished moaning, to halt the cries that alternat-
ingly corded then whipped loose every muscle in her belly and
her chest, until she could bear what was happening to her no
longer, and quite seriously fearing that the absolutely crippling
linked-chain explosion of those murderously multiple orgasms
were *never* going to stop, at least not before they had killed her
outright, she leaned forward—a lighted taper melting, melting
—until she lay collapsed upon him, limp, sweat-soaked, trembling, her pale eyes rolled back into her head like those of a
slaughtered animal, blood flooding her chin where she had
bitten her lower lip almost through—

And he frozen and paralyzed by purest terror had to try
three times before he could get her name out, before he could
scream: "Ana!" in a voice that was high and thin wailing—a
castrate's soprano, really, emasculated as he was, by his horror
and his grief. Or by his anticipation of them both. Because her
pale eyes fluttered open, vacant and mindless. Dazed. Stricken.
Stunned.

"Ana!" he wept.

She tightened her arms about him.

"*Now* I can die. Now I can, Diego!" she said.

"Call her," Diego said.

"No," Ana María whispered, "it's too early. She won't even be home from work yet."

They were in a motel about ten kilometers outside of Madrid, and it was the night before what they both thought of as M-Day. That, of course, in English, would have come out as D-Day. But although Ana María spoke English almost perfectly, she seldom had occasion to use that language, and therefore didn't habitually think in it, while Diego's English was frankly bad. So D-Day, Death-Day, was to them both, M-Day, *Le Jour de la Mort; El Dia de la Muerte,* which made it M-Day in both of the two languages they were completely at home in.

"*Can* you talk?" Diego said, staring at her mouth.

"Yes. I mumble a bit; but the swelling's going down now . . ."

"*Merde!*" Diego said feelingly.

She grinned at him through her grossly swollen lips. "What did you want me to do? Or rather what would you have preferred me to do: bite my lip or scream the damned roof down? I can just picture *that!* People bursting into our room to save the poor girl who's getting murdered, and finding me lying on top of you, both of us stark naked and the room smelling like a cheap whorehouse and—"

"Not a *cheap* whorehouse," Diego said; "a high-class whorehouse. You smell good, Anita *mía.*"

She cocked one thick black eyebrow at him.

"How do I *taste?*" she said.

"Now don't you start *that* again!" Diego howled.

" *¡Ay, mi pudico!* What makes you such a prude, *Diegito mío?* While I am a vicious one. *¡Muy viciosa!* Shall I demonstrate to thee how vicious I am? Teach thee two or three hundred charming little perversions?"

"Two or three *hundred,* Ana?"

"*¡Sí! Dos o tres cientas. Por ejemplo, se puede—*"

"Oh, no, you don't!" Diego said.

"*Lo malo es que no puedo.* The bad part is I *can't.* My damned mouth's too sore."

"Yes," he said slowly, "which means I'm going to have to do the job alone tomorrow. Just as well. Better that way."

"Diego!" she cried. "You'll do nothing of the kind! We started this together, so now we're going to finish it together —no matter what!"

"Ana—think. The essential part of our getaway plan is that a heavy, pregnant blonde in a black maternity dress goes down to the ladies' restroom, and a slim brunette in a light-colored dress—wearing those dark glasses for the *first* time, because your eyes *won't* attract attention under that blonde wig—comes back out of it. Therefore, those two women must have *nothing* in common. But if they *both* have lips that look like they're made of *morcilla,* blood pudding, what becomes of the disguise?"

"*¡Mierda!*" Ana swore. "I *have* screwed things up, haven't I?"

"That you have, *chata*; that you have," he said.

"Diego—call the bar. Tell them to bring us up a bucket of ice."

He stared at her.

"It will bring this swelling down pronto. By morning it won't even be noticeable."

"But—" he hesitated, "those—teeth marks, *mi pequeña masochista?*"

"Sí. I am a masochist. And thou art *un sadico.* Would you like to beat me a little now?"

"No. Nor do anything else to you, either. Tomorrow, *niña, my* legs, anyhow, have to be in shape to do some running. To haul my *culo* the hell away from la Calle de Esparteros as fast as possible. It's not much of a *culo,* I'll admit, but it's the only one I've got . . ."

"Don't call your cute little *culo* a *culo,*" she said solemnly.

"You look like an Englishman anyhow, so call it an 'arse.' Or a 'bum.' Diego—call the bar. Ask for that ice."

"But the teeth marks?" he insisted.

"We'll get some Band-Aids. You know—the flesh-colored kind. Cover them with that."

"It'll still be—a detail in common," he said.

"But a small one. Almost unnoticeable. And even if someone does notice that both of us—of *me*—have got adhesive tape on our lower lips, the sudden departure of three or four kilos of unborn fetus will make him assume it's a mere coincidence and—Diego—Diego *mío—mi amor*—d'you think we *did*?"

"Did *what*?" he said.

"Made our baby last night? Started him, anyhow?"

"Her. It's going to be a girl. And look just like you."

"A fate worse than death! I wouldn't wish that off on my worst enemy. A face like this—"

"Flower eyes. Lips of a *negresse*. Monkey face," he said. She cocked that eyebrow at him again.

"And that's supposed to be a compliment?" she said.

"It *is* a compliment. You're—beautiful, Ana. To me, anyhow. To me, you're the most beautiful girl in all the world."

"Dee-ay-go—" she said. "You've *still* got to run tomorrow. And your legs have to be in shape. So stop tempting me."

"I wasn't!" he said.

"I know. Not consciously, anyhow. But when you say things like that to me, in that tone of voice, I start—wanting you. Very badly. And automatically. Conditioned reflex. Now go call for that ice. Maybe I can spare one cube to put somewhere else. Cool *me* off a little."

"Ana," he groaned, "must you always be so outrageous?"

"Yes. Or otherwise I wouldn't be me," she said.

Federico Sales Ortega drove his own personal car, a Seat 124 Sports Coupé, up la Avenida del Generalísimo until he got to the section of the wide and imposing boulevard above that vast sprawl of pearl gray buildings called *Los Nuevos Ministerios,* the New Ministries, because most of the departments of the Government had been moved into them only a few years ago, on one side of the avenida, and also above the football stadium de Bernabéu on the other. This section was called "Korea" because, during the Korean War of the 1950s, for some obscure reason, a number of North American generals, admirals, minor diplomats and businessmen—and absolutely no Koreans at all—had lived there. Which was, Fredi reflected, a fine example of the oblique tangents along which *Madrileño* humor works.

He parked the car in one of the diagonal parking places let into one of the avenida's islands, those tree-shaded walks that divide the two one-way lateral side drives from the immensely wide center of the avenida, which, unlike the laterals, is a two-way street, locked the handsome silver coupé and went into the really luxurious building where Amparo lived.

She couldn't afford to live in a building like this one. Or rather, she couldn't have afforded it if he hadn't paid the rent for a furnished flat whose decor was twenty-first century, really. It always reminded him of a Hollywood movie set. Its luxury was so—so blatant, somehow. White and crystal furniture. Black, purple, dark green, blood crimson walls. Abstract paintings on them. Even more abstract statues in the niches.

No, Amparo couldn't afford a place like that. No single woman could unless she were an heiress, and if she were an heiress, she wouldn't stay single long enough to even find an apartment, Federico thought: 'Madrid's hordes of totally unscrupulous fortune hunters would see to that.'

He paused, smiling at this thought, despite the weight of weariness in him that was almost pulverizing his bones. "It is, then, unscrupulous to seek to marry a fortune—as *you* did, my fine feathered friend!" he mocked himself. "But it is *not* unscrupulous to keep a poor working girl as your mistress in a luxurious apartment, to which you have the only other key? You *hope!*" he added sardonically.

But he did more than hope. He knew. He would have put Amparo's fidelity even above his wife's. Because Amparo was the most nakedly sincere woman he had ever known, while Consuelo's fidelity was based upon resignation, acceptance, and a want of imagination. 'Or rather upon the wrong kind of imagination,' he thought bitterly. 'She imagines that she loves me, but what she loves are the Sales Ortega family names, and my great-grandfather's coat of arms. Say I hadn't proposed the night I did. The next night Willi-Guillermo Gutierrez O'Conner surely would have, and she'd be living just as she is now, being just as faithful to Willi, and just as sure she loves *him.* And *he*'d be cheating on her, just as I am—just as, in sober fact, he is deceiving his own poor Marta. *¡Santa Madre de Dios!* What a people we are! Do I know one single faithful husband among my circle?' He stopped, frowned with sudden wonder. 'By

Jove, come to think of it, I do! Quite a few of my friends are being faithful to their brides these days—thanks to our dear little Arab friends! Mistresses are a luxury damned few of us can afford in these days of financial crisis. Even those angelic-looking little *putitas* over on the Costa Fleming are beyond our means as well—at least so nearly so to be more than an occasional recourse—'

As he walked towards the lifts he saw the porter peering at him from the glass window cut through the foyer's wall so that the porter could watch the entrance from his own living quarters even at such times as he was not at his desk in the foyer itself. Fredi stared at him hard, and the porter turned away.

That the porter *knew* who he was, there was not the slightest doubt. But he pretended stoutly he had never seen the young Minister's picture in the newspapers, seen his image and heard his voice—over television *española* addressing los Cortes, of which august body he was also a Procurator, in one of those discourses that even his worst enemies admitted were absolutely brilliant. In another country, Fredi realized, the man might have tried a little quiet blackmail. But in Spain the power of the rich, the aristocracy, the nobility was too great. A man of *las clases humildes* knew only too well what the limits and risks were.

'Besides,' Fredi thought, 'whom would he sell his information to? In Spain, *chantajistas,* blackmailers, starve to death. Say a *type* like me is caught out—that some *envidioso, resentido social* like that porter knows where the dirty linen's hid. Say he—upon my refusal to pay *chantaje*—took his paydirt to some scandal sheet. They wouldn't print it. They wouldn't dare. They'd know that the *Censura* would bar that whole edition if they tried it, causing them to loose a stack of money. All our scandal sheets print is tales about actors, actresses—tales supplied by said actors and actresses themselves who find the free publicity attendant upon a nice, juicy scandal a godsend—but anyone connected with the government can get away with murder. Why, if Amparo and I were to suddenly feel the urge right in the middle of the Gran Via, the traffic police would direct the traffic around us, while the police armada would form a ring around us with their backs chastely turned to provide us with the necessary privacy!'

His antic joke pleased him, the more so because he really didn't know to what extent, if any, it was true.

'Have to try it sometime,' he thought, and pushed the call button on the *ascensor.* Lights flickered on, illuminating numbers in descending order from twelve on down. In seconds *el ascensor,* the lift, the elevator, was there.

Fredi shook his head admiringly. He was old enough to remember the time when there was no such thing as a lift in Madrid that worked all, or even most of the time. When the ancient, creaking birdcages crawled upward so slowly that if one were in a hurry, it made more sense to take the stairs even when *los ascensores* were in working order, a condition one almost never had to consider, for all of them were festooned with *¡No funciona!* signs day in and day out.

But now this one whooshed him upward so fast he had to wait on the landing before it on the ninth floor, where Amparo's flat was, for his stomach to catch up with the rest of him. When it had, he walked over to her door and fumbled in his pocket for his key.

As he was turning the key in the lock, he reflected suddenly, oddly, upon the peculiar form of slavery that being a rich man's mistress in Spain actually was. Amparo really couldn't go anywhere unless he took her. She was condemned to wait, night after night, not knowing—because he, himself, very often didn't, and *couldn't* know—when he was going to visit her. And since a kept woman's only means of keeping the favor of her married—and adulterous! he thought wrily—lover were chiefly *sus encantos físicos,* her fleshly charms, she couldn't so much as put on an old, comfortable housecoat, or stick her feet into rundown, worn easy bedroom slippers. He realized that never had he caught her with her hair in paper curlers, or her face smeared with cold cream. No. She was always—perfect. He realized, and admitted to himself, that she wasn't really a pretty woman. She looked every day of her thirty-three years. Even the perfection of her grooming, her exquisite taste in clothes, the haunting delicacy of her perfumes didn't hide that.

'No,' he thought. 'She's not pretty. She's—beautiful. In the spiritual sense, anyhow. *Su alma*—her soul is beautiful. By too much suffering refined. To me, now, she even looks beautiful, because I love her so—'

Then he saw her. She was sitting on one of those outrageously extravagant freeform stools and talking over the telephone. She was saying, sharply: "No! And don't call me anymore!"

Then she turned and saw him standing there. And her lips went white. Even under her make-up, he could see that. Or perhaps they had already been white before she turned.

He said softly, slowly, sorrowfully: "Amparo, who was that?"

She stood there looking at him; then she said quietly: "I don't know, Fredi."

"You don't know?" he said.

"No. He was a stranger. He refused to give me his name. And I have never heard that voice before."

She was telling the truth, he realized at once. But something in her voice awoke unease in him. A nagging disquietude.

"What did he *want*, Amparo?" he said.

"To know if *you* were coming here tonight."

"*¡Dios!*" Fredi said.

"*¡Amen!*" Amparo said. "Fredi—you've never had anything to do with those *Vasco* trials, have you? With ETA, I mean? With the prosecution of——?"

"No. You know I haven't, Amparo. Those things don't fall under the jurisdiction of my ministry, my dear. ETA is the business of the *Ministerio de Justicia*—or the Army. I have nothing to do with them."

"That's a relief!" she sighed. "But, *cielo,* tell me: Have you *done* something—anything, here of late that might have offended someone? One of the two extremes, say: the lunatic Left, or the rabid Right? He sounded distinctly—menacing.''

"Not that I know of—say! There is one thing. I intervened on behalf of that young priest out in the Moratalaz District. Talked to the *Director General de Seguridad.* And to the Minister of Justice, himself. Got the young ass off with a suspended sentence, a warning, and a stiff fine—''

"One of our growing flock of *curas rojos,* no doubt? One of those young Red priests who are out to demonstrate that the church does stand behind social justice and will not desert the poor?''

"Exactly. Only this one was even wilder than the usual. He flatly refused to celebrate the habitual funeral mass for the salvation of the soul of José Antonio, Primo de Rivera, on the anniversary of his execution by the Reds. Said he'd be damned if he would consent to pray the soul of a Fascist murderer out of the Hell in which it jolly well belongs.''

"And you got him *off? How,* Fredi? Truly you amaze me!''

"As a matter of fact, it was quite easy. I say, darling, do you have any objection to our sitting down? I'm *dead.*''

"No,'' she said nervously. "No, of course not! Forgive me, Fredi. I'm not usually so inconsiderate, am I? You do look like the bad death, you poor old dear! Come let me take your shoes off. Or would you rather—''

"Rather what?'' he said.

She blushed vividly. It was one of the things he loved about her: that she could blush. That she *still* could.

"Would rather—that we—that we went straight to bed?'' she whispered.

"*Amparita, niña,*'' he groaned. "Tonight I'd disappoint the living hell out of you. Let's just sit here awhile, shall we? And you might fix me a stiff whiskey. Straight. No—on the rocks.''

"Can do,'' she said gaily; then seriously: "Fredi—you *never* disappoint me. No matter what you do—or *don't* do. Some of my finest memories are of you—really worn out by one of your terrible days at the ministry—sleeping like a baby in my arms . . ."

"You should find yourself a younger lover, *niña,*" he said.

"No. We're right for each other, Fredi. Ten years between husband and wife—oh! I am sorry! Please forgive that, Fredi—it was a slip of the tongue. I meant—"

"Husband and wife. We're going to be. For all intents and purposes anyhow, my *vida.* Consuelo has finally consented to give me that legal separation. So—"

She stood there looking at him. Started to cry.

He leaped up from that chair. Took her in his arms.

"Amparo, *Amparita mia*—please!" he said.

"Stupid of me, isn't it?" she said brokenly. "But I can't help it! I'm *too* happy, Fredi! So don't try to stop me! *Let* me cry! Let me cry it all out! If you knew how I've suffered—"

"I do," he said. "I'm not worth it, Amparo. No man is."

"*Thou* art!" she stormed. "Oh, Fredi, Fredi, thou art worth my life! When I think that in two more days I was going to have to die—"

"Amparo!" he said. "Don't say a thing like that! Separation is not death in the worst of cases. And even if you'd had to go out to *Libano,* I'd have found some way to—"

"Would you, Fredi?" she whispered. "But—how? Of course—my body—my poor self-slaughtered carcass!—wouldn't have been that far away. Just in the civil cemetery because I'd have forfeited my right to be buried in the normal one, wouldn't I? But *me, I, who* I am? Where would that be, Fredi? In hell, surely, calling your name forever—even there."

"Amparo," he got out. "You mustn't—you wouldn't have—"

"I would have," she said. "I was going to. I am simply incapable of living without you, Fredi. Nothing or no one could make me do that. Not even the President. Now, turn me loose. I'm going to fix you your drink. Tonight I'll even join you. We do have something to celebrate, don't we? Sit back down, love. I'll be back in a minute. Then you can tell me about your little Red priest. It may be important, Fredi—"

Again that wave of uneasiness hit him. She had mastered herself too quickly. Gone from wild tears to utter calm—in seconds. It wasn't like her. Of course her self-control had always been admirable, but this—

She came back with the drinks. Sat on the floor on the deep pile rug with her head resting on his knees and listened very quietly to his tale of how he had demonstrated to both the Director General and the Minister of Justice the utter folly of making a martyr of that young fool of a priest at this ticklish political juncture.

"They got it, not being idiots," he said. "Remember the potash mining case? The miners making their sit-down strike in the very bowels of the mine, and twenty of these damned young hippy priests barricaded and starving themselves to death in the parish church in defense of the miners' right to strike in a country where all strikes are illegal! We can't afford things like that, *Amparita*. Spain has too bad an image now in the community of nations. We paid an awfully high price for Franco's vaunted thirty-six years of peace."

"I did, anyhow," she whispered. "My father's life—and my mother's. For it was her grief that killed her, finally."

"I know," he said sadly. "But the nation as a nation paid for it, too. By our reduction in the eyes of the world to a third-rate power. No—say a fifth-rate one. And to hell with it!"

"Fredi—you're in a mood tonight, aren't you?" she said.

"Yes. Forgive me, will you? I really shouldn't inflict these things upon you, my dear."

"That's what I'm *for*," she laughed. "Drink up! I'm going to drag you off to bed—and cheer you up, somehow!"

He smiled at her.

"You usually manage," he said, "but tired as I am tonight, it's going to cost you! Well then, come on—"

"No. Wait. Fredi—who paid the Red priest's fine? You?"

"Yes," he said. "The long-haired young beggar—except for his tonsured spot!—hadn't a centimo. But that was kept strictly a secret."

"Fredi—maybe we'd better get out of here. Go to a motel, or—"

"Why?" he said.

"That call. Maybe the rabid Right is going to pull one of *theirs.* It has to be them. Your little hippy priest was a *Red,* so—"

"Did he make any threats?" Fredi said. "The man who called, I mean?"

"No. Not really. Just asked whether you were going to visit me tonight."

"Hell, *niña*—that could be one of Consuelo's private eyes still hanging in there trying to earn his fee."

"True. Still—"

"Still nothing. Tired as I am, they could blow me up and I wouldn't even feel it. The only reason I don't go home right now and leave you in peace is that I'd rather rest a couple of hours and let the traffic die down somewhat—"

"Oh, no you don't! You're spending the night with *me.* All of it!"

"But, *queridísima,* we're seeing each other tomorrow, aren't we? At that seafood bar you swear is so wonderful. It had better be! I haven't had any decent shellfish in so long, that—say, what's that name again?"

"La Marisqueria Principe, en la calle Esparteros," she said, slowly, clearly, her voice rising, becoming a little too loud.

He stared at her. Saw that her eyes had gone very dark. Widened. Were staring into his own as though she were trying to force him to read her mind.

"Fredi—" she got out; then, abruptly, she laughed. Freely, gaily.

'Or is it—hysterically?' he wondered.

"Oh now I know what to do with you!" she giggled. "Come on. Get up. That's it! Now come with me—"

"But where are we going?" he said.

"To my bath. We're going to take a shower together!"

Tired as he was, her antic notion was appealing. Then he remembered something. Like most members of the upper middle class, who, in Spain, would never dream of combing, waving, curling, or setting their own hair, she almost never took showers, preferring a tub bath, because showers, even when a showercap is used, play havoc with that weekly or even twice-weekly professionally set coiffure that cost her—or rather him —a young fortune.

"But—your hair?" he protested.

"Doesn't matter! I've got to cheer you up somehow!" she said.

In the bath, she turned on the shower full force, carefully adjusting the hot and cold faucets so that the water was something less than scalding. Whirled upon him, tugged at his buttons, laughing, laughing. But her laughter was strained, a little hysterical, he thought. Yet, even so, he could feel life stirring in his loins. He leaned back, let her undress him.

She pushed him away from her, began—with the same oddly forced gaiety—to hum a popular tune. He recognized it. It was the fast paso doble, with just a hint of a rhumba-meringue beat thrown in at the appropriate spots, to which the choristas of Pasapoga, a night club on La Gran Via, did their bumps and grinds, in that god-awful, poor, pitiful imitation of a strip-tease, which always ended with their still keeping on a hell of a lot more underthings than even modish grandmothers wore nowadays. But the censor—the almighty censor!—wouldn't permit any more than that in Spain. Amparo's parody of the chorus girls' act was a masterpiece, and a vast improvement.

"Now, come on!" she said, and dived into the shower.

He followed her. Under the shower, she slipped into his arms, moving into him, fitting, arching, locking her heels be-

hind his, so that there was not one millimeter of their flesh that
did not touch. He moaned a little from the sheer pleasure of
it.

"Fredi," she said quickly. "Listen to me!"

"Listen?" he said. "Good God, Amparo!"

"Yes. I brought you in here—not—not to do what you're
starting to do to me now. Although I love it—love you—and
it feels—wonderful—"

He stopped. Said: "Then why, Amparo?"

"Because—a shower makes a sufficiency of noise—enough
so that—that man—who called me—can't hear what we say.
Through the microphones they've got planted all over the flat.
So this conversation—¡por lo menos!—won't be recorded on
tape. As every word you've said to me all these months has
been. And every one I've said to you. Even the ones that were
not even—words, really. The sounds—that any—hembra—
makes—when she's being—serviced. Gloriously serviced, in
this case . . ."

He pushed her away from him. Hard.

"You little bitch!" he said.

She bowed her head. The swirl of water silvered her hair's
inky blackness. When she looked up, he thought she was crying. But in the shower, he couldn't be sure.

"I was planted in your office, Fredi," she said slowly, flatly,
even quietly, her voice just loud enough to be heard above
the shower's whistling rush, "to seduce you. To betray you.
Paid for it. Paid well. Though I must say I've enjoyed my
work—"

What clawed at his guts then wasn't really death. But it felt
like it. That is, if death feels like anything. 'Dying does,
though,' he thought, 'the act of dying—before all feeling stops.
And what it feels like is this—is this!'

"Fredi," she said. "If you think—if you believe—for even
one second—what I see in your face—kill me. Now. At once.
It's—kinder."

Something exploded inside his brain, destroying in that instant his thinking mind. The ancestral ape stood up and roared through his blood. A curtain of red crashed down between his eyes and her already mist-blurred form. He heard the wet, sick, smashing sound his palm made connecting with her face. Again, again, again. Then his eyes cleared. Powerless to stop himself, he saw how her face jerked right then left then right again under the ceaseless rain of his blows. She made not the slightest move to ward off those crushing, flesh-purpling slaps. She hung there, her hands dangling at her sides, the tears jetting from her eyes under the impact of his big, hard sportsman's hand, flung out with such force that he could see the semi-circular jeweled spray they made cut through even the shower's mist-steam torrent.

And stopped it at once, nausea pooling in his gut, the ice-cold sickness rising in him. It was the first time in his forty-six years of life he had ever struck a woman. It was going to be, he knew then, with absolute certainty, the last.

"Amparo—I'm sorry!" he groaned. "I—"

"It's—all right, Fredi," she said slowly. "Feel better now? I hope so, because there's no time. Fredi—that place tomorrow —there's going to be—a bomb in it. I was supposed—to bring you there. Then I was to—to excuse myself. Got to the rest room. Out the back door—escape—leave you—to die . . ."

He stared at her. Her face was a mess. Blood was coming out of both corners of her mouth. Her left eye was rapidly closing, the flesh puffing about it, turning dark. Even the shower's spray didn't help.

"And—you—you—couldn't do it—" he whispered, then, his voice rising, breaking. "You *couldn't* do it! And I—and I—"

"Have—beaten—the—thing—you *own,* Fredi. Your *hembra.* Your she-thing, bitch-thing. Yours—to do what you like with. Even—that."

"Amparo!" he got out. "How on earth—"

"Wait! When we come out of here—say—loudly—that you're hungry—that you're starving. Offer to take me to a restaurant—and—"

"With *that* face?" Fredi groaned.

"He won't be able to see my face, the man who's listening —the obscene voyeuristic swine! But we must get out of this flat, Fredi. Go—not to a restaurant—I couldn't eat if you *paid* me to! But to *our* motel. We'll talk in the car, though—because they may have the motel *intervinido,* wiretapped, implanted with hidden microphones, by now, since there's absolutely nothing about us that they don't know—"

"Amparo—who are 'they'?" Fredi said.

"Tell you in the car!" she hissed. "Now, come on!"

But, as they came out into the living room, dressed finally, which had taken them some little time, since Fredi had spent the better part of a half hour applying ice packs to her swollen face to reduce the swelling and she had done what she could with astringent lotions, leaving her poor, battered face still a mess, but even so, considerably improved over the way it had been, the telephone was ringing—again.

He nodded. She went to it, picked it up, said:

"*¡Diga!* Speak!"

Fredi crowded in close to her, put his big hand over her slim one, pulled the phone a little way from her ear so that he could hear her caller's voice, too.

"Amparo?" a woman's voice said.

"*Sí. Al aparato. ¿Quien es?*" Amparo said.

"I am—Angela," the voice said. "And Jorge is with me. You know—your friends from—Paris. Is everything all right for—tomorrow?"

Fredi's eyes took fire. He jerked out his ballpoint pen, bent to the note pad on the telephone table. Wrote, in huge letters: "Speak *French* to her!"

He knew she could. That was one of the reasons he had hired her.

"*Mais non,*" Amparo said, "*je regrette, mais je ne me rapelle pas de vous. Vous êtes Angela, vous dites? Angela qui?*"

"*Ça n'a aucun importance,*" the voice said. "*Ceci que je trouve vraiment important c'est si vous avez arrangé ça—ou non. Ce déjeuner si charmant demain—avec votre encore plus charmant ami . . .*"

Fredi nodded vigorously.

"*Oui,*" Amparo whispered. "It *is* arranged, Angela. That charming lunch. With my charming friend. At the place— agreed upon. At the agreed time."

"*D'ac! À demain . . . drôle de petite poule! 'Voir!*"

"She called me—" Amparo gasped, but Fredi's big hand clamped down over her mouth.

He wrote: "We'll talk in the car! Now answer *only* what I say to you!"

He said: "Amparo, *niña,* I'm starving! You wouldn't have anything eatable in the *frigorífico,* would you?" He shook his head rapidly from side to side, indicating that she should say no.

"Oh dear!" Amparo wailed. "You see what an *awful* housewife I am? It's a good thing you *can't* marry me!"

"Doesn't matter. Breda will still be open. I'll take you there."

"Well," she said, laughing, "I could *eat.* What I'm not sure I can do is walk. You, *¡tu brutote!* have left me so sore that—"

"I'll carry you downstairs in my arms," he said.

"With that *curioso* of a *portero* we've got? Not on your life. I can make it—I think. To the lift, anyhow. And from the lift to your car. It's not parked too far away, is it?"

"No. I was lucky. It's just in front. Now, come on!" Fredi said.

"Fredi," she said, when they were outside in the car, "she called me a *whore.* With contempt in her voice!"

"I know. I heard her," Fredi said grimly. " '*Drôle de petite poule!*' And if she's who I think she is, she has no right. For if there ever were a dirty little bitch in this world—"

"Fredi—you—you *know* her! That was why you told me to speak French, wasn't it?"

"Yes, to check. But I *don't* know her. Over the *maldito* telephone, how can one tell? But it did *sound* like her. A lot. A ruddy lot. For one thing she—if she *is* the girl I think she is —is the only young Spanish woman I've ever met—except of course one or two who were accidentally brought up in France, which *she* wasn't—who can manage both the Spanish *and* the French 'R.'"

"Her French was perfect," Amparo whispered. "Far, far better than mine."

Something in her voice caused him to turn, look at her. She was crying.

"Amparo!" he said.

"One of—*yours*, eh, Fredi?" she said bitterly. "That— hurts. That hurts a great deal more than that beating you gave me did. Oh, all right! Who am I to—"

"You're my life," he said flatly. "All my life from here on in. And she's *not* one of mine, even if she's who I think she is. What's more, she *never* was. She was, when I knew her, En- rique's. In Paris. *Sa*—so very French!—*petite amie.* His mistress. I freely confess I liked her. She was utterly charming. So very charming that I checked on her to see if poor Enrique was in as great a danger of doing something foolish as it seemed to me he was. Because, you see, he was absolutely *mad* over her, in spite of the fact that she's an ugly little thing, a quarter of a kilo of bones, with a monkey face and—and—No! Not and, 'but—'"

"But what?" Amparo said, miserably.

"Her eyes. Absolutely the deuced most amazing eyes you ever saw. Lavender, so help me. A pale lavender in a face quite as black as an Andaluzian gypsy's. And that mouth! *¡Jesus hijo de María Virgen, que boca!* The definition of sensuality. Of volup- tuousness. So even skinny and flat-chested as she was, with hips like a boy's, I was afraid Enrique was going to go off the deep end, leave Matilde and the girls and—"

"Fredi," Amparo said, "open the door. Let me out of this car. Now. This minute!"

" *¡Amparo, por el amor de Dios!* It's *not* the same thing! It's not at all. In the first place Consuelo is not Matilde Gil Patricio —not by a long shot! Enrique's wife was *worth* keeping—keeping at any cost. In the second, *you* are not Ana María Casaribiera, who is certainly the biggest Spanish whore to hit Paris since la Belle Otero! Hell, the only man in Paris she *hasn't* gone to bed with is the late General de Gaulle, and I'll bet she did one jolly fine job of polishing his ancient knob for him, if they ever left her around the old boy for as long as five minutes flat—"

"Fredi!" Amparo said, her voice shame-rent, stricken.

"Sorry again. Nor is *that* the same thing. Between lovers, real lovers, anything they both enjoy is permissible, my dearest. And—*¡Jesus del Gran Poder!*"

"Now what?" Amparo said.

"It just hit me! Amparo tell me—and for God's sake don't lie!—who are—'they'?"

She bowed her head. Looked up again.

"The PCE.," she whispered. *"El Partido Comunista Español . . ."*

"Then it can't be Ana. Why would a girl of her background, heiress to one of Spain's greatest fortunes, to one of its noblest names—" He stopped, whispered very, very softly: " *¡Jesus, María, y José!* She *could* be. A member of it, I mean. It would be just like her. She's been doing the exact opposite of what she ought, of what anyone would expect of her, all her ruddy life! Say—she *is.* Say they sent her—to lead Enrique Ximenez, the best friend I've ever had in this miserably, execrably sodomized world, to—"

"His death. Just as they sent *me* to lead *you* to yours. Yes. Very likely."

Fredi sat there.

"I'll get her," he whispered. "Even if I have to do it myself. With my own two hands. Even though she's an untouchable, I—"

"Untouchable?" Amparo said bitterly. "From what you've

just said, it appears that practically *everyone* has touched her—except you. And you—wanted—want to!"

"Wanted. Past tense. I'll admit that much. It has nothing to do with you, with us. When I met Ana María, I had yet to meet you, remember? But want—present tense—no. Except to see her dead and in hell!"

"Why do you call her an 'untouchable,' Fredi?"

"Family. You know Spain. She has Borbón blood from the distaff side. Male ancestors of hers married female Borbóns—Bourbons, for some of the women involved were French. But basically it's the same family. So she's related distantly—but actually—to both branches of our royal house, the *Carlista* Borbóns, and the *Alfonista* ones. More specifically, she's the daughter of the Counts of Casaribiera, who exiled her *themselves,* because she wouldn't quit screwing even their valets and *campesinos*! She's the worst little nymphomaniacal bitch since Isabel *Segunda* and—"

"Fredi," Amparo whispered. "Don't sound quite so—jealous. Please?"

"*¡Mierda!* Now look, Amparo, it seems to me it's *you* who're—"

"Jealous? Of course. I admit it. Sick with jealousy. Now, this minute hurting. But then, I have some right to be haven't I?"

"In the sense that we belong to each other now, yes. Belong to each other—forever, Amparo *mía*. But in the sense that I've given you any grounds to be, no. Absolutely not!"

"Fredi—you spent your vacation in France with your friend who was killed, almost a year ago. You, yourself, told me that. And yet you recognized her voice *instantly*—a telephone—"

"I didn't recognize it. I'm still not sure. Still—"

"Still what?" Amparo said.

"Ana María has a rather striking voice. Startling in a girl so small. A true contralto. Atonal. A trifle harsh. An instru-

194

ment designed to play both Bartok and Stravinsky on. And it did sound like her. Especially in French. If she had trilled that 'R' the way we do, instead of swallowing it the way they do, I would dismiss her as my chief suspect. But she's a born linguist. She even speaks English like a British duchess. And, truthfully, I spent a good many hours in her company. Mostly lending her my shoulder to cry on. She was—or had convinced herself she was—quite dreadfully in love with Enrique. Which could be a motive. For her getting him—murdered, I mean. Hell hath no fury like a woman scorned, y'know.''

"Well," Amparo said, "I hope that while you were drying her lonely tears, the two of you at least remained standing up . . .''

"Oh God!" Fredi said. "Now hear this *mujer*! I have never so much as kissed Ana María Casaribiera y Borbón Galvey Canto, let alone removed her frilly little *bragas*! If you want me to, I'll swear it on my mother's grave!''

"No. Don't swear. Just take me out to *our* motel. And make love to me. Be quite brutal about it. Wear me out. So I can sleep. So I can forget what your voice does, saying her name . . .''

"Lord, *Amparita,* I'm the one who's worn out! I've had a rough day. Especially at home. But if that's what it takes to—''

"Ease me? Yes. That and a few other things. Things you may not even have in you to give me—yet. Belief in me. In *us* as a combination that can work. Trust. Faith. Though I've given you very little grounds for any of those things I—I *need,* Fredi. But I will. These—and any other—pledges—proofs—of how much I love you—how helplessly, hopelessly—slavishly even, without either pride or dignity!—you'll ever require of me. Up to and including my life. But I've done that already, haven't I? Offered you my life. Even offered up my life for yours . . .''

"I don't understand you, Amparo. You're being awfully cryptic, you know!"

"True. And it's just as well. In fact, it's better that way. Now start the car, Fredi. We really must go . . ."

But when they entered that quiet pool-side room in the comfortable motel out near the Barajas Airport whose owner was both pleased and flattered to have them as steady clients for that meant that the young Minister trusted his, the owner's, tact and discretion absolutely, the first thing Federico did was to cross the room and pick up the phone.

Amparo stared at him, her dark eyes enormous.

"Fredi," she whispered, "whom are you going to call?"

"The *Dirección General de Seguridad,* of course," he said, already dialing swiftly as he spoke. "Tell them to send the bomb squad to that place to—"

But she was beside him in two long strides, pushed her finger down hard upon the contact of the phone's cradle, breaking the connection.

He stared at her. Said: "Amparo—"

She put her index finger vertically across her lips, nodded her head in the direction of the swimming pool. He hung up the phone at once. The two of them went out into the night, moved to the far side of the pool away from the brighter of the lights, and away from the people, nearly all foreigners, most of them Germans and Swedes who were still splashing around in the pool, even as late as it was.

"You think that even this place is under electronic surveillance, too?" Fredi said.

"I don't know," she whispered, "but they know too much about our habits, Fredi. We can't take the chance. Listen to me, love. It's no good to send the bomb disposal squad. That damnable thing is not even there yet, and it won't be until about five minutes before *we* arrive. That's one thing—"

"And another?" he said harshly.

She bowed her head. When she looked up again the pool

lights poured white fire into the tears in her eyes. Set them ablaze.

"Fredi," she said quietly. "Do you really want me? I mean —want me by your side—forever? Because if you do—if you truly do, you've got to—keep me alive . . ."

"Amparo, don't start that suicidal rot again!" he said angrily.

"It isn't rot, Fredi. I *would* kill myself if you left me now. I'd have to."

"Now, Amparo!"

"Hear me out. Not because of anything so romantic as my broken heart, my grief at losing you. Though I'm quite sure that both would kill me eventually—or at least drive me mad—without my having to lift a hand against myself. No— it would be because I couldn't stand waiting for the one *they* 'll send to come. To loop a nylon cord around my throat. Jerk it tight, biting into my flesh. Hold it hard—until my face turns black. And all my sphincters loosen. I don't know why, but that detail especially distresses me. I've always been so—so fastidious, say. And being garroted—is such—a messy way to die. . . ."

He stared at her. Whispered: *"¡Santa Madre de Dios!"*

"Or perhaps he'll simply push one of those flat long-barreled pistols. they usually use—Mausers they're called, I think—through a half-opened window. And it will have a silencer on it, so the noise it will make won't be loud. Splat! Splat! Twice. Like that. Only twice. When I was training, I saw their experts at target.practice. Two shots were always enough. They never needed more. But, however they do it, I shall have paid the price—for putting my love for you above my duty to our cause. For betraying *them,* the penalty's always—death, my heart . . ."

"Amparo, for the love of God!" he said.

"All right. I'll stop it now. I've tortured you enough. Strange—I *know* you love me—and yet I had to do this—say these things—to assure myself—to reassure myself—because you talked—too warmly—about a woman I've never even seen —and—"

"So," he said gravely, "they weren't even so!"

"No, Fredi, they *are* so. Unless we play our hands right tonight, tomorrow, and the day after, I won't be alive another week. Do you believe that the people who planned Carrero Blanco's murder, who splattered twelve or thirteen people to bloody rags in la Calle de Correos will play by the rules of Anglo-Saxon sportsmanship?"

"*¡Siga!*" he grated. "Go on!"

"All right. Fredi—here's the funny part. The insanely ironical part, really. It will be your—wrecked career, your loss of—of importance, that will save me—"

"Why, Amparo? I don't see—"

"I know you don't. But first we've got to attend to the immediate danger. Fredi—you've got to arrange me *una coartada*—"

"An alibi? Why, Amparo? For what?"

"For our not showing up at the Marisqueria Principe at two thirty tomorrow afternoon so that you, my love, can be splattered all over the walls and the ceiling in a million bloody bits! A provable, demonstrable reason why we *couldn't* get there. Could you do something to the motor of the car that would make it break down between here and there?"

"I doubt it. My knowledge of mechanics is zero-minus. But why should I? Wouldn't it make more sense to have a couple of plainclothes boys stationed before the door of that place, with a perfect description of Ana María Casaribiera, or even a photo of her, which we could get from one of those idiotic woman's magazines, considering how often a picture of her— usually accompanied by someone else's husband!—has been in them, and—"

"Fredi—*she* won't come. She'll send her *cómplice,* a man we don't even know."

"Have them stop anyone who goes into that place with a bag or bundle big enough to—"

"Fredi, they're experts. He'd spot the detectives a block before they ever saw him. Never show up. Or pull the firing pin on the damnable thing, and stroll by, and throw it into that place, killing your fine detectives along with everyone else in the Marisqueria. And you're forgetting the principal thing— which is an indication, perhaps, of how much you love me—"

He stared at her, whispered, *"¡Dios mío!"*

"¡Amen! Because *who* else could have told you? Believe me, *amor mío,* I wouldn't stay alive a week. Not even if you set the entire *Cuerpo de la Police Armada* to guarding me night and day. All that would mean would be that a number of handsome young policemen with all their lives before them would die along with me. I shouldn't like that, you know—"

"Then what—"

"Mi coartada. My alibi. We've got to make it look like I tried and failed. Because that bomb must go off. After—I hope! —we've got all the people out of there. At the last possible minute. No more than two minutes later than my call to a man I don't know, have never even seen, informs them that you and I are stuck somewhere on some miserable road in *un coche averiado*—a broken-down car."

"But—the place will be wrecked, and—"

"It's probably insured. If not, you, as a Procurator in Cortes can propose a bill before the government to pay the owners for damages suffered in an attempt upon the life of a Minister of said government. *Your* life, Fredi."

"I see," he whispered, "but I don't like this, Amparo."

"All right. Do it your way, Fredi. You *will* put some flowers on my grave, won't you, dearest? That is—if I even have a grave. If they even leave enough of me to bury."

"Oh, Jesus, Amparo!"

"Do you think I could be guarded, protected better than the late Admiral Carrero Blanco, then President of the Government, was? Do you think you can stop the people who planted a bomb in the Café Rondo, across the street from *La Dirección General de Seguridad* itself? Fredi, Fredi—the only reason why they haven't killed Franco, himself, is because they don't want to! They don't want to make a martyr of him at the last, awaken public sympathy for the poor tottering old man, cause people to forget all the quite horrible things that were done at his orders. It's my *life* I'm begging for, Fredi! And that only because I think you love me. Though I'm rapidly beginning to doubt it. If you don't, say so. Then I'll just sit quietly—in my room—and wait for my—executioners—to come. In fact, I'll even—welcome them."

He stared at her, said: "All right. You win. What in heaven's name or hell's could I do to the car that—wait! I've got it! The tires! The tires, Amparo! I stop by the roadside, pretend to look at them, stick a nice hole in one of them with—hell, I haven't even got a pocket knife!"

"Order steak tonight. Purloin a steak knife, Fredi. Now, tell me, how long does it take you to change a tire, *cielo?*"

"A matter of minutes. I'm good at *that,* at least—"

"That's *bad.* We've got to be stuck, really stuck."

He thought. Said, finally: "I've got it. I'll loosen the valve in the spare. By morning all the air will have leaked out of it. So when I go to change the punctured one, I'll have nothing to put in its place. It's a thing that frequently happens . . . and then?"

"You leave me in the car while you go call for one of those highway aid trucks. Call for it first. *Then,* at two twenty, say, *not* before, you call the Marisqueria. Tell them to get all the people in the place out. Don't identify yourself."

"They'll think I'm a crank, and—"

"No they won't. Not after the Admiral, and the Café Rondo. The one thing I'm afraid of is that the person who answers the phone will run out of there screaming and start a stampede. Try to talk some sense into whoever answers. Tell *him* to advise the police. Don't *you* do it!"

"I see. All this is so rare, Amparo. Makes me feel like a criminal, a conspirator—"

"You'll be conspiring to save my life, Fredi. Remember that."

"And thereby—mine." he said, "I couldn't live without you, Amparo. I literally couldn't."

"You won't have to. Fredi, by day after tomorrow, your resignation will have to be in all the papers."

He stared at her. Said: "All right. But why so soon?"

"And you'll have to have moved into the flat with me."

"Same answer. Same question. Why, Amparo?"

"So that when they call me, I can give them the *right* answers. For they'll already have checked the *Ayuda en Carretera* people and found out that I was telling the truth when I call them about three, three thirty, and tell them why we couldn't get there in time to blow you up."

"And?" he said.

"I'll point out to them that I have removed you from the political scene even more effectively than killing you would have. That I have disgraced you, besmirched your good name, hint that I've caused all your faction to fall under a cloud of suspicion and doubt—"

"Amparo," he said sadly, "you sound awfully professional now."

"I am professional. They taught me to be. What they didn't realize was that they were also teaching me to hate their bloody guts in the bargain. Another thing, you know anyone in *Segunda Bis*?"

"Counterespionage? Yes. Why yes, of course. A couple of their head chaps were in law school with me. Why?"

"Well, tomorrow afternoon, after this is all over, you drop in on *La Segunda Bis, Brigada de Contraespionaje.* Give them your key to our flat. Have them send one of their electronic experts over to pass one of those little black boxes all over the place.

You know. The ones that go 'Beep! Beep! Beep!' every time they come anywhere close to a microphone?"

"To debug it? Of course! Jolly good idea, in fact. But, anyhow, we're going to have to move. I won't be able to afford that kind of rent anymore."

"You poor old darling! I have ruined you, haven't I? Now, come let's go back to the room—so I can ruin you a little more."

"Amparo, at the risk of reminding you what a tired old party you've fallen heir to, how many times do I have to tell you I'm *dead*?" he groaned.

She laughed. Kissed him. Said: "Go let the air out of the spare tire. Then come to bed. Don't worry, I'll let you sleep. In fact, from now on, I'm going to *insist* upon your getting your share of rest. Sleeping nights. Eating well. Taking care of yourself. D'you know *why, mi amor*?"

"No, Amparita—why?" he said.

"Don't panic, Fredi! It's because I am—after all—a *Spanish* woman. *¡Muy española!* and I want—oh Fredi, please!—*us* to have a child. Two children, anyhow."

"Or eight. Or ten. Or eighteen! Oh God, why wasn't I born in Sweden!"

"In Sweden? I didn't know you liked blondes. Consuelo isn't. Nor am I. Nor from what you've told me is the murderous little aristocratic *vagabunda* you and Enrique Ximenez were both gone over."

"Well then, not Sweden. But some place—any place— where the women have some goddamned sense! Now come on!" he said.

I t doesn't make any sense, that business of holding up in one of those ETΛ-type concealment cells until the heat is off," Diego said. "In the first place, the police know they exist, since those *Vasco* cretins blew their cover—as usual—after the Café Rondo case. So finding the one we'd be in wouldn't even cost them too much time. In the second, since we're *not* going to splatter this *type,* the heat is likely to stay on for weeks, because he's going to be around to set up one hell of a howl. And you can bet he's got connections, Ana. Nobody gets that far up in Spain unless he's *enchufado*—and plugged into the *right* lines at that . . ."

"So," she said tonelessly, "you go. Leave me—"

"Ana," he said, "would you rather have a *live* husband, or a *dead* Communist martyr? Once you walk back up those stairs from the ladies' room, leaving poor little *Tripas de Goma*—"

"Leaving *whom?*" she gasped.

"Tripas de Goma," Diego said, poking her once again noticeably swollen middle with his finger, "*nuestro hijito.* Poor little Rubber Gut, our baby son . . ."

"Oh!" Ana said. "What a thing to call our poor unborn child!"

"I'd rather call him that than *Diegito,*" Diego said solemnly, "or *Anita,* either one. At the moment, anyhow."

"Me, too," Ana María said. "But I could be; ever thought of that? Pregnant, I mean. My next period's not until—Jesus! I don't remember *when* it's supposed to be. You, you angelic-looking swine, have got me so mixed up I've lost count."

"Ana, for God's sake pay attention! And stop worrying about my leaving you. Temporarily. For a while. For once you walk back up those stairs leaving poor little Rubber Gut stuffed down behind the toilet, you're safe. Nobody's going to connect the daughter of the Counts of Casaribiera with a stupid *Vasco* bomb scare—"

"Diego!" she said. "Suppose they *find* my poor little rubber imitation pregnant belly? And this damned wig? And the dress? They'll put two and two together and—"

"They *won't,*" he said. "Because I'm going to leave this lovely little package in the men's john. Right next door to the ladies'. There won't be *anything* identifiable left. Say, Anita, what do I order? Jesus! I've forgotten the names of shellfish in Spanish!"

"You don't. I'll do the ordering. You keep that adorably angelic mouth of yours *shut, Diegito mío.* When you say anything to me—because if anyone else addresses you directly, I'll swear you've got laryngitis and can't utter a mumbling word!—say it in Spanish; but in a very low tone so that no one will catch *cet enmerdeur accent français* of yours! Because, afterwards, the mere fact of there having been a foreigner in that place would direct the police's attention to—Diego, kiss me! Kiss me hard!"

"In the street?" he said.

"In the street! *¡No seas tan malditamente pudico!* If I could, I'd lean back against a wall, pull up my dress, yank down my *bragas* and make you get to work! A little *calmante vitaminado, mi amor! ¡Un tranquilizante un tanto físico!* That would calm me.

Because those damned pills you gave me certainly haven't. Oh Jesus, Diego, I'm shaking! I'm so damned scared that—"

"Ana, please! Why the devil do you have to go and get scared *now?*"

"Because *that's* it. That place right across the street. Kiss me, Diego."

He bent, kissed her lightly, briefly. But she clawed him, mauled him, dragged into her arms, glued her big, absolutely scalding mouth to his, kissing him like a starving cannibal.

Turned him loose at last, sighed. Said, "I'm—all right now, Diego. Let's go . . ."

"No, wait. See that bar down there? On this side of the street?"

"The Bar Superstar. Yes. Why, Diego? Oh I get it! From there I could—"

"Watch for me to come out of the Principe. Now you wait here a minute. I'm going into that bar, buy a package of cigarettes. See if they've a public telephone."

"Oh they *will,* Diego! Nearly all bars do."

"We'd better make sure, Ana."

"Then I'll come with you!"

"No. They mustn't see us together. And my accent won't make much of any difference there. That a foreigner came in to buy a pack of smokes isn't *that* unusual, is it?"

"No. Not at all. But afterwards, when the *Police Armada* comes around asking questions?"

"They'll say a young foreign hippy with long hair, a mustache, and a beard came in to buy a pack of Chesterfields. There will be nothing to connect said hippy with what's happened. At least not completely. So he was in *both* places? What does that prove? Only that he was in both places, not that he blew one of them up. So the police start looking for him? They don't find him because he—or at least his chief identifying characteristics: the long hair, mustache, and beard—have ceased to exist . . ."

"A pity. I love *tu melena, bigote y barba,* Diego! All right, go see if there's a phone. 'Cause it would be too awful if—"

He was back in minutes.

"There *is*," he said. "Now, come on!"

They crossed the street. Entered the Marisqueria Principe. Sat down at a little table near the door. No one paid them any special attention, not even the waiter, who finally ambled over and said in a weary voice:

"*¿Sí, señores?*"

"How're the *cigales* today?" Ana said.

The waiter opened his half-closed eyes. Stared at them. Took in every detail: Diego's shoulder-length, light-brown hair, his mustache, his beard; Ana's little round belly, that smart, really lovely blond wig, her strange, pale, almost lavender eyes.

"Great!" he said. "The best! Flown in from Vigo this morning by airplane!"

"Show us two big ones," Ana said.

"*¡Sí, señora! ¡En seguida, señora!*" the waiter said and dashed off.

"We've done something *wrong!*" Diego said into her ear.

"I *know!*" she wailed. "But *what?* This is the way you always order *mariscos* in Spain, and—"

By then the waiter was back with the two *cigales,* big, saltwater crayfish from the Galician coast. They were huge. As big as lobsters, even.

"How much?" Ana said, miserably aware that every living soul in the Marisqueria Principe was staring at them with frank curiosity now. She was still doing everything exactly right, the way things are always done; the way she, as an almost native *Madrileña,* knew they had to be. And yet, within minutes of their having entered that shellfish bar, they had, for some unknown reason, committed what is to any political activist, any terrorist, the worst error possible, or even conceivable: They had attracted attention to themselves.

"Have to weigh 'em," the waiter said. He went to the bar.

Every eye in the place turned longingly toward the scale. The needle spun, quivered close to a full kilo for each of the two crayfish.

The waiter came back to their table.

"Lady," he said slowly, sadly, "that'll be—a thousand." He paused, added still more sorrowfully: "Each."

Then it hit Ana María. She had noted when she came into the place that no one had more than a handful of boiled or grilled shrimps on his plate. And that the Marisqueria was three quarters empty. That, in a city where shellfish bars are always jampacked, where the native citizens eat shellfish from noon to night, as casually as other peoples eat potato chips, say, should have warned her. But it hadn't. She'd been away too long. So now she knew what she'd done wrong: She had ordered close to the most expensive shellfish there were, without having previously inquired into this one small detail likely to wreck them, by awaking not only the vivid curiosity of the always curious *Madrileños,* but the active envy of one of the most envious races on earth. She hadn't because she had assumed— stupidly—that her native Spain was somehow immune to the economic disasters rending and shaking the rest of Europe, and hence had not troubled her little head to find out what shellfish now cost. So she hadn't known that in the late summer of 1974, to eat any kind of shellfish at all in Madrid, you needed to *own* the *Banco Hispano-Americano.* Plus the *Banco de Vizcaya.* And a half interest in the *Banco de Bilbao* wouldn't have hurt.

Then she set about righting things, aided by her gut-deep, *womb*-deep feminine instincts: "What!" she shrieked. "A thousand pelas for one miserable little *cigal?*"

"Lady," the waiter said, "you talk Spanish real good. But you aren't from *here,* are you?"

"I was born here!" Ana said. " *¡En la Clinica de Nuestra Señora de Loreto!* You're talking to an authentic *Madrileña,* friend!"

She was thanking the God she still occasionally believed in, especially when the going got to be as rough as it was now, that she'd said "pelas" instead of "pesetas." That was pure, *castiza* Madrid talk, on an order with *"pitillo"* for *"cigarillo."* Or *"treinta duros,"* "thirty hard ones" for a hundred and fifty pesetas; a "hard one" being what *Madrileños* call the five-peseta coin.

"And since I'm from *here,*" she went on furiously, "I know a thousand pesetas for one *cigal* is armed robbery!"

"Lady, *con perdon,*" the waiter said patiently, "you happen to be wrong now. If you're from Madrid, like you *say,* you must have been outa town a *long* time. . . ."

It was time, Ana María decided, to beat a graceful retreat.

She said, all the anger gone out of her voice, "You're right there, camarero. My husband and I just got back from Germany yesterday. Madrid surely has changed."

And came within millimeters of blowing their cover completely.

For the waiter heard her lisping, trilling, staccato Castilian, as different from the Spanish *he* spoke as an Oxford don's English is from that of a Cockney born within hearing distance of the old Bow bells. Stared at her. At those eyes. At that mouth. At that wig that cost more than he earned in a month, at that black silk *prenatal* dress that cost more than he was paid in six. And wondered what the hell a girl who had aristocracy written all over her, who dressed like a millionaire, talked like *una maldita duquesa,* a goddamned duchess, ever had to go to Germany *for?* The boy, yes. *Gallego* or *Asturiano,* surely, to be so fair complexioned, light-haired, blue eyed. And poor. The poverty ground into him until it showed. 'But how, *en este jodido mundo,* did a poor *paleto* like this *chaval*—his hippy hair don't make no difference, every damn *peon de abañil* wears it that long nowadays, so much so that the *verdaderos hijos de Papa,* the real rich boys, are beginning to cut theirs short again—*ever* get hooked up with a classy article like this little *bonbon?*'

Seeing his eyes flicker from her face to Diego's, Ana felt

pure panic knotting her middle, fluttering her throat. 'We've blown it,' she thought. 'We've really blown it! And I don't even know why or how!'

She said, "What's the matter, *camarero?* Is there something wrong—about us?"

"No, lady," the waiter said. "But, begging your pardon *humildemente—raro, sí.* Odd."

Diego's blue eyes opened very wide. Ana caught his hand. Her nails bit into the flesh of his palm.

"Odd—how?" she said. Then she smiled pleasantly, turning on all the formidable warmth of her charm: "You can speak freely. We don't mind. We run into this sort of reaction *all* the time."

"Lady, I was born in *España.* Lived here fifty-eight years. And this is the *first* time I've ever seen *una señorita* like you with a boy like *him.* Begging your pardon, mister."

She got it. Tried to salvage what she could.

"We—we eloped," she whispered. "And we—we're hoping *mis papas* will—forgive us now."

"You ain't seen 'em yet?" the waiter said. "Then *chiquilla,* take an old man's advice. Don't for a few more days. Get him a haircut. Shave off the fringe. Oh you can leave it long, son; but not *that* long. Trim the mustache neat. And buy yourself a good suit. Conservative cut. *Then* you kids go to see the old folks. You got a fine advantage now, lady. With *su señora madre,* I mean. A grandchild on the way makes most older ladies plain *melt.*"

"Thank you," Ana said softly, her eyes misting over, moved by the man's real and sincere kindness. "You're *very* kind."

"I know life, lady. Well, what'll it be?"

"Bring us anything that's cheap," she said. "The money we made in Germany has got to last us a while . . ."

"Barrato, para decir barrato, no lo hay, señorita," the waiter said sorrowfully. "Cheap—to say *cheap,* there ain't really any-

thing, little lady. Not in the shellfish line, anyhow—''

"You mean to tell me that shellfish have gone up *that* much?'' Ana María said.

"*Sí, señora,*'' the waiter said. "First off those big oil tankers have killed off most of the *mariscos* by fouling up their breeding grounds with all that filthy muck they're always spilling into the water. 'N next, the fishermen don't even go out after 'em much these days. What with what fuel oil for the diesel motors of their boats costs now, they'd have to put a price on 'em they *know* the public wouldn't stand for.''

"Does the public stand for the ones you're asking now?'' Ana María said.

"To tell the truth, no. I'm afraid the *patron*'s going to have to close up in another month or two the way business is falling off. Then I'll be outa work. Tell me, how are things in Germany, son?''

"He can't talk,'' Ana said quickly. "Not today, anyhow. He's got a bad case of laryngitis. And things are bad in *Alemania.* We got laid off.''

"You *chavalines* have got it rough, haven't you?'' the waiter said. "Tell me, *chiquilla,* how much do you think you can stand?''

"Say—three hundred pesetas,'' Ana said.

"That means *gambas,* little lady. And not too many of them. How do you want 'em? *¿Cocidas? ¿A la plancha? ¿Al ajillo?*''

"Divide them up,'' Ana said. "Weigh all the shrimps we can get for that much, then bring them all three ways: boiled, grilled, and garlic broiled . . .''

"The boiled ones are already done,'' the waiter said, "but I'll divide the raw ones up in two lots, and tell the cook to fix 'em up. Won't take long. And I'll bring the boiled ones so you can pick at 'em while you wait . . .''

"Oh, Diego! Diego!'' Ana said as he shuffled away. "Let's get out of here! Right now! We've blown it! We've blown it sky high!''

"No," Diego said, "not really. We may even have done it *right,* Ana. Called so much attention to ourselves the way we are now that nobody'll believe we're the same people if they ever see us again the way we really are."

"But my eyes! My *malditos* Siamese kitty cat's eyes! He was looking at them the whole damn time!"

"*Tus ojos de flor.* Thy flower eyes," Diego said, and kissed her mouth.

"Hmmmmmn—sweet! Do it again! Kiss me some more. A lot more, *Diegito mío.*"

"No we don't! Besides, who's going to show him a photo —a color photo of la Señorita Ana María Casaribiera y Borbón for him to identify this fat knocked-up blonde as her?"

"I wish I were. I hope I *am* knocked up, I mean. I don't want to be fat, ever. Or a blonde. You're blond enough. Diego —if we've made *una niñita*—a girl baby—would she be blond? I'd like for her to be. And to be pretty—like you!"

The waiter came back with the shrimps, the cold, boiled ones, anyhow. He smiled at them paternally.

"Devoted young couple, ain't you?" he said. "That's nice. So few young couples are these days."

"We try to be," Ana María said.

"What'll it be to drink?" the waiter said.

"Beer. *Dos jarras*—two mugs," Ana Maria said.

They waited until he brought the rest of the shrimps, grilled, piping hot, and the rest in two earthenware bowls, sizzling in a flood of boiling olive oil, with chunks of the stinkingest garlic and the hottest peppers imaginable floating among them, and the beer.

They noticed with relief as they ate that the other clients had lost interest in them. After all Ana María had behaved with *casta* by protesting at those outrageous prices. And that the young couple were too well dressed didn't bother them. It had been quickly whispered around the bar by those close enough to hear her say it that they were just back from Germany. And most returning workers splurged on clothes, and even, when they'd been there more than two years, and hence were allowed to bring it in without paying the hellish importation tax, as big and expensive a car as they possibly could. What really saved them was the fact that their waiter—who had worked several years for a catering service which provided part-time waiters for the fiestas of the *very* rich, the people who lived in Puerta de Hierro, Somasaguas, Casquemada, La Florida, Conde de Orgaz, and Moraleja—was the only man in the house who had been around that kind of wealth frequently enough and long enough to recognize the exquisite quality of Ana Maria's clothes and, what was even worse, accurately estimate their cost.

To the rest, she was just a little working girl indulging in the characteristic Spanish vice of *luciendose,* showing off. They even sympathized with her for that, for 90 percent of the men in the bar were still paying *letras*—installments—on cars that they really hadn't been able to afford in the first place, and had to leave parked on Madrid's automobile-choked streets most of the time because gasoline now cost twenty pesetas the liter, or roughly one dollar forty-five cents American currency the gallon. Nor did Diego's appearance trouble them. There were five or six other young fellows in the Marisqueria with hair as long as his. Two of them even sported beards. Nor was his Nordic coloring a topic for speculation. While comprising a rather small minority, blonds really aren't all that rare in Spain.

In fact, they'd won ground back. It was actually going well. 'If,' Diego thought, 'we can dominate our nerves, we'll pull it off. We're past the worst part now . . .'

"I don't see anyone who could be—" Ana María got out in a strangled tone of voice.

"Our target for tonight? I do," Diego said. "That *viejo verde* over there. Typical dirty old man that most bigwigs here are. Well over sixty. And the girl's barely twenty. Twenty-two at most. Must be your friend Amparo."

"She's no friend of mine!" Ana flared. "Filthy little bitch

—luring that poor old granddad to his death!"

"By means of a cute little play toy provided by *us*," Diego said.

"Oh, Diego, let's not! Please! Let's just get out of here and—"

"Become Ernesto's targets for every damn night until his *pistoleros* finally find us and score? No thank you, *chata*! Now shut up. They'll be all right. I'm going to deliver the package now. Set it for half an hour. That'll give you time to give birth, get thin, turn *moreña,* and get out. Go to that bar across the street. Use their phone—"

"All right—" Ana María whispered.

By then, the waiter was there.

"Everything all right, señores?" he said.

"Just—just fine," Ana María faltered. "Bring us two more beers, will you, please?"

"Right away. Say, lady—that adhesive tape on your lip's come loose. Gonna fall off if you ain't careful. Saaay—that's *bad!* How'd *that* happen?"

"My husband—had to—had to slam on the brakes," Ana got out, "to avoid—killing—a dog, and my chin hit the dashboard. My own teeth did that. Went right through my lip—"

"Shouldn't drive so fast, young feller. And it would have been better to kill a mutt than to mess your little wife's face up this way."

Diego nodded solemnly, touching his Adam's apple with his hand. 'Oh, muck you!' he thought. 'Oh a thousand times, muck you. I this into the milk of thy mother! I that upon the grave of thy father, if ever thou didst have a father, thou meddlesome old fool!'

"You got any more tape, *chiquilla*?" the waiter said. "That piece ain't agoing to stick. Too much dried blood on it. If not, I'll go get you some. *Farmacia*'s right across the street."

"No, thank you," Ana María said sweetly, and dug into her handbag. Came out with the little tin box of Band-Aids.

"I've got more right here, see? Diego, go on to the rest room. I will too, after I have one more *caña*. Only, it'll take me longer. Got to fix my face, y'know . . ."

Diego got up, taking the cheap plastic flight bag with him. He tucked it up under his arm so that people wouldn't see the letters on it. TWA, the letters read. None of that bag was going to be left, but he'd just as soon the people didn't see those letters, associate them with him. Then he sauntered over to the stairs, went down them.

The waiter hung around a moment longer chatting with Ana María. Like every human creature even 10 percent male who ever spent five full minutes in her company, he was already a little in love with her.

While he was still there, the glass street doors opened letting a current of hot air flood in, momentarily negating the effect of the air conditioning with which the Principe, like nearly all first-class *Madrileño* bars, was equipped, and a crowd of laughing, talking, well-dressed people flooded in with it, smelling of men's colognes, women's perfumes, cigarette smoke, and—'and whiskey likely' Ana María thought.

In their midst was a child. A small girl child. A tiny, truly angelic vision, all in white: a long organdy and silk dress, a smart little hat with a veil, white silk stockings, white satin slippers, and in her white silk gloved hands, a white satin-covered prayer book, with a rosary wrapped around it.

So what they were celebrating was a first communion, an event in the life of a child that Spanish families willingly go into debt—'Or rather,' Ana Maria thought wrily, 'go much further into debt than most of them already are; because I'll be damned if the people of any other country I know live as far above their means as we habitually do!'—to celebrate. And all those people had been invited to share the family's joy at this new soul saved.

'Or to help them show off,' Ana Maria thought with weary realism, 'and compete with them at it. But where? This place isn't big enough to—' She looked at the waiter questioningly.

"Upstairs," he said. "The patron's got the whole *planta* up there. For weddings, first communions, banquets and the like. Pretty little tyke, ain't she?"

Ana María looked at the little girl and had to clamp her teeth shut to keep from moaning aloud. Because the little girl was not only a beautiful child, but was quite as blond as Diego.

"Like *ours!*" Ana Maria mourned inside her mind. "Like ours is going to be! So we can't! We can't even take a chance on this little angel's life! We've got to stop this! We've got to stop it now!"

"Why—*chiquilla!*" the waiter said. "You—you're crying!"

"She's so beautiful!" Ana María sobbed. "And I'm so hoping that *mine*—that *ours*—will look like that!"

"Oh, she will!" the waiter said, watching the communion party trooping up the stairs. "Your husband's a *real* rubio, like a Swede. So you can count on it. Wait, now, I'll get you a cognac to steady your nerves. On *me*—I mean on the house—"

"Thank you," Ana María sniffed. Then she saw Diego coming back. When he was close enough, she gripped his arm so hard that his too-white skin turned red, leaned swiftly close, hissed into his ear: "Diego, we can't! You've got to stop it! There're fifty people upstairs, a first communion! And the most beautiful blond baby girl you ever saw! Like *ours* is going to be. So stop it, damn you! Stop it now!"

He looked at her, his eyes appalled.

"I can't," he said. "I've set off the timer. There's no way to stop those damned things once you do that. Get up, Ana! Go change. Get to the other bar as fast as you can. Call them. You've got the number written down, haven't you?"

"Yes—" Ana María got out.

"Here's your cognac, little lady," the waiter said.

"Thank you. You can't imagine how *much* I need it!" Ana whispered, and, tilting her head back, threw it down her throat.

"*¡Que buena!*" the waiter said admiringly. "Want another one?"

Diego shook a warning finger. Pointed at Ana's little round belly.

"Oh, it's good for that," the waiter said. "Settles a woman's stomach when she's *embarazada.*"

"No, thank you!" Ana said. "We really must go now—in a minute, anyhow. Diego, pay the bill."

Diego bent until his lips brushed her left ear.

"Don't forget the sunglasses!" he said.

Ana María got up. Went down the stairs.

"Traigame la cuenta," Diego croaked to the waiter, praying that his assumed hoarseness would hide his marked French accent.

"En seguida, señorito," the waiter said. Turned. Walked toward the bar. But before he got there, a woman stopped him, said:

"Give me a *ficha* for the telephone—"

Diego turned away. A young man came into the bar from the street. Through the opened door, the sudden rush of traffic noises drowned out the waiter's voice. So Diego didn't hear him say, "No point, Señora; the *maldita* thing's been out of order for the last three days—"

Coming up the stairs, Diego had passed within less than a meter of the public phone. But he hadn't even so much as looked at it. There was no reason for him to. The only thing that interested him about the phone was the number that it bore. And he had already copied that number down from the telephone book in the motel that morning. So he'd passed the phone without a glance. Didn't, as a consequence, even see the little white card stuck to it with cellophone tape, that little hand-lettered card that read, *"¡No funciona!"*

And now, coming up those stairs, herself again—slim, trim, lissome, her hair black, close-cropped as a little boy's, her belly flat as a table, her miniskirted dress a powder blue, her pale eyes hidden behind those dark glasses—Ana María didn't see it either. But for a different, much better reason: she *couldn't.* The holes Diego had punched through those thick plastic lenses sharply limited the angle of her vision, narrowed it to a zone almost dead straight ahead of her. She had all she could do to keep from falling over her own feet.

As she came through the bar, Diego was paying *la cuenta,* the count, or bill. But the waiter stared at Ana María.

"Didn't see that one sitting anywhere," he muttered. "Hope she's not leaving without paying her bill. Women do it all the time, you know."

"No," Diego croaked. "Just came in. Went downstairs to the ladies' room, I guess."

"Don't try to talk, son," the waiter said. "Laryngitis is a hell of a thing. Well—here's your change."

Diego tipped him generously.

"Saaay!" the waiter said. "She's gone! Funny thing—in a way she reminded me of your wife."

Diego shook his head. Made a great looping curve with his two hands in from of his own flat belly. Wigwagged his finger in front of the waiter's face.

"Oh I saw that one wasn't," the waiter said, "but all the same, something about her face, her mouth—"

Diego pointed to the waiter's ballpoint. Took it from the man's hand, wrote on a folded paper napkin: "Got to see a man about a job. And I'm already late. Tell my wife to wait. Be back in ten minutes. All right?"

"De acuerdo," the waiter said. "And thanks for the tip. Hope you have luck. Your little bride is *really* something!"

"¡Gracias!" Diego said and went through that door.

As he passed the Bar Superstar he lifted his arm. Waved. Went on.

Ana María waited, holding her breath until he had rounded a corner, was out of sight. Then she let her breath out in an audible rush and flew to that phone.

But she was instantly confronted with the fact that she could not see to dial through those damned little holes Diego had punched through the plastic lenses of her *gafas de sol,* so she took them off. And both of the two bartenders in the Bar Superstar saw her eyes.

"*¡Madre mía!*" one of them said. " *¡Que ojos!* A fellow could fall into 'em and drown!"

"And die happy!" the other one groaned. "And that mouth! I tell you, Miguelito, a girl who's got a mouth like that has just got to be a hot little number!"

"Skinny little thing, though," Miguelito said. "I like my women to have meat on their bones. *Metida en carnes. Llenita,* anyhow."

"Hell, you like 'em *fat.* Now just you tell me one thing, Miguelito *mío;* you ever see a *fat* filly win a race?"

Ana was dialing, desperately.

She waited. Heard: *Dee-dah! Dee-dah!*

"Oh, God!" she wept. "The busy signal! Someone's talking over that phone!"

She tried it again. Again. Twenty times.

Turned to the bartenders, wailed: "I can't get through! And I must! It's very important!"

"Maybe you ain't dialing right," Pepe, the older bartender said. "Give me the number, señorita; lemme try it."

Ana passed it over.

Pepe dialed, much more slowly than she had.

Dee-dah! the sound came over. *Dee-dah! Dee-dah! Dee-dah!*

"*Esta comunicando, señorita,*" Pepe said.

"I know *that,*" Ana said. "But I don't believe it! It's been going on too long!"

"People talk a long time, sometimes, señorita. Say—what happened to your mouth?"

"My boyfriend bit me," Ana said venomously. "He gets a little too excited, sometimes."

"Can't say I blame him," Pepe grinned, "for if there ever was a girl who looked good enough to eat, it's *you,* señorita!"

"*Dios mío!*" Ana wept. "I've got to get through! I must! You're sure this phone's all right?"

"Was this morning," Miguel said. "Hey! Maybe the one you're calling's out of order. When they are all you get is a busy signal."

"Oh Christ!" Ana said. "How can I find out?"

"Call *averias*," Pepe said. "The number's oh-oh-two."

Ana dialed the three numbers, got another busy signal, as you always do in Madrid. And very likely in any city of over three million inhabitants. By the very law of averages it was probable that enough people will be calling to report out-of-order phones at any one given moment to tie the lines up for some considerable time.

'I'll have to go over there,' Ana thought, 'warn them myself. Accept the consequences. A prison sentence. A long one. And—Diego's gone. Oh God I—I'll try it one more time!'

Out on the Madrid–Barcelona road, Federico Sales Ortega stood in the foyer of the Chuletera Osborne and dialed that same number. He had already dialed it more than twenty times. But now he looked at his watch. Saw that there was no time. Did then at once the right, the obvious thing, the thing he had to do:

He dialed the *Dirección General de Seguridad.*

"This is Federico Sales," he said, "Minister without Portfolio. Put me through to the Director himself! If he's *comunicando*, break through. I'll assume the responsibility. But break through, man! It's a matter of life or death! So get through to him. That's an order, *sargento*!"

Two kilometers down the road, Amparo sat in Federico's car. She was crying, praying, trembling. And hoping. Desperately hoping. 'Four totally absurd emotions,' she told herself, 'in an equally absurd, abysmally merciless world. But still, God, hear me. If you're enough like us, your creatures, to even have ears. If mercy is one of your attributes, though I've seen no evidence of it, so far! If—pity is. Forgiveness. Please, God, please . . .'

By then, Ana María had got through to *averias,* the section one reports out-of-order telephones to, or asks whether a number one cannot reach belongs to a non-functioning phone.

"Yes, señorita," the *telefonista* said finally, after having taken a gut-wringing age to look it up on her list, "that one's out. Been out three days. We're doing what we can, but—"

Ana María slammed down the phone. Ran through that door. The shock wave of that explosion reached her before she was all the way across the sidewalk, even. Slammed her up against the iron pole of the street lamp, knocked her unconscious.

When she came to herself, she was back inside the Bar Superstar, lying on the bar top. The bar hadn't any windows now. It was powdered five centimeters deep in broken glass. Miguel and Pepe were both bleeding from dozens of small cuts in their faces, necks, chests. But they were bathing Ana's face in cold water and paying absolutely no attention to their own hurts.

"How long was I out?" Ana María said.

"Twenty minutes," Pepe said. *"¡Dios mío!* but you had us scared, Señorita Condesa!"

"¡Señorita Condesa!" Ana said.

"Yes. We looked in your handbag—for your *documentación* —in case you passed on—Señorita Condesa! And we found your *Carta de Identidad.* With the names of your parents, naturally, Los Señores Condes de Casaribiera y Borbón. And— another one, with your picture, too; but different names— printed—in French, I think, anyhow—"

"That one doesn't matter," Ana said. "Could you call me a taxi?"

"Yes, Señorita Condesa," Miguel said, "but it won't come. The police have both ends of the street cordoned off. We tried calling an ambulance, but we couldn't get through. Every *clinica* in town has its phone *comunicando,* now. Lots of bad hurt people over there. Lots of—dead—"

"Oh, Jesus!" Ana María said, and sat up. Her head reeled, dizzily, then it cleared. She leaped down from the top of the bar, raced to the door. Hung there, unbreathing.

They were bringing people out of the Marisqueria Principe. Or rather out of what was left of it, which wasn't much. They were burnt black, most of them. Covered with blood. Ana thought they were all dead at first. But they weren't. Because now they brought a man out with his head covered with a sheet. Or one of the bar's tablecloths, maybe. Another. Another. Another. Ana counted them. Got up, unbelievably, to thirteen.

Then they brought one more out. A tiny bundle, white-covered. One little hand dangled from beneath the sheet. It had a rosary twined about its plump little wrist.

Ana stood there, staring, her eyes and mouth opened wide. Her knees doubled under her. She went down on the sidewalk. Bent over. Vomited up the remains of the *gambas* and the beer. Pounded her fists into the white drifts until they were reduced to bloody mush. Screamed until she couldn't scream any more. Moaned until her moans became less than silence. Turned her mad, streaming eyes toward the smoke dirtied, stinking sky.

Whispered: "Kill me. If you're merciful, kill me. Or if you're even—there . . ."

After that, she fainted.

When she came back this time, a face she'd never seen before was peering worriedly down into hers. A man's face. A very handsome face, her endlessly feminine mind told her at once, in spite of the circumstances. Dark. A well-trimmed mustache. Upon his black, curly hair, a cap. A gray cap with a red band around it. A member of the *Police Armada,* she realized.

"Just relax, Señorita Condesa," he said pleasantly. "We've called for an ambulance—though there'll be quite a wait, I'm afraid. But you don't seem to have any broken bones. A bit of concussion, maybe. And your hands . . ."

Ana looked at her hands. They were thickly bandaged. They hurt.

"I did that," the *sargento* of the Armed Police said with a little laugh. "Not a very good job, to be sure. Strange—they're the only place you're hurt . . ."

"She cut 'em up like that herself, *sargento!*" Pepe said. "When they brought that poor little dead baby girl out. She started screaming and pounding her fists into the broken glass, and—"

"Shut up, you damned old fool!" Miguel said out of the side of his mouth. "That there's ¡alta—alta sociedad! You don't want to get mixed up in it—"

"Get mixed up in what?" the sergeant said.

"Nothing, sir!" Miguel said.

"*Sargento*—" Ana whispered, "could you—you, yourself —take me home? I don't need to go to a hospital. Besides they're all too busy—with really serious cases, I mean. And—and *mis padres* will be so worried, and—"

The *sargento* thought about that. About five seconds. Which was longer than he really needed to think about any request that came from a girl with a name like Casaribiera y Borbón in Spain. Besides, he knew she hadn't any broken bones. He had felt her all over to make sure. And enjoyed it. But she still could have internal injuries. The shock wave of an explosion did absolutely the damnedest things at times. He told her that.

She said: "*Sargento,* at home, I'll be attended to faster than I would be in *any* clinic right now. And better. Our family doctor will be there in minutes, after my father calls him . . ."

Which, the *sargento* reflected, was sure to be true. He said: "Well, if you won't be embarrassed, or los Señores Condes, *sus padres* won't, by a patrol car's bringing you home—it'll attract a lot of attention, you know—"

"*Mis padres* will be very grateful. They'll thank you in person. And—and speak to your superiors about you—"

The *sargento* stretched up to a full one meter ninety, at least eight centimeters taller than his normal one eighty-two. He even blushed, a fact that Pepe and Miguel noted with astonishment. Like all lower-class *Madrileños,* they held the firm conviction that the members *del Cuerpo de la Police Armada* weren't even human. And *la Guardia Civil,* even less.

"Oh, that won't be necessary, Señorita Condesa! I'm only doing my duty!" *el sargento* said.

The President of the Government stood there in the Calle de Esparteros looking at the wrecked bar. The Minister of Justice was at his side. The Minister of Information and Tourism. The Minister of Education and Science. The Minister of *Hacienda,* an office roughly corresponding to the Treasury Department in other countries. *El Alcalde*—the Mayor—of Madrid. Several of the more important of *Los Procuradores en Cortes* —legislators, say. But the *Director General* of *Seguridad* wasn't there, which struck the President as odd. Even the *Jefe del Parque de los Bomberos*—the Chief of the Fire Department—was there by then.

The President turned to the Minister of Justice.

"Don't see the Director General," he said.

"I don't either, Your Excellency," the Minister of Justice said, then: *"¡Dios mío!"*

"Why 'My God!' Pablo?" the President said.

"Maybe this is an all-out thing, sir! Maybe those Red swine have—got him! I can't think of any other reason why the Director General—"

The President's face turned gray.

"Get on the phone, Pablo!" he said.

But before Pablo Lascalles Martinez, Minister of Justice, could even cross the street to the Bar Superstar, a *teniente* of the *Police Armada* came up to him, saluted, said: "Your Excellency, the Director General's on my car's radio-phone. He wants to speak to you—or to the *Presidente,* if he can—"

"To both of us," the President said. "Come on, Pablo! Where's your car, *teniente?*"

"Right this way, Señor Presidente!" the lieutenant said.

The President took the car phone that the driver sergeant handed him. Leaned into the car to cut out the babble of excited voices in the street. Barked into the mouthpiece: "Ricardo! Are you all right?"

"Why yes, Señor Presidente!" the head of all the Spanish Police said, recognizing that well-known voice at once. "Could you come over *here,* Your Excellency? And bring *el Ministro de Justicia* with you? Believe me, it's important. Your young friend, Federico Sales Ortega, *Ministro sin Cartera,* is in my office. And he's yelling the place down. Demanding that we arrest—a certain party from circles we ordinarily don't touch, sir. Says he has hard evidence that she's the one who planted that bomb—or at least aided the actual culprit in planting it—"

"Can you tell me her name?" the President said.

"Over the *radio,* sir? Why half the ham operators in town are tuned to the police frequencies by now!"

"I see. All right, Ricardo. Pablo and I are on our way—"

"Fredi," the President said, "it makes more sense to arrest —your Amparo. In fact, I'm afraid we'll have to."

"Do that. Maybe in the Woman's Prison she'll be safe. Maybe those Red murderers can't get to her there—to strangle her. To garrote her for telling me the truth. You know whom that *maldita bomba* was supposed to eliminate, sir? *Me.* And you were right. Amparo *was* planted in my office. To lead me on.

To invite me to *una mariscada*—a shellfish feast—at La Marisqueria Principe, at two thirty P.M.—today! Only, being a
woman—"

"She let her heart get ahead of her head," the President
said.

"Or more likely, another part of her anatomy," the Minister of Justice chuckled.

Federico whirled upon him.

"Sir, men have been killed for less than that!" he said.

"Fredi, calm down!" the President said wearily. "Look,
my boy, we can't do this. We simply cannot arrest Ana María
Casaribiera on the basis of what you *believe*. That she killed—
or rather led—poor Enrique to his death. That she's the girl
someone phoned this office from Paris about. Still later, from
Perpignan. Gave a rather detailed description—"

"That fits her!" Federico howled.

"Of a presumed female terrorist on a mission into Spain.
Another of her *cómplice,* a blond boy of about twenty-four. Our
unknown informant—a woman, it seems—gave a description of
a car, a Peugeot two-oh-four, old model, Paris license four-five-
three, two-two-two SM seventy-five. But our men at the fronter
all inform us that no car of that type—the old model two-oh-
four hasn't been manufactured in years, Fredi; you ought to
know that, so it would have stuck out like a sore thumb!—ever
crossed any of our customs controls anywhere on the French
frontier. That *matricula* was *never* noted—"

"Which only means that Ana María and her latest *paramour*
found out they'd been informed on. Ditched the car. Took a
train. A plane."

"But you only heard her voice!" the President said. "Over
a telephone at that. Goddamnit, Fredi! We can't arrest a girl on
that kind of evidence!"

"If she were a shop girl," Fredi said, "our kind and genial
friend, Don Ricardo, would *already* have her here. In one of
those soundproof cells in the basement. With the floodlights in

her eyes. By now, she'd have already talked, unless she were made of sterner stuff than most women are. Or unless she *couldn't.* Which happens, sometimes, doesn't it, Don Ricardo? Your young gentlemen of the Interrogation Squad sometimes forget themselves in their enthusiasm for their work, their professional zeal to obtain results, I'm told. Señor Presidente, I'm out of your august and almighty government. My resignation will be on your desk, with a copy to every newspaper in town—stating my reasons!—by tomorrow. Now are you going to put out an order for the arrest of that murderous little aristocratic *zorra,* or do I have to leak this story to the foreign newspapers?"

"I think," the President said wearily, "that I'm going to have to place *you* under arrest, Fredi. Hold you *incomunicado* until you calm down."

"That's a life sentence, sir! About *this,* I'll never calm down."

"Fredi, for the love of God!" the President said.

"Wait," Federico said. " *¡Que estupido he sido!* What an ass I've been! Sir, if we can *get* some hard evidence, what would you do?"

"Have Don Ricardo here pull the young lady in, of course. Discreetly ask her a few questions, anyhow."

"Good enough! Look, Don Ricardo—*mira, mi General*—send some of your better-looking boys, discreet types who know how to ask a question without swinging their blackjacks *first;* those, if such there be in this splendid *Cuerpo!,* who have brains enough to find their way to the nearest métro entrance without getting lost—"

"Get on with it, Fredi," the President said. "Insulting the police will get you nowhere, you know."

"Right. Send, *mi General,* your plainclothesmen around to the offices of all those idiotic magazines which print detailed stories about what color *bragas* Elizabeth Taylor and Sophia Loren are wearing this week. About the posh, veddy, veddy, strictly U wedding of the daughter *de los Duques de Tanta Mierda*

to the son of the *Marqueses de Muy Mala Leche—*"

"Fredi, for God's sake!" the President said.

"*O séa, La Prensa Sentimental.* The Sentimental Press. Our latest euphemism for those distributors of undiluted fecal matter. Excreta. Sugar coated, though. And with *nata batida* on it."

"Perhaps you should consider emigrating to the United States. Working for the North American presidency. Your gift for undeleted expletives would be highly appreciated over there, *Señor Ex-Ministro sin Cartera,*" the Director General said.

"I just get tired of being buried in it. Eating a ton of it every day," Federico said. "It's our national diet. Oh, all right! One of those filthy scandal sheets is *sure* to have a photo—a *color* photo—of Ana María Casaribiera in their files, due consideration being given to her *usual* style of living! Then have your boys show it to the survivors. To the people in the other establishments along that street . . ."

"Fredi, we don't know if Ana María Casaribiera is even in Spain," the President said.

"That's easy to check, sir. Call her *house.* Ask the *mayordomo.* Or the downstairs maid. Or whoever answers the goddamned phone," Federico said.

The President nodded.

Ricardo Ruiz-Salado, *Director General de Seguridad,* picked up his phone. Spoke into it briefly. Said: "Get me the residence of Los Condes de Casaribiera. Yes, in Puerta de Hierro. Ring me when you've got it."

He hung up. There was a silence. It went on and on. A very small aeon. A tiny, nerve-cracking age. Then the phone rang.

Don Ricardo picked it up, said suavely into the mouthpiece: "This is the *Director General de Seguridad.* There's been an accident—a bad one, unfortunately—in a midtown bar. And we've been told that your young mistress, la Señorita Ana María, was seen going into that bar. But she's not among the people who were hurt—or—"

"What's that? She's *there?* At *home?* And she *was* hurt, you say? Her *hands?* Oh, I see! Cut by the flying glass? Why didn't she wait for an ambulance, then? The doctor says she's in shock? Quite natural, under the circumstances. What's that? The *police* brought her home? Tell *el Señor Conde, no hay de que.* He's quite welcome. It's part of our duties, after all. Oh no, I hardly think we'll need to bother the little lady *today.* But we would like her impressions of—the accident. Most of the people who were in that bar were too badly hurt for us to question them yet, so anything she could tell us would be extremely valuable—"

He hung up. Looked at the President. The President sighed.

"Oh, damn women, anyhow! Arrest her, Ricardo. Arrest her now," he said.

The *mayordomo* of the Villa Marguerita in Puerta de Hierro looked at the three men in the doorway. They were very well dressed. Soft spoken. Polite. But he didn't like their looks, He didn't like their looks at all.

"I'm afraid you cannot see la Señorita Ana María," he said. Being a well-trained butler, he didn't make the common error of calling Ana María the countess that she *wasn't,* and wouldn't be until her mother died. "She's lying down. In fact, she's under sedation. You see—"

"We know all that, Señor Mayordomo," the eldest of the three men said. "But, unfortunately, we've an order for her arrest. And we'd prefer as much as you—or los Señores Condes would for us to—to handle the matter quietly. She won't be harmed. We've even brought a trained nurse along to take care of her until we get her downtown."

"Show me your credentials!" the butler snapped.

The three men brought their leather-cased detective badges out; their police identity cards. The butler stared at them. They were from the Political Action Squad, which was grave. Very grave.

"I—I'll have to consult with el Señor Conde!" he said. "Wait here, please!"

He was back in seconds.

"Come in!" he said.

Felipe Menguado, Conde de Casaribiera y Borbón, waited for the plainclothesmen in the big salon. He had married very late and sired his only child later still, so he was old. Old enough to have been Ana María's grandfather instead of her father. He stood there, trembling a little, leaning on his cane, a hint of tears in the pale, off-blue eyes his daughter had inherited from him.

"Gentlemen, what has my daughter done *now?*" he said.

They explained as best they could, embarrassed by this tired old man's shame and grief—"Certain accusations—a matter of asking *la Señorita hija del Señor Conde* a few questions, nothing more. . . . A matter that the Lady Daughter of the Lord Count could clear up in minutes, likely. . . . The Director General requests that—"

The Count of Casaribiera crossed to an old-fashioned bell pull. Yanked it. A pretty, uniformed maid appeared as if out of thin air.

"Go wake la Señorita Ana up," the Count growled. "Tell her to come down here a minute." Then to the *mayordomo:* "Eduardo, bring the whiskey, and some brandy. *Hine. Courvoisier. Bisquit.* And some *Carlos Tercero* in case some of these gentlemen prefer the Spanish. It's *orina de caballo,* but they might . . ."

Strictly speaking, the three plainclothesmen were on duty and hence weren't supposed to accept the offer of a drink. But there were times when the rules had to be bent a little, if not broken. This, their policemen's instincts told them, was one of those times. They accepted the drinks that the butler pushed into the salon on an Empire period serving cart with grateful murmurs of thanks.

"Señor Conde," Capitan Barberios of the Political Squad said uneasily, searching for a way to save his own neck however the axe should fall: "We have orders to bring your señorita daughter down to Headquarters. And we *have* to comply with those orders, *su Gracia.* But I've been thinking—if you'd prefer to bring her downtown yourself, we'd be happy to permit that —as long as one of my men came along in your car. A mere formality, your Grace! He could ride up front with your chauffeur . . ."

"That's handsome of you, Capitan!" the Count said. "I have no doubt that Ana's done something outrageous again. When hasn't she? All her life she's been in hot water. One horrendous scrape after another. But I should prefer to bring her downtown myself. Present my apologies to His Excellency, the Director General, in person. Tell him I'm perfectly willing to make restitution for whatever damages that rebellious little idiot of mine has caused . . ."

'The damages,' the Capitan thought grimly, 'are fifteen dead—so far. Thirty-seven injured. Eighteen of them, gravely. Three, *gravísimo.* If they make it 'til tomorrow, it will be a miracle of God. And if it were *my* daughter involved, instead of *yours,* Ilustrísimo Señor Conde de Casaribiera y Borbón, Hidalgo y Grande de España, she'd already be downtown— and already crippled for life by the polite and gentle methods of our interrogators—"

But he didn't say that. He smiled thinly, said: "My man will have to ride in your car, Señor Conde. Or else *I'll* be in hot water. And with His Excellency, the President of the Government, not to mention my chief, the Director General!"

"Of course, of course! No objections at all, Capitan! The rules are the rules, after all. Well, Pili?"

For the maid was back by then. Her face was very white. She looked as if she were going to faint at any minute.

"La Señorita Ana's not—in her room, Señor Conde!" she got out, "nor in her bath, either. I—I looked, sir!"

"Then she's in her mother's. Crying on my poor Vicki's shoulder. As always when she's in some hellish mess! Go call her, Pili! This is serious!"

'I'll say it is!' Capitan Barberios thought.

The pretty little maid scurried away. Didn't come back this time. Instead it was the Lady Vitoria Galvey Canto, Condesa de Casaribiera y Borbón, who came.

The three detectives bounced up out of their seats. El Conde got up more slowly.

"These gentlemen—" he began.

"I know," the Condesa cut him off. "They've come after Ana. Felipe—she's quite hysterical. Keeps sobbing that she— murdered a baby. A little *rubia. Una niña en su primera comunión.* And she swears that the dead child's *hers.* That she—that she —forgive me, Felipe, but these *caballeros* will understand—had her by a *chico rubio* named Diego. Diego Fernández. Which isn't very likely is it? There's no family in our circle named Fernández is there? Dreadfully common name! And blond?"

"She's mad!" the Count said.

"*¡Un trastorno mental!*" the Capitan said. "That's an excellent defense, Señor Conde! And I and my men will be happy to swear before the *juez* we heard you say it! How long has your daughter's behavior seemed to you—well—odd?"

"All her damned life," the Count said. "Where is she, Vicky?"

"Locked in our bathroom. I've tried and tried to persuade her to come out, but—"

Capitan Barberios stiffened. Came up to Ana's mother. Bowed.

"Señora Condesa," he said quietly, "I beg your permission —and the Señor Conde's—to break down that door . . ."

"Now see here, my good man!" Don Felipe said. "My daughter's no common criminal. I won't have—"

"I know she's not, Señor Conde," the Capitan said, "and, begging your Grace's pardon humbly, that is not my point. But —your señorita daughter is, as your *distinguidísima e ilustrísima dama* just pointed out, hysterical. Perhaps—emotionally disturbed, or even—temporarily, of course!—mentally deranged. And bathrooms, *su Gracia,* are infernally dangerous places. For instance, I'll wager that her Ladyship has—some *somnifers* in there. Sleeping pills. Twenty of which, sir, swallowed—cause—a rather rapid paralysis of the lungs—"

"I do!" Ana's mother said. "Barbiturates. My doctor prescribed them for—"

Don Felipe stared at Capitan Barberios. Extended a trembling finger, said: "Up—those stairs. It's the third door to the right. Yes. please do break it down, Capitan—and fast, *¡por favor!*"

Then he collapsed into a chair. Buried his tired old face in his thin, age-mottled, wildly shaking hands. And it came to Captain Barberios for the very first time that, *en este perro mundo* —this dog of a world—there actually were occasions when wealth, and even titles didn't serve for much, either.

'Poor old fellow!' he thought with real pity. *'Tan jodido como cualquier hijo de su madre—'* 'Just as fucked up as any other mother's son—'

"Shall I shoot the lock off, Capitan?" Teniente Jacobo said.

"No, fool! We'll just force it. They hear gunfire and the two of 'em will die of heart attacks. Poor old parties! All that money, and rank, and what have you—and what have they got, really? Their daughter—their only child—won't see daylight without bars crossing it, in less than thirty years—"

"That's what you think, Cap'n!" Lieutenant Jacobo said. "Five'll get you ten she's out next *week!*"

"You're on, Teniente! You just don't understand today's political climate. They *won't* spring her. They won't dare. All right, sargento, give it a good kick!"

Sargento Tomás lifted his huge, booted foot. Crashed it into the bathroom door. Again. Again. Again. The door was very stout. It held.

Captain Barberios lifted his hand. All three of them hung there, listening. No sound came out of that bathroom. No sound at all.

"Come on!" he grated. "All three of us together. Ready? Now!"

The door burst open. They almost fell into that bathroom. Again Capitan Barberios held his hand up. In the silence, they could hear the footsteps of the Countess coming up the stairs, coming with a surprising speed for a woman of her years.

"Tomás, go stop her!" the Captain said. His voice sounded strange. As though he were strangling.

Sargento Tomás turned. Raced to the head of the stairs. They could hear his voice, pleading:

"Please, Señora Condesa! I beg of you, Señora Condesa! Don't go in there, Señora Condesa! *¡Por favor! ¡En el Nombre de Dios, Padre,* Señora Condesa! Please . . ."

While they, the two of them, Capitan Barberios and Teniente Jacobo Milar, were reading the words scrawled across the mirror. In lipstick, both of them had thought at first. Then saw, even their policemen's cast-iron guts knotting up on them, that it wasn't lipstick. Lipstick doesn't—drip—and run—and coagulate, slowly.

"*Diego, te quiero—*" Capitan Barberios read slowly, "*hasta —siempre—Ana—*" The name wasn't finished. It had only the first two letters: "*An——*" The final "a" was a long, long streaking blur smeared downward, downward—

"Diego, I love you—" Teniente Milar repeated it after him, "until—forever—An—"

Then he too followed the Capitan's slowly, reluctantly downward sweeping gaze. Stopped his, too, where the Capitan's had already stopped. Whispered: "*¡Dios mío!*"

Bent, stretched out his hand toward that old-fashioned straight razor, which lay centimeters away from those slim, red-clotted fingers, flung out in a gesture calculated to stop any man's mind, his heart. Even a policeman's.

"Don't touch it!" Capitan Barberios snarled. "Don't touch anything! The *forense*'s got to—"

"*¡Señora Condesa!*" poor Tomás moaned. He was actually crying. The Spanish are an emotional race.

But Vitoria Galvey wasn't used to being ordered about,

especially not by the lower orders. She stormed into that bathroom. Stopped. Stood there. Her hands came up. Her beautifully manicured nails dug into the thin, blue veined, sagging, old woman's flesh of her cheeks. Brought blood.

Then loudly, terribly, she screamed.

H e had been in Lisbon three days, and it was beginning to look to him as if he'd never get out of it. He was even conceiving a totally unreasonable dislike for that rarely lovely city. In the first place, he hadn't wanted to go there, but to Tangier. Not that he was especially fond of Tangier, either. But he knew that city, had Party connections there he could call on for help, and best of all, could experience the blessed relief of speaking a language he really knew, since most of the people in the North African city were French-speaking.

But when he got out to the Aeropuerto de Barajas after leaving Ana María—"Keep her safe! Bring her home to me!" he prayed to the God he swore he didn't believe in—he found out that there wouldn't be a plane for Tangier until day after tomorrow, because one of the things that neither he, nor his doctrinaire spy master, Ernesto, with his insistence that the unforeseen must be eliminated from a serious action, had counted upon was that due to the vast increases in the prices of *anything* derived from petroleum, as the kerosene used in jet motors was, the airlines had had to cut their flights drastically.

He had almost panicked, was actually heading for the Hertz car rental desk to rent a car and head directly for the French frontier, with the wild and practically unworkable idea of abandoning the car near it and going up over the Pyrenees on foot, when he saw on the bulletin board, or rather on the closed-circuit television network that serves as a bulletin board at Barajas, as at most modern airports, that there was a TAP flight to Lisbon in twenty minutes.

That time, the unforeseen was on his side. Because, by then, air travel had become so damned expensive that most international flights were taking off from half to three-quarters empty. He had no trouble at all getting aboard.

But once in Lisbon, his troubles started. He asked a taxi driver to take him to a hotel, speaking to the man in Spanish on the reasonable assumption that the two Iberian languages were closely enough akin for the man to understand. He was right, for all the good that did him.

The taxi driver, with a snarled: *"Sí, Senhor!"* took him to the Francfort on the Rua Santa Justa, the biggest, and one of the most expensive hotels in Lisbon. But, figuring that he'd only be there overnight, Diego stayed. And the next morning a strike of airport porters, office personnel, and the radio and radar operators of the air traffic control halted all flights out of the Portuguese capital.

So he was stuck. He spent the next two days reading every Spanish newspaper he could get his hands on, which in practice mean *Ya* and *ABC,* in the hope—and fear—that they'd print something about Ana María. That she was visiting her parents say, had gone to a party; had been entertained by—the things they usually printed about her, for she was, after all, something of a celebrity in the modern jet set sense every time she came to Spain.

But there was nothing. It wasn't until the third morning that, going to the corner kiosk to buy the two Spanish newspapers once more, he saw the Lisbon morning daily. That picture on its front page. It looked just like— He bent closer.

Looked like, and was. Ana María's clear, pale eyes, their tender intensity undiminished even by the miserable quality of the paper's half-tones, stared back at him with grave reproach. Next to her picture was a smaller photograph of a *cura*—a young priest with the face of a fanatic and a madman's gaze.

And it all caught up with Diego Fernández. He realized in that one heart-stopped instant that he had been wrong to buy the Spanish papers, because the Spanish censor damned well had no intention of letting any of them print a story calculated to drive the Monarchists straight up the nearest wall and give aid and comfort to Spain's increasingly bold and restless Left. He didn't even need to read the headlines to know that it had all gone wrong, was shot to hell. The mere fact that Ana's picture was on the front page, instead of the society pages told him that.

He dug into his pockets with fingers gone dead, lacking both strength and tactile sense, dragged out an escudo, gave it to the news vendor, staggered over to the nearest bench—he was in the Parca do Comerico in front of the Rio Tejo, and a fairish number of benches were available—and slumped into it.

He found, to his anguished sorrow, that he could read that newspaper with scarcely any difficulty at all. If you can read Spanish, you already have 60 or 70 percent of Portuguese's vocabulary, once you've caught the trick of compensating for the slight difference in spelling *coã* for *ción,* for instance. And if you also know French, you've added another 15 or 20 percent, because nearly all the words in Portuguese that don't look or sound like bad Spanish look or sound like worse French.

The Portuguese correspondent in Madrid had had himself a *fiesta.* And, being, as he was, a secret member of the Portuguese Communist Party, he had slanted his story to embarrass the Catholic Church, which is any Communist's favorite indoor sport.

Entitling his story, "Scandal in Madrid," he had all but

ignored Ana María's alleged connection with the bombing of the Marisqueria Principe. Employing his subtle language's immense capacity for irony, he had given an almost heartbreaking description of how Ana María's coffin had lain outside the doorway of the Church of San Jeronimo el Real in a pouring rain, while the *Obispo*, himself, stood in the doorway and flatly forbade her body's being so much as brought into the Church, not to mention the celebration of the normal *Misa de Cuerpo Insepulcro*, on the grounds that she had died both unconfessed and unshriven, was probably a murderess, and certainly a suicide, both mortal sins, which placed her totally beyond any hope for salvation, even if he conceded that the charges that she was both an atheist and a Red had not yet been completely proven—

Diego sat there. That was *all* he did. He sat there. Then, sometime later, he read on.

"Thus," the Portuguese reporter wrote, "this poor little rich girl, known to have been deeply disturbed emotionally, very probably in need of competent psychiatric care—her nymphomaniacal tendencies being one of the *alta sociedad Madrileña's* worst-kept secrets—became a victim of the Church's unceasing, and totally hypocritical efforts here of late to woo the working classes of Spain. For the first time in Spanish history, very likely, an aristocrat, and the daughter of titled personages, was refused Christian burial precisely because she *was* an aristocrat and the daughter of nobility, the comforts of their religion being denied her aged, weeping parents only because the archbishop wished to demonstrate that the new, self-styled democratic Church was not to be influenced by such mundane considerations as titles, position, or wealth . . .

"Or, may we add, by simple mercy, which is supposed to be an attribute of the Christ it serves . . ."

There was more: How, at the last moment, a young, liberal priest had openly defied the *Obispo;* had carted the whole funeral cortège off to his dingy little modern-style church in the *barrio* known as Moratalaz, had celebrated the funeral mass there, for which he had been promptly excommunicated by the archbishop, removed from his church, forbidden to say mass, or preach anywhere in the diocese—

And still more: How, when the family had finally arrived at the Cemeterio de la Almudena, where they had their immense family pantheon, thinking to lay the remains of their only child there in the shelter of that imposing mausoleum, they found the bishop's representatives there before them, standing before the cemetery gates, to refuse them entrance, since la Almudena was *campo santo,* and the corpse of no damned soul could be permitted burial in holy ground . . .

"So hence," wrote the reporter, "off once more to the civil cemetery, reserved for Protestants, Jews, heretics, atheists, and other assorted outcast scum, where poor Ana María Casaribiera y Borbón Galvey Canto was finally laid to rest in a simple grave lacking even a tombstone.

"And that night, vandals—said by the malicious to have been members of the Cuerpo de la Policia in civilian clothes— stripped every corona, wreath, and single flower, from the poor demented girl's poor barren grave . . .

"It is, of course, scarcely likely that the wild rumors being circulated around Madrid that the deceased was one of the pair of ETA Fifth Assembly Terrorists who placed the bomb in the Marisqueria Principe in la Madrileña Calle de Esparteros, which cost seventeen lives, have any foundation in fact. We are pleased to report that all thirty-five survivors are now out of danger. . . ."

Diego sat there. He didn't move. He did not tremble, vomit, shake, or cry. The expression on his smooth young face did not change. He got up from there, walked all the way back to the Hotel Francfort. Went to his room. Went to bed. He took no supper. Nor did he eat breakfast the next morning.

The only thing he did was to call the airport. And learning that the strike was finally over, he took a taxi out to it, leaving all his clothes in the closet, and his unpacked bag in the hotel room. Besides his passport, his identity card, the clothes on his body, and what little money he had left, the only thing he took was one of the two Belgian-made Browning automatics that Ana María had smuggled into Spain in her kangaroo pouch.

At the airport he bought an airplane ticket.

A one-way ticket to Madrid.

In the offices of *la Dirección General de Seguridad,* the phone rang. An Armed Police sargento picked it up. Said: *"¿Diga?"* in a bored tone of voice, then *"¡Un momento! ¡Por eso tengo ordenes de ponerse con el Director General, mismo! ¡Espere!"*

He punched a row of buttons built into the base of his phone. On the Director General's desk, another phone rang.

"¡Diga!" the Director General said.

"¡Mi General!" an excited voice said. "He just came through! *¡El terrorista!* The blond boy called Fernández! Even used his own passport, sir! I know you gave us orders not to touch him, but we could grab him so easy, now. He's wandering around looking dazed—"

"Don't touch him, you fool!" the Director General said. "Hang a tail on him, that's all. Discreetly. Why should we be content with one terrorist, when he'll probably lead us to five or six of his co-conspirators before night? That's it! Hop to it, Teniente!"

He hung up the telephone. Looked at his visitor.

"You were right—*again,* Señor Ministro," he said.

"Ex-Minister, *mi* General," Federico Sales Ortega said.

"I doubt that the President is going to accept your resignation," the Director General said. "You're far too valuable to him. And if he does, you've got a job waiting for you—with me. *En la Segunda Bis."*

"No, thank you, *mi* General. I should prefer to remain— a human being," Federico said.

"Oh, come off of it, Sales! The police are absolutely necessary, and you know it!"

"So are garbage collectors. But I shouldn't like to *be* one," Federico said.

"Damned if you aren't the prickliest character I ever met!" the Director General said.

"Self-defense. Part of my efforts to remain a human being," Federico said.

"Still—your head *works*. You solved the Marisqueria Principe case for us before it was really even over—"

"Much to my sorrow," Fredi said.

"Why to your sorrow, Sales?"

"My wife, as you probably know, is suing for a legal separation. And—my mistress—has become my *ex*-mistress because of my intervention in that bloody case."

"*¡Que raro!* Why should she do that? After all, she warned you what they were planning, didn't she?"

"Yes. But she claims that my subsequent actions lacked—humanity. That I persecuted poor little Ana María. Was small of heart. Narrow of soul. Was vindictive. In short, that I drove that poor little half-crazy bitch to her death."

"She's wrong. The poor thing's own conscience did that. She saw them bring out the body of a child. Eyewitnesses, among them one of our own officers, swear she knelt on the sidewalk and pounded her own fists into the broken glass until they were unrecognizable as fists."

"They were in good enough shape for her to hold her old man's razor. Worked well enough for her to cut her throat."

"True. I suppose the glass wounds, while mutiple, were only superficial. Tell me, Don Frederico, how did you know the boy would come back?"

"Because—I remain a human being. I know how a man's guts feel when they knot up on him. When he wants to scream the roof down and can't."

"But what made you so *sure?*"

"An item in the papers: How you—or somebody—sent your bully boys to strip all the flowers off her grave."

"Sales, you wrong me! And I don't defend my morality,

but my intelligence! When have you ever known me to do something as stupid as that?"

"You've a point, *mi* General. You wouldn't. You *are* too smart. Then who did?"

"Our rancid Right. A group called *Defensores de los Principios Fundamentales del Movimiento. Camisas Viejas* and their stupid sons. Of course they're still untouchable, but—"

"All right. You want me to tell you what Fernández will do next?"

"God, yes!" the Director General said.

"There's a catch to it. I'll tell you on one condition—no, two."

"Which are?"

"That your light-fingered boys keep said fingers off their *gatillos.* Even trigger-happy as they are. That they bring him in —alive. That, even though we can't avoid a *juicio sumarísimo*— we're the only damned country on earth where the military is allowed to courtmartial civilians—I want the right to defend him."

"Your last condition's granted. But your first—how could I guarantee that? Suppose he starts shooting? D'you know how many men we and the *Guardia Civil* have lost this year?"

"Yes. Too many. All right. I'll modify condition one. That your men don't shoot first. Because if he shoots, it will be because he wants to die. The ultimate right of a man. Even his ultimate privilege. I'd be the last man on earth to deny him— or any poor hopeless devil!—that . . .''

The Director General peered at the ex-Minister without Portfolio narrowly. Started to say something. Changed his mind.

"Fair enough, Sales!" he said. "Agreed. What will our little blond terrorist do?"

"First, he'll go to a florist's. Buy two dozen blood-red roses. Or maybe he'll buy only a single, perfect rose. Then he'll go to the civil cemetery. Lay them—or it—upon her grave.

When he comes out, he'll surrender, very quietly. Or else he'll come out shooting. If he does come out shooting—kill him. It will be a kindness. Believe me, I know . . ."

He stood up. Put his hand in his pocket. Felt the two keys. The one that was his. And the one that Amparo had given back to him when she moved out of the flat.

"May I go now, *mi* General?" he said.

"Yes. Why, yes, of course, Don Federico! I only called you in to express my thanks—my profound thanks for your help in the bombing case . . ."

"*De nada. No hay de que. ¡Hasta—siempre, mi General!*" Federico Sales Ortega said, and walked out of there.

After he had gone, the Director General touched a button on his desk. In less than a minute, a young teniente appeared, saluted smartly.

"There's a woman we've been keeping under discreet surveillance. Her name is María del Buen Amparo Leal Solana. You'll find her current address in the files. Arrest her. Bring her here. By here I mean directly to this office, not to the detention cells downstairs," the Director General said.

"*¡Sí, mi General! ¡A la orden, mi General!*" the young teniente said.

Capitan Barberios picked up the radio telephone in the patrol car. Put it to his ear.

"We're in la Plaza de Roma," a husky voice said, whispering, he was sure. "He just stopped his taxi, and he—he's getting out! Shall we grab him?"

"Look at the taxi," Captain Barberios said. "Is it moving off? Has the driver put the *Libre* sign back up?"

"No. Seems to be waiting," the husky voice said.

"Then leave him the hell alone, will you?" Captain Barberios said.

"Cap'n!" the husky voice said. "He's going into a florist's shop!"

"Move in as close as you can. See what he buys," the Captain said. Waited. Several minutes.

"Bought himself a rose, Cap'n," the husky voice said. "Just one. Wrote something on a piece of paper—put it in his pocket. *¡Que raro!* You'd think he'd tie it to the rose, wouldn't you?"

"Don't think. Causes headaches and dizziness in types like you. Break off contact. Give me the taxi's *matricula,* then break off. We know where he's going. We'll be waiting for him there."

"It's M five-five-one, four-two-three, and the hack's a one-two-four, not a fifteen hundred."

"I didn't ask you that, but thanks anyhow. There are a few less Seat one twenty-four taxicabs than there are Seat fifteen hundreds, I suppose. Break off now. Don't follow him. Over!"

"Roger, Cap'n. But if you're guessing wrong I sure wouldn't like to be in your shoes!"

"I'm not guessing. I was told what to do. By an expert. And so far he's called it right down the line. Now break radio contact, will you? Sometimes those taxis have a gismo on their sets that can tune us in. Maintain radio silence until I call you. Over."

"Roger, Cap'n Barberios!" the husky voice said.

So when Diego came out of the civil cemetery, they were waiting for him there, three patrol cars blocking every angle he could run. He no longer had the rose in his hands. He had left it on Ana María's grave. So she would have that one anyhow. From him.

His mouth was dirty where he'd pressed it against the earth covering her. His blue eyes were red streaked. Swollen almost shut. He had been able to cry, finally. Not that that helped anything. Or changed anything either.

He stood there very quietly, waiting.

"*¡Alto!*" Captain Barberios barked. "*¡Manos arriba!*"

But he didn't stop; didn't put his hands up. Instead he drew the Browning and started shooting. Aiming high, far above their heads.

He saw the linked blowtorch splutter of the submachine guns start. Something slammed into him and another and another so fast that they seemed one continuous blow. He hurt. He hurt so very badly that he had an almost uncontrollable desire to scream. He jerked the trigger of the Browning, heard it roar, felt it smack back against his palm. Then things were slamming into him, mule kicks, hammer blows, breaking him all apart inside himself, and a hot wetness was flooding out of him, and he felt very weak but *¡Que raro!* he really didn't hurt anymore. And now, suddenly, it was very dark. And a split second after now, he was suddenly very cold. Then gravely and quietly and contentedly he realized he was beginning not to feel anything anymore. And then he didn't. Not anything in this world.

Captain Barberios stood there looking down at the body.

"What's that in his hand?" he said.

Sergeant Tomás bent, pried those still flexible fingers open, took that piece of paper out, read aloud: *"Aqui yace polvo, cenza, nada . . ."*

"Poor little bastard!" Captain Barberios said.

" 'Here lies dust, ashes, nothing'—now that was a hell of a thing to write!" Teniente Jacobo said.

"Yes. Isn't it? Especially when you mean it. Now go get on the radio. Tell them to send an ambulance. And the coroner. Hop to it, will you?" Captain Barberios said.

Federico sat on the sofa in that movie set of a flat he had never even gotten to really share with Amparo.

'Couldn't have kept it, anyhow,' he thought. 'I'll never be able to afford a place like this again. But, then, what *can* I afford? Not even my next breath, really—'

The phone rang. He let it ring. It kept on ringing. On and on. He got up and answered it.

"¿Don Federico?" a man's voice said.

"Speaking," Federico said.

"This is Capitan Barberios—of the police. I'm sorry, sir—

but he came out shooting. There really wasn't any way to—"

"All right, Captain. I suspect that's the way he wanted it."

"I know it was, sir, if that's any comfort to you. You see, he left a note—"

"What did it say?" Federico said.

Capitan Barberios told him.

"Thank you, Capitan," Federico said, and hung up the phone. He went to the bar, poured himself a stiff Scotch. Straight. Went back to the sofa. Sat there, the Scotch untasted. He didn't know whether he was trying to think or trying not to think. He knew that all the things he had to think about were very bad, and all the things he didn't even want to think about, a good bit worse, and that thinking about the one and not thinking about the other, or vice versa, or thinking about them both, or thinking about neither of them wasn't going to solve a bloody thing in this miserable, *realmente jodido* world.

'Life is totally absurd,' he thought. 'I wonder if death is any less so?'

It was then that he heard the doorbell. He didn't get up to answer it. He sat there, lost in himself. *Ensimismado,* the Spanish call it.

The doorbell was one of the new electronic models with a soft, melodic chiming sound. But even so, after a very few minutes, it got to be maddening. He stood it as long as he could, then he got up, went to where the chimes themselves were, above the kitchen door, and yanked the wires loose from them.

He sat back down to enjoy the blessed silence. Sipped the whiskey. But now someone was pounding on the door and calling his name. The pounding went on and on and on and kept getting louder and louder and the voice that came through the door climbed straight up off the tonal scale until it was screaming in pure aching anguished terror and through it, he could hear the babble of his neighbors' voices saying: "Call the Police! *¡No, los Bomberos!*"

He sighed deeply, said to himself: "You're being a bastard now, Fredi."

And got up and opened the door. He was aware of his neighbors hastily shutting theirs, but not all the way. He held his open, said: "Come in, Amparo."

She came into the foyer. Stood there looking at him. Or rather trying to look at him because she was crying so hard he was sure she couldn't see much of anything. Then she sank to her knees and held her hands out to him. They were covered with blood from the way she had broken all the flesh on her knuckles hammering on his door.

He said: "*¡Dios mío!*"

Then he saw what she had in them. A cassette tape. The kind you use in small tape recorders. And even in some big, expensive, high fidelity decks, now.

"What's this, Amparo?" he said.

"Your voice, Fredi," she whispered, "saying what you said in the Director General's office, two—no, three—hours ago. Predicting what that poor, utterly damned boy—would do. What he actually *did* do—"

"So that microphone on the Director General's desk was live, eh?" Fredi said.

"Yes. That's routine down there. They tape *everything,* you know. Then he had me picked up. Brought to his office. Forced me to listen to it. To the things you said. The *way* you said them. So now I've paid for all the sins I've ever done. And all I'll ever do. Except one, maybe—"

"And that one is?" he said.

"Hers. Ana María's. The one I'll do if you put me out that door. And the little Red priest from Moratalaz is gone. I'll just have to lie there, Fredi. In the rain."

He caught her by her wrists. Drew her slowly to her feet. Kissed her mouth with aching pity. For her. For himself. For all damned souls wandering all over the nightmare landscapes of their self-created, private hells. But not for Ana María who, in the end, had at least had a rose from the hand of her Diego, and the two of them were out of it now, anyhow, and—he hoped!—at peace.

He led Amparo to the sofa. Sat there with her, his arms around her, her head pillowed against his shoulder.

"Fredi—" she murmured. "Do you know much I—"

"Don't talk. Just sit here. Hold me. Let me hold you. So the world won't slide out from under us again, maybe. But, for God's sake, Amparo, please don't talk!" he said.